About the

Erinna Mettler's first novel, the Brighton-set *Starlings*, was published in 2011 by Revenge Ink and was described by one reviewer thus: 'We read this and feel as though we know Brighton intimately, just as we get to know Baltimore inside and out in *The Wire*.'

Erinna is a founder and co-director of the spoken-word collective Rattle Tales and the newly established Brighton Prize, the city's only short-story competition. She is also an experienced tutor and mentor.

Erinna's short stories have been shortlisted for the Manchester Fiction Prize, the Bristol Prize, the Fish Prize and the *Writers' & Artists' Yearbook* Arvon Award. Her stories and poems have been published internationally in journals such as *Riptide*, *Swamp* and the *Manchester Review*. She has a special interest in writing for performance and her career highlight so far was having a story read by a *Game of Thrones* actor at Latitude Festival.

To Allie
we rule!
Mettler

FIFTEEN MINUTES

FIFTEEN MINUTES

ERINNA METTLER

Unbound

This edition first published in 2017

Unbound

6th Floor Mutual House, 70 Conduit Street, London W1S 2GF

www.unbound.com

ISBN (eBook): 978-1911586357

ISBN (Paperback): 978-1911586364

Design by Mecob

Cover images:
© iStockphoto.com / RyanJLane
© Shutterstock.com / Jade ThaiCatwalk

Printed by Clays Ltd, St Ives plc

For Rob, Noah and Gillespie.

Dear Reader,

The book you are holding came about in a rather different way to most others. It was funded directly by readers through a new website: Unbound.

Unbound is the creation of three writers. We started the company because we believed there had to be a better deal for both writers and readers. On the Unbound website, authors share the ideas for the books they want to write directly with readers. If enough of you support the book by pledging for it in advance, we produce a beautifully bound special subscribers' edition and distribute a regular edition and e-book wherever books are sold, in shops and online.

This new way of publishing is actually a very old idea (Samuel Johnson funded his dictionary this way). We're just using the internet to build each writer a network of patrons. Here, at the back of this book, you'll find the names of all the people who made it happen.

Publishing in this way means readers are no longer just passive consumers of the books they buy, and authors are free to write the books they really want. They get a much fairer return too – half the profits their books generate, rather than a tiny percentage of the cover price.

If you're not yet a subscriber, we hope that you'll want to join our publishing revolution and have your name listed in one of our books in the future. To get you started, here is a £5 discount on your first pledge. Just visit unbound.com, make your pledge and type FUTURE15 in the promo code box when you check out.

Thank you for your support,

Dan, Justin and John
Founders, Unbound

Super Patrons

Bethan Roberts
David Robson
Jay Rooke
Edward Rowe
Olga Ruszczak
William Shaw
William Smith-Bowers
Jamie Steane
Polly Stebbens
Valerie Tatum
Sue Teddern
Ashley Vaughan
Anja Vipan
Graham Walker
Susannah Waters
Amanda Welby-everard
Rebecca Whitney
Will Wood

In the future, everyone will be world famous for fifteen minutes.
Andy Warhol, Stockholm, 1968

Contents

1

Sourdough

I found my spot early, just after dark, tucked away in the thin line between two apartment blocks on a fire escape someone had forgotten to push back up. Just when I thought I was gonna drift off I was jolted awake by the bangs, four or five of them, like a car backfiring or something. Then there were the sirens – more than usual – and people shouting and running along the street. Try as I might, I couldn't ignore it. I opened my eyes and turned my head to the end of the alleyway. Blue flashing lights flickered up the road and bounced off the water-smeared walls. Bulky shapes darted past. There was screaming – a woman. Something big must've kicked off all right, a shooting I guess. It all died down pretty quickly; besides, it had nothing to do with me. Once I'm hunkered down, I don't move until morning. It's the only way to keep from freezing. Every night I stow my most precious belongings in my lap, pull my sleeping bag up to my chin and then don't move an inch. Not unless I really have to. This part of town is usually quiet enough, even at this time of year, just three weeks short of Christmas, when the world has gone seasonally insane and crowds fill the streets day and night. It can make you jumpy, all those extra bodies milling about. Accidents waiting to happen. So, like I said before, it's less frantic up here. The office parties all go downtown, and the fruit loops and the junkies tend not to come up – the police are real hot on them in this neighbourhood. If I can find the right spot, hidden from view, I can sleep safe and sound all night and be up early enough to catch the rich folks on their way into town. It's not that they're especially generous up here; though there's a lot of money about (bankers, celebrities, folks that have everything they could ever want), I can sit there for hours and not even get a glance. Every so often I'll get lucky; someone will remember the spirit of Christmas and they'll try to salve their conscience by digging deep into their pockets. If this happens, I'm set up for the day – a couple of hot meals and a bottle, maybe even a bed someplace. It didn't happen yesterday.

I get up, stretch and wriggle the pins and needles from my toes. I roll away my sleeping bag, stuff it into my biggest carrier, pick up the rest of my things, and shuffle out of the alley and along the sidewalk to the corner of 71st Street and the park.

There are a lot of people about today. Too many and too early, and not your usual commuter, fewer suits and briefcases. I wonder what's going on? Some kind of citywide celebration? It's a little short of seven but already it feels like it's well into rush hour. Everyone is moving in the same direction – north along the park – like they're being called by something. Entranced. I stand still to cough as my lungs catch up with the exertion of the day's first steps. The pain in my sides is almost unbearable today. It depends on the weather and it was a cold one last night, that's for certain. I suppose I should go to the ER but I don't like hospitals. I've had friends on the street who didn't make it out, and others who got sent back out with a painkiller for cancer because they didn't have insurance. I don't trust hospitals. People jostle me as they pass like they can't see me; one sends my shopping bags spinning so the handles twist like knives into the skin of my fingers. I did have a pair of gloves but they were stolen in the last shelter. I cough thick gunk up from my chest and splatter it onto the sidewalk. A man in a suit looks at me, then looks quickly away. I know what he's thinking.

As I start to walk again, I notice that nobody is talking. It's real eerie. Some folks walk together holding hands, some are carrying flowers. Their faces have a haunted look, like photographs of children in wartime. I walk along with them, and for the first time in years I feel like I'm just one of the crowd; suddenly a part of something. A young man with long hair and little round sunglasses stops in front of me and hands me a flower. It's a marigold, small but fluffy, and as yellow as the sun. I can feel myself smile, using muscles that haven't worked in months. The man nods, then walks away.

I carry on walking but watch him over my shoulder as he hands out flowers to people in the crowd. A woman crosses quickly in front of me so I don't see her until it's too late. She recoils as I crash into her. The impact knocks my bags from my hands; they fall at her feet, their contents spilling onto the ground.

'Watch it, mister,' she hisses.

I look up from her spike heel as I try to gather my belongings. Her legs go on for miles and she's real pretty, but her make-up is thick and dark roots are showing in her bleached blonde hair. There's a hole in her black stockings, just below the hem of her leather miniskirt, exposing a circle of bright white skin. She's got a faraway, spaced-out expression, looking over me as if I'm not even there. I know the type. The memory makes me smile.

2

'Okay, princess,' I say, straightening up.

She stares at me as though she really is a princess and I'm shit on her shoe. As she takes in my appearance, her face is transformed by sudden anger. Her pretty blank features contort into ugliness. She narrows red-rimmed eyes into lizard slits.

'Fuck off,' she shouts, almost screams. 'You stink!'

Her words echo like a shot through the still December air.

People stop and stare at us. I'm not part of the crowd anymore. I know what they all see – a bum harassing a vulnerable woman. I hunch my shoulders and drop my gaze to the sidewalk. She carries on shouting for a while but I don't move. Finally, I hear her heels clatter away. I stay as I am until I'm sure she's gone. When I look up, no one is paying any attention to me anymore; they are all intent again on their silent migration. I'm shaking but I cross the street unhindered to where I can see Cyril Patel and his pretzel cart.

I like Cyril and I'm glad to find him so close. It looks like business is good for Cyril Patel but then it usually is. He must be the only Indian pretzel pusher in Manhattan; it's a novelty and people like him cos he's always smiling, showing off his tombstone teeth like he has the best job in the world. Once, when I passed him in a snowstorm that was smothering the city in a cotton-ball blanket, and he greeted me with his usual huge grin, I asked him how come he was always so happy.

'Things could be worse,' he said with a giggle, his brown face almost entirely covered by a fake fur hunting hat. 'Things can always be worse.'

Things could certainly be worse today; even though the morning has barely begun, there's already a huge queue snaking along the park railing. Something big is happening. I can't work it out. Across Central Park West, a crowd spreads out from the doorway of the corner mansion, spilling in clusters onto the road. West 72nd Street is blocked to traffic by two patrol cars parked nose to nose. A cop leans on the open door of one, speaking into a walkie-talkie with a stern expression, the metal on his cap and shield glinting in the sun. There are other cops dotted around the crowd trying to control everything and achieving nothing. News vans line the left-hand side of the street, stripes of red, white and blue with little satellite-dish hats; each has its own reporter and cameraman, the same scene repeated over and over like the hall of mirrors at Coney Island. The reporters hold microphones out for people to speak into. I can hear the low rumble of voices and the insistent caw of car horns frustrated by the hold-up along the park, yet at the same time everything seems unnaturally quiet.

'Hello, Jimmy,' says Cyril as I approach. He's sweating, despite the cold.

'What's going on?' I ask, as I sit down on the sidewalk beside his cart. This spot is my regular home most mornings. I take off one of my hats and set it down in front of me, then I take the cardboard HAPPY CHRISTMAS sign from my inside pocket and lay that in front of the hat. You need a sign. Without a sign, you're nothing. Without a sign, folks don't notice you at all and simply walk on by as if you are vapour on the sidewalk. This one's made from the lid of a shoebox I found outside Macy's. It had shoes in it but they were too small, so I left them on top of the dumpster for someone else to find. I look up at Cyril.

He works like an octopus. Blasts of hot, salty air billow from the cart as he opens the top to take out the fresh pretzels. He carefully wraps one in a napkin and holds it out to a wispy girl at the front of the queue wearing an Afghan coat.

'Some nut-job shot John Lennon,' he says without looking back down at me.

On hearing the news spoken aloud the girl sobs. Her boyfriend puts his arms around her and kisses the top of her head. They turn and walk away, leaving their pretzel in Cyril's hand.

I rub my beard. The smell of the salted dough makes my stomach rumble.

'What? Last night?'

Cyril nods. 'It was on the radio around midnight. I got here at five – the place was already swarming. All lit up with candles like Diwali.'

He breaks from his work just long enough to hand me the unwanted pretzel and a coffee.

'Well,' I mutter, 'that explains the screaming.'

I eat quickly, without tasting. The coffee is too hot to drink, but the cup warms my hands as I look at the feet tramping the frosted leaves on the sidewalk.

All morning I sit next to Cyril Patel's pretzel cart and watch the heartbroken at the Dakota building, as they lay flowers on the steps, light candles and scrawl messages in chalk on the walls. Regular commuters stop on their way to work. There's a real mix of young and old, hippies and suits. Every so often, part of the crowd starts to sing a familiar tune and the sound rolls from one end of the street to the other, then it's quiet again.

They say if you can remember the Sixties, you weren't there – well all I can remember is being out of it, so I guess that's true. I turned 21 in 1960. I spent the entire decade in a psychedelic whirl of drugs and sex and rootlessness.

They didn't get me with the draft because I was of no fixed abode. I disappeared into a family of friends. Didn't have a ma and pa to start with; I was one of Saint Bartholomew's lost boys. Thing was, one of the brothers, Brother Randall, he didn't have any trouble finding us, every opportunity he got. I left as soon as I was 16.

It's all in the past now; no point in dwelling on it. I was lucky, I guess. I had fun – wild chemical fun. And I didn't die in a foreign war, though sometimes I wish I had. Hush now, Jimmy – it's a sin to be talking like that; death is never better than life. Trouble is, it's not the Sixties anymore, and I'm certainly not 16. The street is my home and the street's no place for ageing bones.

I wasn't really what you'd call a Beatles fan but a song starts in my head. I think it's 'A Day in the Life'. The lyrics tell me the story of a man reading the news and thinking about graves and photographs.

At eleven o'clock Cyril closes the cart lid and says, 'I'm out.'

The queue lets out a collective grumble and merges with the crowd. I have just one dollar ten in my hat.

'Hey Cyril,' I say. 'Do you have a pen?'

He stands by as I write, looking at the pilgrims across the street.

'He was a good man,' he says. 'He never once walked by without saying hello. One day he said to me, "I've always liked the Indians, Cyril. They're so much better than the cowboys."'

His impersonation is so good several people turn around to see if John isn't still with us, after all, but it's just Cyril and his big smiling face. He laughs and mouths 'sorry' to the disapproving stares.

I show Cyril my new sign.

HAPPY CHRISTMAS (WAR IS OVER.)

Cyril takes a twenty out of his top pocket and drops it into my hat. He doesn't meet my eye or say anything and I don't either. I'm sure he knows I am grateful and one day if he needs my help I will give it freely without question and without the need for thanks. I watch him push his cart away along the park and turn left through the first set of gates until the bare black bones of the trees hide him from view.

It only takes a minute but when I look back down at my hat I have three more twenties.

2

A Blaze of Green Light

She heard it in the quiet of another lonely afternoon. A noise like footsteps running across an upstairs room; but she was always the only one home since Oscar had died. Her husband was there at night, of course, but only in body. More and more he got back from work after she'd gone to bed and left early in the morning before she admitted to wakefulness. Sometimes he slept in the spare room so he didn't 'disturb her'. Increasingly he would find an excuse to stay in town on weekdays. It was how he coped, she knew that, but still she felt abandoned in a house too full of memory.

Her son, Oscar, was with her still, despite his lack of corporeality. His smiles inhabited every room, so she wasn't particularly surprised to hear his footfalls upstairs as she re-polished the already spotless coffee table. She listened, duster in hand. The house was old and settled itself throughout the day; she was familiar with its conversation but this was something more. Something solid. There it was again. A light-footed tripartite, a child running this way and that. Her heart mimicked its notation. She put down her duster and pulled herself to her feet. Hesitating, she saw dead leaves spinning around the garden in an autumnal whirl. A form emerged, complete with wizard's hat and cloak, and she wondered briefly if her imagination had conjured the sound upstairs too. Tap tap tap. It was real. She was certain it could only be Oscar and she was smiling as she hurried to the stairs.

Oscar's room was in the attic, fitted with Velux windows and oak flooring. It was reached via a spiral staircase at the end of the landing. In his short life, it had gone through several transformations – blue aeroplanes, dancing octopuses, Thomas the Tank Engine. The last was Harry Potter. Stars, moons and dragons trailed its walls. The Gryffindor shield stood proudly above Oscar's bed, time kept by a clock depicting the Weasleys' Ford Anglia.

Oscar loved his room and spent most of his time there. She would often take up post-school milk and cookies and sit on his bed listening to him talk about his day. The conversation would inevitably turn to the adventures of

Harry and Oscar's encyclopaedic knowledge of the latest book or film. Oscar's friends loved his room too; they often sprawled on the floor to play DS games and paw over Lego.

Oscar had wept when the brain tumour banished him from his room. One day he had tried to lift his foot to the stair as he had always done and had simply been unable. 'Mummy!' he'd cried. A plaintive, anguished sound like a bird call across a lake, so heartbreaking it had made her drop a cup, shattering it on the kitchen floor. She'd found Oscar shaking, tears in his eyes, staring up at the entrance to the room he would never go into again.

They refurbished the guest room, using the same designs as the attic. They dismantled and reassembled their boy's furniture, arranging his bed and desk exactly as they'd been upstairs, laying out his spinning globe and telescope. By the time they had finished, it was a pretty good simulation, but it wasn't Oscar's room. Its traditional, wall-bound windows opened onto trees rather than sky. Something in the light was wrong, as if the very essence of Oscar's room had depended on its proximity to the heavens. Their son smiled weakly as he sat on his bed and ran a fingertip along the books on his bookshelf. He didn't take one down to read. The boy previously so immersed in the tales of the young wizard didn't even have the heart for that distraction.

'I will later,' he said, seeing her concern. 'I'm tired now.'

Looking back, she wondered if Oscar's eyesight was failing then – if he'd kept the worst symptoms secret from her as long as he could and hadn't wanted to read then because the letters were already merging into one another, incomprehensible. He only lasted a matter of weeks.

Now excitement overtook her. If Oscar was up there, her life would change. She could say all the things she'd remembered when it was too late; all the protestations of love that had been lost in the practicalities of caring for a dying child. A child who had died sooner than the doctors expected. She could be his mother again.

She presumed the dead were cured of earthly ailments. Her son would be well. His face round and rosy. His hair lustrous. If he looked the same as he did when he died it would be heartbreaking, but more heartbreaking still if it wasn't him at all. She stood, her foot on the first step, unable to ascend. Then she heard it again – tap tap tap – and she knew she must see.

At the top of the stairs she peered nervously from side to side like a mouse checking for the house cat. She was surprised to see the Ford Anglia clock, now ticking the wrong time on the far wall. They must have forgotten it in their haste to move Oscar's things downstairs. The wooden floor was no longer shiny; dust patches blurred its corners. The window caught her eye, wide open, its glass a guillotine of reflected cloud. She wouldn't have left it open like that. She hadn't been up here for months. In the first few weeks after his death it was here, not the refurbished guest room, where she'd spent all her time, convinced she'd somehow be closer to Oscar in his old room. She could smell him in the air, but as each day passed his presence grew fainter and after a couple of months she couldn't sense him anymore. Her husband had become worried for her sanity after coming home and finding that she had cried all day, curled foetally on the bare floor. He begged her to stay away, to try and get on with her life. There was grief counselling and goal setting and Oscar's room was placed out of bounds. The counsellor suggested they redecorate but neither of them could face that. Oscar's father didn't come up here anymore either. These days he couldn't even bear to look at the staircase.

A sudden breeze shook the window, turning the glass into a breached lake. As it juddered, she saw a face reflected in it, wide and white, fuzzy around the edges. The eyes, yellow and as round as new moons, blinked and disappeared into a snowy dome.

She jumped back, almost losing her footing on the stairs, and grabbed the rail. It wasn't Oscar she'd seen. It wasn't a child at all. It was inhuman and yet, in that brief glimpse before the wind shifted the window, beautiful. Her heart raced. She stepped fully into the room and crossed to the window. First she checked behind her, a chill dancing over her shoulders. She expected a phantom to appear, a white-headed revenant. Grateful to discover the room was empty, she bobbed her head out through the frame, looking right onto rain-slicked roof tiles. Nothing. She heard a sound to her left – a mousy scratch – and turned, worried what she might see. She gasped.

An owl blinked at her with steady eyes.

It was the size of a medium dog and only a few feet away. Its head and chest were entirely white, flat feathers fanned the eyes, a cluster fell like whiskers over its curved beak. Great wings rested at its sides, sweeping in ripples of black tips, a triangle at the neck, feathered boots encasing the legs.

They each stood perfectly still looking at the other.

The owl's gaze was mesmerising. She didn't dare breathe for fear of spooking him. He shifted his feet on the tiles, clacking stone on stone, blinked fathomless eyes and turned his head to peck at his back. She let herself breathe out and the owl's face took on a quizzical expression. She smiled at him. He accepted her smile and settled himself, closing his eyes against the wind. She wanted to reach out and sink her fingers deep into his warm down but she didn't dare. Instead, she watched. As she studied him, taking in the intricacy of each feather, she felt calmer than she had for years. Time seemed to stop.

She must have watched him for hours because now the sky was shifting into dusk. The owl opened his eyes and looked around; he hobbled scratchily towards the gutter, then spread his enormous wings and whooshed into the sky. He soared effortlessly, turning on the breeze to head into the trees. She watched him go for as long as she could see him.

'Don't be silly,' her husband said, unusually home in time for dinner. 'You're talking about a snowy owl. There are no snowy owls in Scotland, it's too far south.'

'I know,' she said excitedly. 'I spent hours on the internet after he'd gone. He shouldn't be here but sometimes they go off course, looking for food. There have been some sightings in recent years. Just single birds though, lost on their way to somewhere else. It was him I heard walking around upstairs. He must have flown in through the open window. I really thought a person was walking about up there.'

Her husband raised an eyebrow and poured himself a second glass of Rioja.

She continued to rattle off details, the bird's size, eyes and markings.

'It was so relaxing watching him. Much better than that bloody therapist. It was like having a conversation with Mother Nature.'

Her husband stabbed a piece of pork with his fork, chewed thoughtfully and took a big slug of wine.

'So, a snowy owl blew off course, came into our house for a little rest and had a chat with you on the roof for several hours.'

'You think I'm making it up.'

'No. No. I know you're not making it up but is it possible that you could have had a nap and dreamt it?'

'Dreamt it?' She pushed her plate away. 'I know the difference between fantasy and reality.'

'I know, darling, but dreams can be very vivid. You're here all day long on your own. Perhaps you fell asleep and didn't realise. The mind can play tricks on you when you're tired.'

'But I'm not tired.'

'Well, you don't sleep well, do you? And you won't take those pills the doctor prescribed.'

'Like you'd know. I'm usually asleep when you get in – if you get in.'

'Yes, but you get out of bed and pace around all night like Lady Macbeth. It's no wonder you're exhausted.'

'I'm not exhausted!'

They held each other's gaze for a while, then she stood and pulled the plate from in front of him, scraping the contents onto her own barely touched food.

'Hey, I haven't finished.'

'Oh, I think you have.'

She went straight to bed after that. They hadn't argued so openly in years; maybe it wouldn't have stung so much if they had. As she lay in bed alone, unable to close her eyes, she wondered if he could be right. Was she so purposeless that she could invent the events of an afternoon? The whole thing sounded fanciful but the owl had been so real, she could remember every feather of him. She couldn't have made him up. Could she?

She heard the muffled TV cease and her husband's uneven steps on the stairs. She turned to face the window and closed her eyes. He came into their room and sat heavily on the bed. She could smell wine and whisky on him as he bent to kick his shoes off, sending each one thudding into the wardrobe.

'Sshh,' he told himself, then he rested his hand delicately on her hip.

'I'm shorry, darling.'

She could hear the crack in his voice but as usual she didn't stir and eventually he took his hand away and left the room.

In the morning, Oscar's window was closed. She couldn't remember closing it. Her husband had left before six. Could he have closed it? Perhaps he was right. Perhaps she was losing her mind. Nerves bubbled in her stomach as she turned the handle on the window and shoved it open. It was unlikely the owl would be there again. She should have taken a photograph of him as proof. The RSPB website explained that snowy owls stayed in one place for a few weeks during migration in order to take full advantage of the food supply. He could still be around, hunting at the edge of the woods. She closed her eyes, dipped her head out of the window and wished on all the stars painted on Oscar's bedroom wall. When she opened them, only the sky and the wood stretched ahead, void of snowy feathers. Disappointment caught in her throat and she fought back tears. Then she heard a voice to her left, soft and familiar.

'It's all right, Mum. I'm here.'

Turning, she saw the owl sitting a little way up the roof, huge and majestic, whiter even than she remembered, the feathers around his beak looking for all the world like a smile.

Oscar jumped into his old room through the open window. He was almost too big for the gap, but with some ungainly manoeuvring he managed to land. His talons skidded on the floor and she had to steady him, her hand light on his chest, the beat of his bird heart radiating into her palm. A tear welled in her eye. Oscar looked up into her face, his deep eyes filled with sadness and wonder.

'I'm so glad to see you, Oscar,' she said.

'Yes, me too.'

It was odd hearing Oscar's voice coming from the owl's mouth, but each word was comfort and each facial tic a confirmation. He cocked his head to get a better look at her.

'You look tired,' he said.

'Not you too!'

'Dad? He'll be worried about you. I was. That's why I came back.'

'Oscar, how did you come back? I'm so very happy you did but I have so many questions.'

The bird shrugged.

'I'm not really sure. I remember going to sleep. You and Daddy were there and I could hear you and I wanted to tell you that it was all right. I couldn't feel any pain. I was happy. I heard you say, "I love you Oscar", and then I was flying through a snowstorm. The flakes were so thick that I could only see white. There weren't any trees or houses, the sky and the ground looked the same. I was frightened and I started falling fast but then somehow I righted myself and soared.'

He flapped his wings to demonstrate and giggled.

'The wind keeps you up; she helps you, gets you where you need to be. I wasn't cold; my feathers are as warm as a ski suit. After a while, I came to a massive pine forest. It was getting dark so I stopped on a tree for a rest. I caught my first meal there. A mouse.' He shuffled self-consciously and looked briefly at the floor. 'Disgusting, I know. But Mum, it tasted so good!

'I stayed in the wood for a while because it felt safe and there was food. Every day I'd sit on a branch and watch the creatures below – mice, foxes, even reindeer. Everything smelt of snow and pine. It felt like Christmas. I was getting used to it. I could have stayed for ever but then the wind told me about you, struggling, and I had to come and find you.'

He smiled his strange, beaky smile and widened his eyes.

'I flew for weeks and weeks through the snow. The wind guided me but the land didn't change. I got so tired I thought I'd die again. Then the snow stopped and I could see green patches on the ground. Eventually, there wasn't any snow at all and I could see roads and farms and sheep and rivers and then there were the woods near our house and then there was you.' He took a deep breath and coughed. 'I'm not used to talking anymore.'

Engrossed in his story, she had forgotten to offer him anything.

'Shall I get you a drink? What do you drink? Are you hungry?'

The bird nodded.

'A bit. I've been catching mice and small birds but it's not as easy as it looks. I just drink water.'

'There are some sausages in the fridge – would they do?'

'Yes, I should think so, and maybe some cheese. I fancy a bit of cheese.'

She smiled. Feeding her son was a gift she thought she would never experience again. When he'd been ill, he'd lost the ability to relish his food. Even his favourites brought him no joy. In the end, his food had to be delivered directly into his stomach through a tube.

As she made her way to the stairs, Oscar called after her.

'Don't cook them,' he said.

She took out the packet of sausages and snipped them into bite-sized pieces along with some extra-mature Cheddar, then grabbed a bottle of water and a saucer and carried it all back upstairs. The bird had his back to her, pacing in a figure of eight and looking up at all the stars on his walls. He turned when he heard her.

'Harry Potter,' he said. 'I just remembered. We used to read together and watch all the films.'

Not quite all. They had watched the first film when Oscar had been five, snuggled on the sofa during a snowstorm. He had cried at the end. It had surprised her. He had never cried at anything other than scraped knees before, but here was empathy for a boy less well off than himself, a boy without parents. Oscar was becoming fully formed. He watched the film every day for a week, then started on the books. Every bedtime was taken up with one or two chapters. Even when he could read them himself, he still wanted her to read to him and urged her to do different voices for all the characters while he spoke Harry's words. They laughed and gasped and cried through them together. The owl, Hedwig, was his favourite.

'I'd like an owl as a pet,' he'd said after they'd seen the second film together at the multiplex in Dundee.

'A big white snowy owl with a bad temper, that eats mice when they're still alive!'

They'd danced to the car, squawking and flapping their arms.

It became a tradition to see the films on the weekend of release. Her husband was content to let them go together, sensing it was their thing.

Oscar grew with the characters, infant school became junior school, he made the football team, got the lead in the school play, even made friends with a girl. One day he felt unwell, a slight headache, a fluctuating temperature, probably just a cold. But he didn't get better.

He'd missed the last book and three films. She went to see the last one on her own but left after 20 minutes, unable to bear the emptiness of the seat beside her.

They talked all day and neither noticed the sun go down. Oscar heard the car first, turning his head towards a sound beyond her perception.

'Dad,' he said.

She was flustered; rushing to the window, she saw the car swing up the drive. 'What should I do? Should I bring him up?'

'No,' said the owl firmly. 'He doesn't need to see me. I'm only here to see you.'

The car drew to a halt and she heard the door slam.

'Will you stay?' she asked, scared that the answer might be no, but the owl nodded.

'Of course, for as long as you need me to.'

She pointed to the plate of half-eaten sausages. 'Didn't you like them?'

'No, not really. They were a bit bland. I've got used to bones, perhaps you could bring me a chicken leg tomorrow? The cheese was nice though.'

Her husband was already through the door when she came downstairs. He hung up his coat and set down his briefcase, kissing her on the cheek, his face cold against her skin. He looked at her suspiciously.

'Are you all right?' he said. 'What were you doing in the attic? I saw the light on. You're not starting all that again are you? Spending all your time up there, getting upset.'

She smiled at him.

'I'm not. I promise. I was just clearing out the cobwebs. I noticed them yesterday.'

'Was the owl back?'

'No. No owls today. I think you were right. It must have been a dream.'

She wandered into the kitchen.

'I didn't know if you'd be back,' she said. 'We haven't much in.'

'I think there are some sausages,' he called as he slipped off his shoes. 'Those will do.'

In the morning, she searched the internet for owl food and then drove to a reptile and aquatics centre near the M90, buying two dozen pinks before stopping off at a supermarket for human food and a Harry Potter box set. The mice were still frozen when she got them home, hairless and raw, their eyes tiny ticks, their paws crossed at their chests like bodies laid to rest. They looked peaceful. She bathed them in warm water until they were soft.

Oscar devoured them, grabbing them one by one from her hand with his beak, making a horrible guttural sound as they moved whole down his throat. She should have been repulsed but it was wondrous to behold her son enjoying a meal.

'Thank you,' he said when he had finished. He smoothed his chest feathers with his beak. 'Was it all right yesterday, with Dad?'

She thought about the previous night – the hunt for the 'missing' sausages, the omelette made together, he whisking eggs, she grating cheese, sitting close in front of the TV.

'It was better.'

After his lunch, they went downstairs and watched *The Half-Blood Prince*. It turned out that Oscar still liked popcorn. He watched intently, not taking his eyes off the television as he bent to peck the corn from the bucket. She took the opportunity to look at this strange bird/son perched beside her. It was his face that intrigued her the most. It was an owl's face, flat and wide, eyes bigger than the sum of it and yet, it was also Oscar's face, his expressions, his frown and smile, his mischievous eyes.

'You're staring,' he said and took a nib of popcorn.

They watched the film to the end, still and silent as the credits rolled.

'I remember it,' said Oscar. 'You read it to me. It was heading towards a very dark place.'

'Yes. You never got to see how it all turned out, did you? You...'
She held her hand to her mouth and sobbed suddenly.
'Died?' he said.
She nodded.
'But I'm here now. I'll always be here.'
She hugged him then, his feathers absorbing her tears and tickling her face.
'Mum?' he said.
'Yes, darling?'
'What happens to Hedwig?'

It snowed heavily that night. She woke into a world of white. There was no getting the car out, so her husband worked from home, taking possession of the desk in the study upstairs. He kept the door open. She couldn't go up into the attic without him hearing her, so she spent the day on edge, taking every opportunity to pace the corridor with a laundry basket at her hip lest he should wonder what she was doing. The attic was silent. She assumed Oscar had flown to the wood to do owl things. In the evening, she and her husband cooked and ate together, talking about the weather and what was on the news. Later, flicking through the channels, they found a documentary about snowy owls. They watched in silence, her heart beating loudly, her breath faint. There was a bit about recent sightings in the UK, several in Scotland. She watched him sip his beer. He held out his hand to her and she took it.

'Okay,' he said. 'It's possible you saw an owl.'

Three days passed, and on the dawn of the fourth she heard a loud, mechanical noise outside. She opened the curtains to see a slick of tarmac curving up the driveway. Their farmer neighbour had used his tractor to dig them out. He waved at her as he drove away.

Her husband said he'd better try to get into work, and as soon as his car had disappeared from view she ran upstairs to Oscar. She'd longed to see him over the last few days. Once, when her husband was in the shower, she'd got a little way up the steps but he'd come out almost immediately and she'd retreated along the hallway before he'd seen her.

The floor was covered with white splashes and the owl was stooped under the eaves. He looked shrunken, yellowing, half the bird he was before.

'You should have left the window open,' he rasped, and taking a step towards her staggered and fell, cradling himself with his wing.

She fed him sugar water with a spoon and a few crumbs of cheese. Though he appeared greatly weakened, his eyes retained their clarity. They were an extraordinary yellow, ringed in black. They reminded her of a photograph she had seen in the paper, the sun through a telescope, raging against the void.

Oscar recovered over the hours, his breath slowly returning to normal.

'I'm sorry,' she kept saying. 'I'm so, so sorry.'

The breeze through the now open window revived him and he managed a couple of the pinks. She scrubbed away the guano and bagged his pellets.

'My feet are itchy,' he said. 'I need to fly.'

'I'll leave the window open tonight.'

He said nothing but the feathers under his eyes quivered.

Her husband was home by four carrying a box file.

'There's no one in the office,' he said. 'I thought I may as well work from home. I'll make you dinner.'

She heard the scream as she dozed on the sofa in front of the blazing wood fire. Her husband came into the living room holding several frozen mice on the flat of his palms.

'What the hell are these?'

She stared at him, searching her brain for a viable explanation as to why there were a dozen mice in their freezer. He looked angry.

'They're for "the owl" aren't they?'

No words came.

'Aren't they?'

She nodded.

'Jesus, are you insane? It's all in your imagination. You shouldn't have gone up there again. There is no owl.'

'There is,' she said, 'but he isn't just an owl.'

She told him everything. He sat on the floor in front of her so she couldn't see his face. When she had finished, he turned to her and she saw that he had been crying. She'd not seen him cry since the day Oscar died, not even at the funeral. She'd often wondered how he couldn't. She knelt beside him and held him in her arms.

'I miss him too.'

He snuffled into her neck like an animal. She could smell the natural odour beneath his aftershave and the memory of it brought tears to her eyes too.

'I'll show you,' she said.

She led him by the hand to the first-floor landing, his eyes wide as a child's as they stood at the foot of the staircase. Her heart beat louder than ever; so fast she thought it might burst. He went up first, the steps creaking beneath him. When he reached the top and had disappeared from view, she followed. He'd turned on the light and was standing with his back to her as she emerged from the steps. The room was still and bright. Oscar wasn't there. The window was closed and there was no trace of feathers or pellets; the saucer stood full on the floor, bluebottles fighting for space on the limp mice and mouldering cheese. She put her hand to her mouth as the floor spiralled beneath her feet and she fell like a dead weight.

'Darling, darling…'

His face came into focus, tender and concerned, his lap a pillow of down supporting her. He smiled and she sat up groggily, remembering everything.

'There was no owl?' she asked.

He stroked her hair.

'Probably not, darling.'

'Am I insane?'

'Maybe there was an owl for you. It doesn't mean you're mad.'

'He was so real.'

'C'mon,' he said, 'let's get you up.'

She was unsteady on her feet but he held her until she got her bearings and then led her to the stairs. Neither of them saw the small white tuft fluttering in the breeze on the window's edge.

They made love that night – a slow and tender coupling – and afterwards, lying entwined in the dark, they fell asleep to the sound of the wind swirling through the trees and, lost within it, a far-off plaintive cry like that of a bird across a lake.

They woke late and, after a hearty breakfast, he held her hand and said he thought they should move.

'Right now. Just pack everything up and go to a hotel in town, then find somewhere to rent until we can sell. I don't want you to be here alone anymore. It's not right.'

'What, just like that?'

'Yes, darling, just like that. We won't forget him. He's in here,' he said, pointing to her heart. 'We don't have to be where he was to have him with us.'

She knew he was right. The house held too much of Oscar in its rooms. He couldn't bear it and if she didn't go with him now, they would drift apart again. He would find excuses to stay in town and she would spend her days talking to imaginary owls.

'Okay,' she said.

He smiled. 'Really?'

'Yes. But there is something we should do first.'

They watched the last two films together, the whole afternoon a rollercoaster of emotion. Both jumped when Hedwig died in a blaze of green light, holding each other tight in an ouroboros against fear, regret and loss.

When it was over, they dried each other's tears with kisses and packed a suitcase of essentials. He threw away all the perishables in the kitchen, including the thawing mice. As he carried their bags to the car she locked up, lingering on the doorstep to look at the empty house. In the attic, beyond the realm of her hearing, the Ford Anglia clock finally slowed to a stop.

They drove away at dusk and she didn't look back, keeping her eyes focused on the road ahead and the tops of the trees jabbing at the yellowing sky.

'Looks like snow again,' he said.

There was a flash of white high above them. She turned her head to look at it. The owl swooped down level with the car and flew alongside her window for a few hundred yards, his wings flapping desperately, his face turned full to look at her, then he flew upwards in a swift ascent.

Her husband stopped the car.

'Can you see him now?' she asked.

He squeezed her arm in reassurance.

'I can see him.'

The bird continued swooping heavenwards, caught on a soaring current, his wings cruciform.

They watched him go, higher and higher as the snow began again. It fell faster and faster until Oscar became one of the snowflakes, just another white dot in the distance, and then he was gone. His parents held hands and watched the snowflakes fall onto the windscreen, momentarily blessing it with their beauty before melting away into nothing.

3

Carbon in its Purest Form

One of the 'Loose Women' announces it, interrupting morning TV's unceasing schedule of misfits, wannabes and celebrity gossip. They don't comment, Ricky and Jean, just glance at each other surprise-eyed for a moment and then turn their attention back to the television, back to the inane reactions of the women on the show, short, sweeping and quickly dismissed by the host.

'I've never liked that Carol one,' says Jean, scratching her nose. 'She looks like a right cow.'

There's a proper newsflash in the break, a few details about where she died (a typically fairy-tale location) and some archive footage of her last public appearance, her hair white and her face slack on one side. Every over-enunciated word from the newsreader's lips makes Ricky's heart beat a little faster.

When that first bulletin is over, before there is time to collect reactions from colleagues and enemies, and the nothingness of morning television resumes, Jean says brightly, 'Want a cuppa tea, luv?'

Ricky nods and she squeezes his knee as she passes into the kitchen, leaving him to watch the elephant stomp around the TV studio, knocking over tables and flattening the guests who are there to talk about fashion and recipes. He can hear Jean humming in the kitchen but he can't make out the tune. She's gone for a good while.

'We had a couple o' Bourbons left,' she says on her return, and lays his Trinity mug in front of him with a chipped saucer of chipped biscuits.

Loose Women finishes and then it's the news proper. Familiar images flicker across the screen; a firework display of camera flashes, those steely blue eyes and that perfectly set hair, brooches of sapphires and diamonds pinned onto a series of smart blue coats, handbag brandished like a weapon. He always wondered what she kept in those monstrous handbags. They were so big they could have housed an axe – and how appropriate that would have been. As he watches, he realises it's been a long time since he's seen any pictures of her on the news.

He picks up his mug and inhales. He can tell Jean hasn't used Aldi own brand; it's a different blend, one the passages of his nostrils recognise of old. She's let it stew so it's a deep orange, the colour of the Spanish sunsets they used to watch together on long-ago family holidays, sangria and sandy feet on sea-facing balconies while the kids slept soundly, two to a bunk.

Jean's not used sweetener either. This time it's sugar, thick and grainy on his spoon at the bottom of the mug. The doctor says he shouldn't have sugar, says he needs to watch his weight, that his blood pressure's too high, but Ricky can barely tolerate the metallic aftertaste of sweetener – a taste that ultimately leaves his mouth feeling the opposite of what it's supposed to. *Sugar's natural, innit? What's wrong wi' sugar?* After he has stirred (seven times to the left) he looks over at his wife. In her late fifties now but still what his mam used to call bonnie, Jean looks to Ricky the same as she did the day they got wed, one bright spring morning in 1974. She wore a lace high-necked dress with bell sleeves and had a crown of silk daisies in her hair, and he wore a blue tuxedo, bow tie and frilly shirt. He inwardly cringes now if he sees photographic evidence of this fashion faux pas – wonders how he ever thought powder blue and long, curly hair were masculine, even with a 'tache. The kids used to roar with laughter at those old photographs, used to get them out of the white brocade box in the sideboard, lift the tissue paper inside and snuggle up on the sofa for a good old giggle. 'Look at me dad,' they used to say. 'He looks like a right ponce.' They'd turn the precious pages and laugh until their sides hurt and their breath would neither go in nor out.

'Gi-oer,' Jean used to say, pretending to be cross. 'If it weren't for us getting wed you lot wunt be here.'

The thing Ricky remembers most about his wedding day is Jean's face. She was just 18 and her skin was peach smooth and flushed, her hair tumbled in shiny waves to her shoulders. She'd had her make-up done professionally at the house, but she could have gone natural because she was lit from within with love. Everyone could see it. She emitted a beautifying glow that made grandmas and toddlers smile when they saw her. Ricky could feel its warmth as they made the journey from the church to the club in a carriage pulled by two white dray horses dressed in brasses and feathers. People came out of their houses to wave when they heard the clip-clop of the hooves on the road and Ricky waved back, safe in the knowledge that he was officially the luckiest man alive.

There are lines on Jean's face now, of course, and grey roots in her hair but, as there has been since the day he met her, there's also carefully applied lipstick and mascara. She's always made up, his Jean, even though she's nowhere to go. *I dream of Jeanie with the light brown hair.* He still sings that to her, his Jeanie, alive with hope after decades of having nowhere to go. God knows why she stuck with a deadbeat like him in a town like this.

She takes a little nibble of a Bourbon cream as if she wants to make it last as long as possible, then a big, crunching bite, washing it down with a noisy slurp of tea. She doesn't take her eyes off the television. They dart unblinking from side to side, following the unfolding events. Her face doesn't betray any emotion; you would think she was just watching a soap ad. Jean sees him looking out of the corner of her eye.

'What?' she says through biscuit crumbs.

He smiles.

'Anyone would think we were celebrating or summat.'

Still smiling, he drinks deeply from the best cup of tea he's had in ages.

They don't talk about it over lunch – an hour later than usual to accommodate the extended news – they don't talk about anything really. He eats beans on toast and Jean has an egg salad. She's watching her weight too, has been all her life, even when she didn't need to, but she can't resist a large dollop of salad cream. The only noise is the scrape of cutlery on their plates and the constant tick of his dad's retirement clock. After lunch, there's more tea made in the same way. When they've finished that too, Jean says, 'You going tut club?'

Ricky rubs the grey stubble on his chin. He doesn't shave every day anymore – there's no need, unless they're expecting company or he's making one of his increasingly less frequent visits to the club. He wonders if he should have one now. He normally would, but it's well into the afternoon and he doesn't want to miss anything. Besides, his chin is past the itchy stage and is now more beard than neglect.

'Aye,' he says. 'Reckon I should put in an appearance at least. Is there a shirt clean?'

Jean hands him his gloves by the front door. They look into each other's eyes for a moment as she ties his scarf around his neck.

'It's still cold out there,' she says. 'You should watch that chest o' yours. You don't want to end up on antibiotics again.'

'Yes, mam.' He winks and closes the door quickly behind him so as not to let the heat out.

The troublesome cough bubbles in his chest when the cold air hits his lungs and he wheezes heavily on the mile-long walk up the hill, past deserted streets and closed doors.

It's grey out, mizzling, and he's eager to get to the sanctuary of the club, to a warm, dry welcome. The clubhouse stands defiant at the end of a row of boarded-up shops, lights shining through barred windows, Christmas decorations still hanging around the red slate roof despite it being April. Most of the big events of Ricky's life have been celebrated in this club, from his christening through his 18th, 21st and marriage, to the birth of his kids and the wakes of his parents and younger brother. The place is nearly full. Men young and old cluster around the TV above the bar. He looks for someone to sit with but none of his friends are there today. They, like him, spend less time here now; a working-men's club should be for working men, so they're probably at home watching it all with their wives. Standing in the doorway, Ricky wishes he had done the same, but he's here now so he may as well stay.

The club's oldest member, Dan, sits alone in his usual spot, scruffy lurcher Jeff at his feet. The dog lifts his head from his paws when he sees Ricky, eyebrows dancing in welcome. Dan's half blind, his eyes opaque with glaucoma, but still he greets Ricky by name when he comes in, always has. Ricky wonders if Dan's other senses have compensated for his lack of sight, if each man in the club has his own particular smell that only he can differentiate. Dan once told him that he didn't mind his sight failing, said the murkiness reminded him of the pit and he'd 'worked in the darkness of t' pit for nigh on thirty-five year'. Said he was comforted rather than afraid, that it was the daylight that scared him.

One of the Parker boys is on Ricky's bar stool but his brother nudges him when he sees Ricky and they both nod in assent and move away to the pool table.

'Usual, Ricky?' asks Louise, the barmaid. Ricky and Louise were in the same class at school. She started working for her dad at the club when she was 16, collecting glasses and heating up pies. Now she runs the place.

'Ta, Lou,' he says and heaves himself onto the stool. His knees lock as he tries to find the cross bar; pain shoots up his right leg and his foot goes numb. His breathing is laboured and sweat collects on his lip. One day soon he'll have to face facts and sit at a table by the window like old Dan. He's had his knee replaced once already and they said another one wouldn't work out as well. *As well as what?* Ricky wonders.

His pint is placed in front of him, as tan as Jean's tea, with froth bubbling up from the bottom like a living thing.

'On the house,' says Louise. 'Just for today.'

Ricky nods gratitude.

The music is loud, boxing with the sound of the TV. The men watching the news cuss and cheer words that Ricky can't make out. His hearing's not what it used to be. Jean's always telling him he needs it testing but he can't face another set of medical appointments, further evidence of the failing of his body. He can guess what's being said from the faces on the screen and the reactions of the men. At one point there's a round of applause, stamping of feet and two-fingered whistles. Ricky looks at the face on the screen, someone he knew from the Union, must be almost 30 years since he last clapped eyes on him. He's sitting in front of a faded embroidered banner, gold tassels on red cloth with a picture of an oak tree in the middle, like something that belongs in a museum. He has Union badges proudly displayed on the lapels of an equally faded jacket and his face looks like Ricky feels.

Ricky wishes he had a fag. He still finds it odd that you can't smoke in pubs and clubs now. For most of his life cigarette smoke hung in a blue fog near the ceiling of the club, day and night. The chemical roast smell of tobacco hit you in the face as you opened the door, an almost solid dryness, pricking your nostrils and reminding you that this was the time to relax, that soon you'd have a pint and have taken that first draw on an Embassy and everything in the world would be well. Ricky misses that smell. Working men and women smoked, that's all there was to it. He hasn't noticed any less of them dying. He didn't even stop when his brother, Clive, died of cancer, but he didn't stop going down the pit then either and they said that had as much to do with it as the ciggies. The only thing that stopped him was Jean, because she wanted him to, and he would do anything Jean asked, no matter how hard.

Those men not around the telly, those playing pool or dominoes are singing along to the music. They seem to know all the words. Ricky recognises the songs but it takes him a while to make the connection – 'Ghost Town', 'Shipbuilding', 'Free Nelson Mandela' – but by the time they play 'Tramp the Dirt Down' he's got it. Ricky hasn't heard these songs in a long while and to him they sound like they belong to another age. *These days it's all meaningless, bouncy pop, innit? Jessie G or whatever her name is.* His granddaughter, Tiffany, likes her – prattling on about it not being about the money to a shiny, bouncy beat. *Yeah right, luv,* he thinks. *Course it's not.*

One of the younger lads stands next to Ricky at the bar as Norman Tebbit appears on the TV. Ricky knew the boy's dad, but he's long gone now; left his missus with four kiddies to bring up.

'They want to come here,' says the boy, cocky as you like. 'I'd tell 'em what I thought of her.'

Ricky finishes his pint and wipes his mouth with the back of his hand. This lad wasn't even born until the '90s.

'They won't come here,' Ricky says. 'Why would they?'

'You were there, weren't you, Ricky,' says the boy. 'Wi' me dad?'

Ricky clenches his fists for a second. He sees flashes of movement in his mind's eye. Disjointed. Uncoordinated. Riot shields and head guards reflect sunlight, their faces mirrored back to them by men in Plexiglas defences. Horses' nostrils flare, snorting smoky breath; steam rises from their flanks in the heat of the sun. He sees raised truncheons and crow bars, cricket bats – anything the lads could get their hands on – the gleam of shiny buttons and police insignia. He sees rocks hurled across a blue expansive sky, bottles stuffed with glittering, flaming rags, limbs flailing in a demonic dance, like a really bad Friday night at the Roxy, boots put in, fists smashing jaws. He sees men dragged from horses, women hit by truncheons, blood streaming into eyes. He hears the overwhelming noise, the chants and battle cries, the clatter of shields and shoes and hooves, the screams and the threats. He smells blood and cordite in the air, mingling with the sweat of desperate men. And they were desperate by then, you could see it in their eyes. It was the desperation that finished it in the end; not the poverty or loss of pride, but desperation pumped directly into living rooms on the evening news. Civilised people don't like to see desperation – it reminds them of how vulnerable they are.

Ricky rests his hands flat on the threadbare John Smith's bar towel in front of him, feels its coarse, damp comfort. He remembers the boy's father; he worked hard and he played hard. He did every shift he could to earn as much money as possible for his family, the family he eventually couldn't provide for. The failure killed him. His heart gave out, too full of booze from the good times – and the bad.

Ricky has watched this kid grow up, from the cheeky toddler kicking a football against the garage wall, to the joyrider terrorising the neighbours, to the grey-faced junkie no one mentioned who lived in the house on the edge of the estate. He got out somehow, cleaned up his act. Lord knows how – a charity or some government scheme that probably doesn't exist anymore; as Jean always says, sometimes do-gooders do good.

The lad blinks at him expectantly.

'Let me get you another pint,' he says. 'Me dad would have wanted me to.'

Ricky's phone rings. 'The Red Flag' – Jason, his eldest, loaded the ringtone before he gave the phone to his father as a present. Thought it was a huge joke. Ricky can't figure out how to get rid of it. A few of the men cheer and beer from their raised glasses sloshes onto the already sticky carpet. But Ricky winces. He's embarrassed by it, and half the blokes in here don't even know what it means.

'Hello, Dad?' Jason's voice sounds tinny and far off. 'I just got out of a meeting and heard the news. You okay?'

'Fine. Why shun't I be?'

'I phoned the house; Mam said you were a bit – quiet.'

Ricky doesn't answer.

'It's bound to drag up old memories.' Jason goes on, unheeding of his father's reticence, his voice exaggeratedly cheerful. 'Made me think about the strike myself, about how our birthday and Christmas presents were all from Oxfam and Sunday dinner was always beans on toast.'

'Happy days,' says Ricky.

Another cheer goes up from the TV crowd, this time it's for Ken Livingstone.

'What's it like at the club?' asks Jason.

'A few silly beggars think it's summat to be happy about.'

'You can't blame people for celebrating, Dad. Not after everything that happened.'

'Some old lady dying in't going to make any fuckin' difference to me or any bugger else, is it?'

Ricky's voice is loud; his words hover over the heads of everyone in the room, cutting across the joviality, gagging conversation, lowering the volume of the music, as if time itself has stalled. Some of the men look over at him, some look at the floor, a couple smirk at each other. Ricky looks down at his pint and time begins again.

'I'll call you later, Jason,' he says quietly. 'When I'm back home. Love tut kiddies.'

Jason got out too, worked hard at school, went to college, lives in London, works in Parliament, if you can believe it. Ricky thinks he might as well be in a bloody foreign country for all t' difference it is to here. They make the journey south sometimes, if Jason sends him and Jean train tickets. Christmas, kids' birthdays and the like. Ricky can't stand the place. All folk do is rush around ignoring each other. He knows people round here think Jason is stuck up, the shop-counter gossips with nothing better to do. He's proud of his eldest though; he may as well be down there as up here in a club for working men who haven't worked in years.

They were a family of miners; generations working in the pits from Durham to the Valleys. As it was, only Ricky stayed the course. Even his father gave up on it, preferring to drive the coal away from the pit rather than going down to dig for it. Ricky's younger brother, Clive, didn't last long enough to see the end – the cancer ate away at his lungs until he didn't have enough air to speak.

On his first day underground, Ricky was so scared he threw his breakfast up into his mam's rose bushes. He'd worked up top since he left school so he was familiar with the comings and goings of the pit, but the thought of actually going down it frightened him more than he let on. His dad stood by until he had nothing left to puke, then gave him first a handkerchief and next a cigarette.

'You'll be all right, son,' he said. 'You've the right stuff for it. It'll suit you.'

As he stepped into the shaft cage and stood beside men the size of mountains (his pristine orange overalls hanging off his greyhound frame), he felt much younger than his 18 years. He looked straight ahead at the yellow bars, his mouth as dry as biscuit crumbs and his heart horse hooves in his chest. They travelled down at rickety speed through the cold to the sweltering heat of the train tunnels and the rumbling conveyor belts to the coalface. Ricky recognised men from the club – neighbours, his dad's friends, all working to the same purpose, all part of the same family. His fear shrank with the daylight. In fact, he felt safer than he ever had in his life, cradled deep in the arms of the earth with his new comrades. Nothing bad was going to happen to him down here. The drill screeched through the pitch and the coal shone in the beam of silver light from Ricky's hat like a billion tiny diamonds melded for ever with the solid black. His dad was right; it suited him. Mining was the only thing he knew how to do. When it was all over, he just didn't take to anything else.

Ricky wishes there was something else on the telly at the club; a diversion from the endless round of archive footage and aging used-t-bes. He reflects that all he does these days is watch the telly, whether he's at home or here, and if they mess up the schedule for whatever reason – the Olympics, royal weddings, even something as momentous as this – it plays havoc with his nerves and fills him with unease. He needs his daily round of quiz shows and documentaries; they have made him an armchair expert on everything, and nothing.

He watched a documentary once about the universe, about how everything in it is basically carbon, and how, in the right circumstances, if you wait long enough, you'll end up with diamonds. That Northern lad that's always on these days said there is a planet in another galaxy that's made entirely of diamonds. Ricky had been struck by that; a diamond planet. Course it would be a rough diamond, wouldn't it? As opaque as Dan's poor old eyes. Ricky had a dream about it – the diamond planet. He dreamt that the beings that lived near it sent a spaceship up to cut and polish it. They took the time to refine it so it reflected light from its sun across their night sky, just so they had something pretty to look at in the dark.

Ricky's grandad had a tiny little rock he told them was a diamond. He used to show it to Ricky and his brothers when they went round for Sunday tea. He said he'd found it in the pit, said there were lots of diamonds in the pit if you looked hard enough – that diamonds were just carbon in its purest form. Ricky was about 14 when he realised it was just a bit of old glass, probably left over from some miner's lunch. Before that, he believed his grandad wholeheartedly, couldn't wait to get down there and start digging for diamonds.

He leaves his pint unfinished on the bar. Jeff, Dan's dog, is the only one who looks up as he leaves, but even he doesn't lift his head. As he stands outside, Ricky hears the men sing louder now he's gone, silly munchkin voices gabbling on about dead witches. Tonight there'll be fireworks and tomorrow sore heads and more debt. Ricky looks up at the heavens. There's a streak of blue emerging from the cloud, a bright sapphire river winding through granite sky. He zips his coat up and pulls his scarf tight because, despite this scant promise of the coming spring, it's still punishingly cold for April.

4

Miley Cyrus Fault

Where Are You

so heavy my head feels like a bag of bricks wed say that after a night on the town bottle after bottle of Cristal line after line so high we always came down with a bang waking up with a head like a bag o bricks our curtained room migraine bright let alone studio whites and strobes at some photo shoot for a lads mag I still remember that stuff which lighting and lenses made me look best less like me and more like someone good you know someone who matters someone people would want to look at know about emulate no one would want to do that now would they look at me a beached whale lump with train track stretch marks and other tracks worse sinister reminders almost faded but there nonetheless the itching talking just below the skin reminding me of what I did of how awful I am unworthy useless senseless stupid mare Ive tried to make sense of it all but I cant I was given a chance and I blew it why would God give me a chance if I was just supposed to end up here in a one up one down on a grimy terrace in Sheffield for fucks sake isnt it meant to be MAL-IBU or CANNES or somewhere I dont know my head is so so heavy and its not HIS fault I know everyone says it is Mum and Kelly and all my friends not that Ive got any of them any more but I did have 350k followers when I came out of THE HOUSE 150K more than the winner that stupid hippy cow with her save the world crap peace love and harmony fuck off I didnt even have the energy to save myself let alone the fucking rain forest 300k more than HE ever got people follow you to vent their hate and sometimes it felt like every single one of those 350K hated me they told me often enough shut up you silly bitch no one cares what you think you shouldnt even open your trout pout mouth youve no right to have an opinion you are a waste of space ugly no talent cunt why dont you just DIE and they turned out to be right about that didnt they I was clever and thin when I auditioned but I was never what youd call beautiful not like ANGELINA or VICTORIA or anyone like that and I didnt have the boobs then and I didnt have the hips and the boys didnt come and call much eight A stars that was the prediction 8 A stars and five years at law school thats what Mum and Dad wanted Id be finished now if Id done what I was supposed to do Im 25 and if Id done what Mum and Dad wanted Id be a lawyer with a swanky flat of my own in town with a concierge called Mack and a new car a PORSCHE or a MERCEDES and holidays in the BAHAMAS and BAJA but I didnt want that when I was 18 back then it looked like a life sentence of hard work and that woman saw me serving coffees in STARBUCKS and singing the orders cos thats what I did when I was a teenager I sang in the hope that constant chirping would stop the dull ache in my chest she had on a cream suit and you could tell it was designer and not knock off and she gave me her card with her long red nails and she said you should make an audition tape back home we argued and Mum cried and I promised that Id take my exams in a year if I got inside because Id make all the money Id need and more to pay the tuition fees cos its not only the show is it its the photo shoots and the articles in *Heat* and the chat shows and if Im lucky record deals and acting jobs thats what I thought anyway a number one single and a few hundred grand for exclusive interviews a regular part in a soap then HOLLYWOOD and Mum and Dad agreed so long as I promised to go back and do my exams and I meant it when I promised but I never did go back I broke that promise right off and I remember Mum coming to the flat one morning after a party and there were bodies everywhere and lines of coke and half empty bottles of Cristal and a pop star passed out naked in the bath and she stepped through it all like a fairy godmother offering me a chance to get out and looked me in the eye and said when are you coming home to take your exams and I just laughed in her face and told her I couldnt I couldnt give it all up and she looked round the place and pulled a grim little face and turned and walked away we made up later when I found out about PETAL and HE left and I really needed her but for a while we didn't talk it was hard and they printed that picture of her in the sidebar of shame coming out of ASDA in jogging bottoms and fake UGG boots and she wouldnt have been seen dead in them if Id been there but HE was everything then and so even though she looked about a hundred years old and was obviously sick with worry I just carried on regardless parties clubs premieres fashion shoots get your tits out for the lads and for thousands in the bank laughing all the way when I was at school the populars used to trip me up pull my hair call me fatso and slag send me texts and leave scary whispered messages on my voicemail this one girl Imelda she was the worst we were friends when we were little but something happened between juniors and seniors and she hated me hated me she was a big boobed cow udders they were and the boys all looked at them bobbing up and down when she walked tongues hanging out and the girls all looked at them too because we couldnt believe they didnt hurt must have been hard for her no one ever looking her in the eye she really had it in for me spread rumours about me sleeping with Kevin Churchill when I was 13 13 for Gods sake I couldnt even look in the general direction of someone like Kevin Churchill when I was 13 I barely had the confidence to speak out in class thats what all my teachers said back then she needs to put her hand up in class we know she knows the answers wish I knew the effing answers now Imelda really had it in for me think she fancied Kevin Churchill though because he got her pregnant when she was 16 we both have babies now no partners and no jobs so I guess we are the same me and Imelda Ive only had three lovers people think Im a slag but thats it three Im not exactly KATIE PRICE am I Im not counting the girl I only did that because HE wanted me to not that it wasnt soft and nice and tender but I wouldnt have done it unless HE asked HE was everything but HE went and told the press about it column inches were important to both of us back then and HE said HE did it for me for us but it was just for HIMSELF really I see that now eyelids heavy Ill text her soon then Ill be all right everything will work out so when I had my 350k followers MAX said I should try for a singing career like Miley Cyrus I could sing Id shown that when I was in THE HOUSE Moon River with Pedro on Spanish guitar saved me from getting voted off one week I think it was that or the bikini that wasnt my idea by the way that was the production company they told us what to do and what to wear a lot of the time people dont realise that but I would have worn normal clothes given the choice I was bloody freezing for the whole five weeks I was in there but the bikinis were part of the deal MAX was part of the deal too they have it all planned they hold your hand as they strap you into the rollercoaster I used to love rollercoasters when I was a kid my dad took me to BLACKPOOL PLEASURE BEACH every year wed go on all the rides and eat candyfloss and then catch the bus up the GOLDEN MILE after sunset THE BIG ONE runs high along the beach so high you feel like youre flying like youre one of the gulls soaring over the irish sea as it churns below and your rickety old car seems to slow down so you can breathe calm and clear air fresher than summer rain then suddenly youre whiplashed to the right ribs bashing against the car against each other and you laugh and you scream until your lungs burst let me off let me off but it doesnt stop it just goes faster and faster and louder and louder scary and hilarious all at the same time but that was nothing compared to being in THE HOUSE and what happens after that THE BIG ONE was the last time

I had a clear head not now heavy now heavy but shell be here soon I cant call 999 myself that wont work and Im sorry for her that shell have to find me like this but it will all work out I just need enough cash to get out of this mess one national exclusive a couple of TV interviews LORRAINE maybe I always liked LORRAINE she never judged and I saw her at a few parties full of fun and love Id like my own show like hers I could do that after Ive never been starstruck so I wouldnt get all tongue tied interviewing anyone famous like MILEY CYRUS I could have her on weve so much in common or we will have when people give a shit again maybe when SHES older me and PETAL can go on the rides at Blackpool and SHELL lift HER arms in the air and scream if you scream if you scream if you want to go faster heavy so heavy its the Nembutal I got it on the internet the doctor told me to get some exercise and eat vegetables hed only give me Temazepam at the lowest dose and that wouldnt have done so Ive mixed them and two bottles of Chardonnay and some paracetamol to make it look authentic like Im serious and my head is almost too heavy to lift so I know its the right dose shell be here soon shes got PETAL and it must be nearly time for HER tea so I know shell check her phone she normally rings me when shes got PETAL and lets HER talk to me I told her I had a job interview I did actually for a receptionist at a dentists I have very good teeth got them all veneered with my first six figure cheque natural though not neon bright like some deranged alien see me coming before Im in the room cant face working in a dentists was all set to go then got caught up reading tweets about MILEY CYRUS Imelda and those bitches she hung out with I went into THE HOUSE to escape all that but I should have known at the interview when they got us to vote each other out of the running asked us questions about secrets and sex and what wed do for money anything I said except kill someone HA! no one mentioned suicide my head is so so heavy now eyelids shell be here soon the crowd brayed for blood when I walked up those steps but they clapped and whistled too and there were lights and flashes and that music and they were all looking at me taking pictures of me and I knew Id be in the papers and Imelda would see and the bitches would see and I liked that idea those cows too green to eat their Special K over the morning news shell be here soon it was their idea to get us to pretend to have sex you all thought we really did it but we didnt they talked about it before we went in told us who and how and how long and you all bought it like the spoonfed morons you are I had the highest IQ of any contestant ever in THE HOUSE they test you when you pass the first interview but it didn't stop me falling in love with HIM did it and it didnt stop me being hated by 2.3 million viewers who all applauded when HE dumped me on air

HE told me they made HIM do that too when we got out and it was all fairy tale for a while but like I said it was only column inches to HIM and it wouldnt have mattered if Id released that single as planned it was okay you know not crap I can sing but PETAL came and that was a shock and Max said I couldnt go on tour with a fat belly or a kid not for a debut and when I wouldnt get rid of her he dumped me they both did the money went quick without Max as back up there were a couple of my heartbreak spreads I did for cash even though I didnt want to go over it all again but I dont get any money from HIM and only the best for PETAL and no one cares enough to pay any more I don't see how HE can bear not to see HER SHES HIS too when SHE smiles its like a hot water bottle around your heart MILEY CYRUS though 15 million hits for sticking her tongue out and her scrawny butt up for all the dirty old men I can do that again I can easily lose this baby fat and Ive got my 34GGs now I can do a diet and exercise DVD Mum will find me and theyll pump my stomach and Ill emerge bravely from intensive care into camera flashes and goodwill on TWITTER my fingers are heavy eyes wont stay open shell be here soon unless cant think about that its all MILEY CYRUS fault

Message Failed To Send. Retry?

5

The Typewriter

His mother tells him his name – Joaquín – means 'God's choice'. Lately, he finds himself pondering the exact nature of this Divine dilemma. Does it mean that he himself is chosen – for some higher purpose? Did Elvira have the heads-up from on high that her only son was going to be someone special? Or is it simply this: that his very existence was not his mother's choice but God's?

He has known for some time that his birth wasn't planned. Elvira refuses to talk about it but in his imagination he has joined the dots in a tale of shame and exile. He knows that his presence in her belly caused her to flee her home when she was only 16 and settle here in the city of Saint Francis. He doesn't know if he was supposed to be born here, but he was, and is that peculiar hybrid – an Amexican.

The overweight couple at the end of the bar drain their cocktails and finish the complimentary snacks. Hubby has beads of perspiration on his pale forehead. His military buzz cut makes his head look like a pencil eraser. He turns his piggy eyes to Joaquín, clicks his fingers and gestures at their empty glasses. He doesn't smile or say a word. Joaquín lifts the grease-stained goblets from the bar and places them under the counter with their last two. They're really going for the two-for-one offer – three margaritas each in an hour and it's not even three o'clock.

The bar is slightly off the tourist track and not on the shopping route. It's small and dingy but the owner has strung it with fairy lights and Day of the Dead decorations, and local artists paint Mexican icons on the outside wall in exchange for beer. In summer it hums night and day with hipsters looking for Latin authenticity, but these guys being here so near Christmastime means they're either lost or slumming it in a cheap neighbourhood hotel. They're not the usual clientele; in their late thirties – at a guess – not yet old but not making the best of themselves either. They are wearing matching Golden Gate T-shirts, which must be XXL, but still strain over their pillow-like chests. The man has boobs bigger than his wife's; hers have been consumed by her belly, his protrude over the sides. The wife is wearing fuchsia lipstick that makes her lips look tiny in the red enormity of her cheeks. The man coughs and, without actually looking at Joaquín, gravels, 'And a mixed combo and a basket o'fries to go with.'

'Oh, sugar,' purrs his wife, pawing his forearm, 'you read my mind.'

Joaquín sighs and writes the order. He'll be 26 next week, and if he's God's chosen one he hopes it's for something more than peddling heart attacks to Midwesterners.

Joaquín has just two hours between shifts but tonight he needs the comfort of home. He rushes up Mission Street and along 18th, his cheeks burning with cold and sweat as he mounts the stone steps to the fourth floor of the red-brick he calls home. Twenty families live here, four apartments on each floor and an attic conversion. There's barely 400 square feet each and he's suffocated by the lack of space. He can hear the mealtime rituals as he passes his neighbours' door, children laughing, pans clinking, Domingo playing his accordion, Anna-Maria singing along. Elvira is cooking too; he unlocks the door to mouth-watering aromas and condensation blisters the windows of their tiny apartment.

'Hi, honey,' chirps Elvira as he comes in. 'Didn't expect to see you this evening.'

The Killers' 'When You Were Young' is blasting from the stereo; Elvira wiggles and joins in the chorus. His mother's youth never ceases to amaze Joaquín; he feels as though he is catching her up and soon he'll be older than she is.

He remembers when one of his college friends came to visit and was waiting for him to finish his shift so they could go to dinner. Elvira had come in the bar to meet them and, not realising she was Joaquín's mother, his friend had pointed her out with some crude sexual intention. The dinner was a disaster; his friend couldn't look either of them in the eye, barely spoke and was never heard of again. Elvira's hot stuff, but as far as Joaquín knows he is the only man in her life and lately this abstinence has worried him. That and the gun he recently found in her closet.

He slumps at the table with his chin on his hands. Elvira pulls him a beer from the refrigerator and kisses the top of his head.

'You look tired. You feeling okay?'

'Mmm.'

'You want something to eat? There's mole.'

Soon they're sitting opposite each other with steaming bowls of chicken and sauce and more beer. The meat is sweet and melts on his tongue with a fizz of spice. He is suddenly ravenous and lifts forkfuls rapidly into his mouth. Elvira watches him like a bird.

'Hey, slow down, you'll give yourself heartburn.'

'It's delicious. You should write a cookery manual.'

She beams at him and rubs sauce from his cheek with her thumb.

'How was your day?'

'Oh man, there was this couple in the bar, they were enormous, big fat pigs, and they must've gone through four margaritas each and two combos and fries. They didn't speak, barely even to each other, just consumed.'

He snorts over his bowl and Elvira laughs.

'You shouldn't be so cruel, they're probably very nice people.'

'Well the only tip they left was to tell me to *cheer up – it might never happen!*'

He wipes his mouth, staining the napkin with piquant flecks.

'How about you; how goes it with the rich people?'

Elvira is a cleaner at one of the grand houses on the Heights. She's worked there for five years; since the green card came through. The house belongs to Reyes Delgado White (Ray), an immensely successful publisher. Ray's father was Fernando Delgado, a Mexican screenwriter with a bunch of Oscars to his name. Fernando was a favourite of Joaquín's. He was jumping with excitement when he found out his mother's new employer was the son of one of his literary heroes. The story is well known; in 1950 Fernando took some friends into Mexico to celebrate New Year only to be refused re-entry to the US. He was exiled for six months while MGM pulled out all the stops to get him back. He used the time to write what many consider to be the great American novel. A study in dispossession so powerful it won the Pulitzer.

Joaquín would kill to be published by Ray. He once persuaded Elvira to ask him to read his manuscript. He had it printed and bound professionally at great expense and gave it to her to take to work the next day. He waited nervously for a week and when no phone call came he asked his mother if she'd remembered to give it to Ray.

'Sí,' she said. 'He said he'd gladly read it and he put it on the very top of his in-tray.'

That was four years ago.

'Ray's got a new piece for his collection.'

Joaquín sits up, suddenly less fatigued.

'When I got in this morning he told me there was a very expensive type-writer on his desk that I wasn't to touch. "Clean around it," he said, "and what-ever you do don't take off the cover." So, I got round to his office and there it was, but it didn't look expensive, it was just a tiny little thing in a blue plastic case, all frayed and dirty at the edges. It didn't look like it was worth anything; in fact, it looked like he should throw it in the dumpster.'

Ray collects literary memorabilia. Elvira told Joaquín about the collection in the office on her first day. Ray had given her the tour so she knew its value. Elvira couldn't tell him much except that the things once belonged to famous authors and that they looked like junk. Some of it was in sealed glass cabinets. There was even a shotgun. He pressed her for information and the next day after work she'd said there was a name on the brass plaque under the firearm. On hearing that name, Joaquín realised that Ray's collection was very special indeed.

'Hmm. I wonder? He couldn't have, could he? You say it cost $245,000?'

'You know what it is?'

'It was on the news. A famous author's typewriter sold at auction to an anonymous bidder. What make is it?'

'Oh wait, it did say on the case – Olivera or something.'

'Olivetti! Oh my God. He did. $245,000! What does it look like?'

'I told you, it looks like doggy do. Why, whose was it?'

'Cormac McCarthy's.'

He expects her to roll her eyes the way she does when she doesn't know what he's talking about, to say *who?* But instead she says, 'The guy who wrote *The Road*?'

Joaquín narrows his eyes.

'Among better books,' he says.

'I don't see how they could be better.'

'*You've* read *The Road*?'

'You're not the only one in the family who can read, you know. I think I taught you.'

'Really? I thought I learnt in school.'

Elvira throws her hands up in the air in mock indignation.

'You could read before you went to school and you didn't just wake up one day able to do it. Do you really think I'm so stupid I can't read a book?'

'Of course I know you can read. I just thought Harlequins were more your thing.'

They glare at each other and Elvira gets up to clear the plates.

'Well, it was on Oprah's Book Club.'

Joaquín laughs. 'Oprah's Book Club! I knew it.'

Elvira slaps the back of his head as she takes his plate.

'Don't be such a little snotnose.'

She clatters the china into the sink and sits back down, bringing a cup of coffee with her.

'Did you see the movie?' she asks.

'No, I didn't see the movie and I won't be seeing it.'

'Why not? It was great, the little boy was unbelievable.'

'Unbelievable isn't good in an actor,' says Joaquín. 'Movies are never as good as the books they're based on – not once in the whole history of cinema has the movie ever come close.'

Elvira stirs sugar into her coffee and screws up her mouth as she does when she's thinking of what to say.

'Ha! *The Wizard of Oz*.' She bangs the table. '*The Wizard of Oz* is a better movie.'

'Yeah yeah and *Toy Story 2*.'

'Well, I liked it. I cried. So sad at the end when the father dies, but happy too because now the boy will be looked after.'

'He will?'

'Si – same as the book. He goes away with the good family and the dog.'

'But... it's still the end of the world! Even if they are good – and that's debatable – no one's going to survive long.'

'Huh? How do you make that out? That boy lives. He's like Jesus, a saviour. The good guys win. It said so on Oprah.'

'Oprah! The boy isn't like Jesus. I didn't think there was anything religious in the book at all.'

'Don't be ridiculous, the boy is the Messiah, he's going to save the world. Besides, Oprah interviewed the writer on television – such a nice old man, so clean and handsome – and he said that the book was religious. His kid goes to Catholic school and he regularly attends Mass.'

'NOW he does, probably because he's REALLY old. There isn't any God in any of his other books and there isn't in this one. I don't even think it's about the future; it's what's happening now, good people getting fucked over by fat-cat cannibals, like Ray for example. You've worked for Ray for five years, cleaning up his mess for peanuts, and he spends a quarter of a million on a typewriter,' he clicks his fingers, 'like it's nothing.'

She takes his hand and studies his face.

'How did my happy little boy get to be so bitter?'

He doesn't answer.

'Ray doesn't pay peanuts. He's a good employer and a good man.'

'Ray, Ray, Ray. I swear to God you're in love with Ray.'

She frowns and then, even though they both know they aren't really talking about the book anymore, she adds quietly, 'Sometimes people are just good, like the boy's father.'

'Well I wouldn't know about that, would I? I don't have a father – good or bad.'

She pulls her hand away.

'Jaq, don't.'

'Elvira, I need to know. I'm a big boy now. I can handle it.'

She is shaking; her crucifix earrings betraying the involuntary trembling of her body.

'I can't,' she says. 'I just can't. Not yet.'

How'd you get to be so bitter?

It's a quiet night at the bar and Joaquín has plenty of time to think about his mother's question between customers.

He was the bright kid at school, after all. An avid reader and writer from an early age, he earned a scholarship to a good school and then went on to Irvine to study creative writing. Even with funding, money was tight and he had to tend bar every night just to get by, but his college years were the best of his life, bar none. His tutors salivated over everything he wrote. He got top marks, edited the faculty journal and was regularly published in minor literary magazines. And the girls! He couldn't believe his sudden attractiveness to women after years of being sidelined as the geek; those beautiful sun-kissed muses who talked about Sylvia Plath into the early hours and then fucked him into exhaustion.

Joaquín left college with a novel his professor described as 'a work of shattering genius' that would, if there were any justice in the world, be 'snapped up immediately'. In the following year, his masterwork was rejected by 104 publishers. He's kept all the letters; they're in a lever file under his bed. His dreams were buried incrementally under a pile of yellowing correspondence. Most of the rejections opened with the memorable words:

We hope you don't take this personally but…

As if he could do anything but that.

After 12 months, Joaquín had stopped writing altogether. He pretends he's still a writer but he knows he's just a bartender, because when he sits down at his keyboard nothing comes to him. He surfs the net, mails his friends, downloads music and porn – occasionally he'll write a paragraph but after reading it through he deletes it.

He's only met Ray the once, on Christmas Eve three years ago. On that day, Elvira had called to say she needed a lift home as Ray had given her a Christmas gift too big for her to carry. Ray's gifts were always extravagant; last year she got a cashmere sweater and at Easter she brought home a chocolate hamper so enormous she had to give most of it away. Joaquín has always been suspicious of Ray's generosity in this regard. He doesn't understand why he just doesn't pay her more instead of all these grand gestures. He wonders what Ray's motives are, if he expects a special something from Elvira in return.

Joaquín resented driving to Pacific Heights because his mother's employer didn't have the foresight to buy her a present she could carry home. He was snippy with Elvira on the phone and when she wasn't outside waiting for him his mood worsened. It was freezing in the car, his breath fogged the air and his fingers throbbed inside his thin woollen gloves. Elvira didn't answer her cell so he got out and strode towards Ray's gate.

'I'm here for Elvira,' he said to the voice on the intercom and the doors swung open with no further question.

He looked up at the tall, elegant house with its blindingly whitewashed walls and art-deco windows and the holly wreath that probably cost a day of his wages, and he felt an extreme resentment that it belonged to Ray and not him.

The front door opened and there was Elvira holding a huge wrapped box. She had her back to him and was chatting brightly to someone inside. He mounted the steps and Ray came into view. He was younger than Joaquín had expected, around 50, a gringo in Ralph Lauren – an open-neck shirt hanging loose over casual pants – effortless but expensive. He had a slight paunch and a full, amiable face surrounded by a mop of salt-and-pepper curls. His arm was wrapped around a thin, blonde woman wearing a black turtleneck and jeans. She was incredibly beautiful; the type of woman you usually only see on the big screen. At that moment he hated Ray more than anyone on earth. To him, Ray had everything he wanted and almost certainly had never worked for any of it.

'You ready,' he said as Elvira turned to his footsteps. 'I'm freezing to death out here.'

Ray and his wife kissed Elvira goodbye and wished Joaquín a merry Christmas, but he was already walking through the gate, leaving his mother to struggle with the box. He opened the car door and turned back to take the gift from his now frowning mother as the gate swept shut behind her.

'I didn't bring you up to be so rude,' she said.

They travelled home in silence and he sulked in front of the TV with a six-pack until his mother went alone to midnight Mass.

When Elvira went back to work after Christmas, she found Ray drunk under his desk, crying for the loss of his wife, who had left him for his latest discovery, a young poet called Elizabeth. This news filled Joaquín's heart with joy.

Joaquín stands on the BART surrounded by shoppers and drunken office-workers. A young woman wearing a tinsel crown and smelling of cherries is pushed up against him so tightly it should be indecent. She smiles and says, 'Merry Christmas,' her eyes full of amusement. He looks away at the advertisements above the train doors. One is for the DVD of *The Road*; boy and man bound together in grainy misery, pale and skeletal, wrapped in colourless refugee clothes. The world burns behind them but they are eternally together, always connected.

Joaquín's footsteps echo on the stone floor of the church. The interior glows with candlelight, organ music reverberates tangibly around the walls – a Christmas carol unrecognisable without the words. The parish priest, Father Miguel, who Joaquín knows as Uncle Mike, is standing at the altar rail talking to a woman arranging statues around a crib. It's as if they are planning a battle. Mike looks up when he hears the footsteps, surprise crossing his face.

'Hi, Uncle Mike,' says Joaquín.

'Joaquín?' he says. 'We don't often see you here. Is anything wrong?' His smile rises and falls with his words.

'I need to know about my father and I'm not leaving this time until you tell me,' says Joaquín abruptly.

Mike shows him into the sacristy, the cold, monastic cell Joaquín came to every Sunday as an altar boy, even when his 17-year-old limbs were too long for the largest cassock. He made the decision not to return the day he left for Irvine, and never has. Until now.

'Please, sit.'

Mike offers him a cigarette.

'Thanks.'

'Shouldn't you be asking Elvira?'

Joaquín's hands shake as he leans forward to Mike's lighter; the cigarette glows like a dying sun.

'You know I've tried, Mike. She still won't talk about it. It's killing me. I can't sleep. I can't write. I feel like I don't belong anywhere.'

'Even so, Jaq, it's your mother's story to tell, not mine. Ask her again.'

'I asked her yesterday. She shut me down immediately. It's driving a wedge between us.' His eyes are desperate, pleading. 'I need to know what was so terrible about my father that she shakes when I mention him, even after all this time. Did you know that she keeps a gun in the closet? Was he a murderer or something?'

Mike sighs and pulls over a chair to sit opposite his nephew.

'I'd hoped she would tell you herself. Be prepared, Jaq. It isn't a pleasant story, but perhaps it is finally the time to tell it.'

Joaquín nods.

'She was fifteen years old. A really clever girl. We all hoped she'd be the first in the family to go to college.

'Papa had a music shop in Tijuana, just off Avenida Revolución. Elvira loved that shop, there were always musicians playing inside. And she loved Papa – she was a real daddy's girl. She often went there on the way back from school to hang out and come home with him when he closed up. On this particular day they had a little row about something – a boy, make-up – it doesn't matter what. Elvira left the shop to go home alone. There were three boys outside, between bars, Americans. Elvira said they weren't much older than she was. They stank of booze and she was afraid of them. She hurried away but they followed her, calling for her to keep them company. She tried to shake them off by cutting down side streets, getting further and further away from home. Eventually, they caught her and dragged her into an alleyway.'

Father Mike pauses; Joaquín's expression doesn't change.

'She was missing for hours. It was brutal, Joaquín. She was unconscious by the end. She said she woke up in the dark and crawled her way into town. A tourist picked her up and took her to the police, who called Papa. A few days later they told him there was nothing they could do. Elvira's descriptions were too vague – three drunk American boys, probably way over the border by then.

'It nearly killed Papa. He felt guilty about letting her leave the shop alone, and, in a way, I think Elvira did blame him a little. She withdrew into herself, didn't go out, didn't talk. The family assumed it was just shock, that with time and care she'd get over it.

'She kept the pregnancy secret for six months. Papa noticed first. One morning in the kitchen, the button of her school dress popped and rolled across the floor.'

Mike picks at something infinitesimal on his trousers before continuing in the same level tone he has used throughout.

'There was a family conference. It was decided to send her here, to have the baby in America so I could find a good family for adoption. By the time she went into labour we had it all set up; you were going to a nice young couple who couldn't have kids of their own. I remember that the husband was a doctor. That way Elvira could go back home, finish school and carry on. But when she saw you that was it. She held you close and said, "I'll call him Joaquín." The couple moved away soon afterwards.'

Joaquín sits in silence. His cigarette is a smoking stub. A tear slides from his eye.

'You pretty much know the rest. She lived as an illegal until you were 21 and could sponsor her citizenship. There was no more school for Elvira, just cleaning for parishioners and looking after you.'

There's a knock on the sacristy door. 'Father Miguel?' It's the woman from the altar.

'Just a minute.'

Mike squeezes Joaquín's shoulder.

'So, now you know what Elvira did for you. It's your story, Jaq, good or bad. Maybe now it's time to do something more with your life than tend bar and screw tourists.'

Joaquín walks home. Finally, he knows who he is – the boy with no father. A maelstrom is pounding in his head. He sees everyone on the streets as potential. He'd be in his forties now. One of three rapists. The one with the most aggressive sperm. This guy here, maybe? A bus passes, scattering water droplets from a puddle onto a traffic cop's trousers. The bus driver? That cop? The businessman obscured by the black windows of his limousine? The chauffeur? This schoolteacher leaving the school gates? Everyone and no one – one drunken attack put down to spring-break high jinks and then a guilt-free life? Maybe he did it every week. Maybe Joaquín has a hundred half-breed brothers. A murderer would have been easier to take.

His heart knocks. He stops to catch his breath by a bus shelter and sees the poster again. The boy and the man look out at him in post-apocalyptic unity.

Elvira isn't home. He runs to her closet and takes down the shoebox. He removes the gun and holds the cold metal in his hands. He's just hidden it under his pillow when she comes in. She stands at his bedroom door chewing her nail.

'I spoke to Mike. He said you visited. He said I should talk to you. You okay?'

She looks like a child and, after years of desperately needing to talk, he can't think of anything to say. Did Mike tell her he knew? What good would it do, making her relive it all now? He nods.

'I'll be okay.'

He can feel the gun underneath the pillow poking into his shoulder. Suddenly an idea comes to him.

'Elvira, will you do something for me?'

Ray's house is quiet. Elvira shuts the door and looks nervously down the hall.

'Ray should be out but you can't stay long. Ten minutes at the most and don't touch anything.'

'I just want to see it. I'll be out in a flash.'

'His office is down there on the left.'

She leaves him in the hall, taking the stairs to what he assumes is the kitchen. He hears the hum of a vacuum cleaner, walks softly towards Ray's office and pushes open the door.

Elvira was right. At first it doesn't look like much. The blinds are drawn, casting light like ruled paper onto the white carpet. There's a large wooden desk in front of the window with an overflowing in-tray. The walls are covered with picture frames and on the left is a mounted shotgun. Two tall glass cases stand between the door and the desk. Joaquín goes over to the first. Inside there's an old leather collar on a plush cushion, sturdy and thick, designed for a big dog. The brown leather has worn into ridges, so cracked in places it's almost white, and the huge brass buckle and lead ring are tinged with green. There's a buffed nameplate elaborately engraved:

C. Dickens Esq./Gad's Hill Place, Higham.

He moves on to the second exhibit: a silver cigarette case propped open on a velvet stand. Small and delicate, the silver pearlised on the inside, still containing two yellow-papered cigarettes. The inscription reads:

To Gold Hat, Always, Zelda.

He walks around the room looking at the frames; letters from Jane Austen and J. D. Salinger, an Arthur Rackham drawing of Salome, a signed photograph of Kerouac, multiple letters of authentication, endless testaments of worth.

To the desk – and there it is.

The cover has been removed. Like Elvira said, it's tiny; a flimsy collection of plastic letters configured on a metal frame, the blue paint worn to silver at its edges. The finger touches of 5 million words are written across it in decay. There's a sheet of paper threaded inside with a line of faint script. Joaquín smiles – Ray's been trying it out. He stretches his index finger towards the I…

'Who the hell are you?'

Joaquín looks up and sees Ray glaring at him from the doorway.

'I…'

He begins to explain but can't. What could possibly justify this intrusion? How could he ever be deemed worthy of occupying the same space as these artefacts? He's lost for words. He reaches into his jacket pocket and pulls out Elvira's gun. Ray starts, his eyes as wide as a bullfrog's, and holds up his hands.

'In,' says Joaquín, gesturing with the weapon like a dime-store hood, 'and close the door.'

Ray does as he's told, but Joaquín can see he's regaining his composure by the second as he takes the measure of the young man before him. He hasn't shaved but he's hardly gangster material; Elvira still irons his T-shirts. Ray's stare is level and there's a hint of a smile on his lips. 'What now?' he says calmly, nodding towards the typewriter. 'You'll have to shoot me if you think you're getting out of here with that.'

Joaquín tries to speak but his mouth is too dry. It was a mistake to come here – with Elvira's gun! A mistake to press Mike about his father. He should have just left it alone. Now there are more questions than answers. What did he think? That the typewriter Cormac McCarthy used to create a modern masterpiece about paternal love would make everything all right? That somehow, possession of it would mean that having a violent rapist for a father wouldn't matter anymore? If he'd taken it as he planned, could he have written his best work? Erased his past with each strike of the keys? Would the resulting manuscript the object of a bidding war, a multi-million bestseller, the subject of endless articles about its genesis? And would Ray have forgiven him? Published his work? Then, a little time later, married Elvira, all of them spending Christmas together at the mansion, Ray treating him like a son?

A ridiculous fantasy. Even if he had managed to get the typewriter out undiscovered, Elvira wouldn't have let him keep it. She'd have made him take it back, like she did when he was seven and stole a candy bar from the local store. Ray wouldn't have been as sympathetic as that shop owner. She'd have lost her job. He'd have gone to prison. But for a few hours, all Joaquín could think about was picking up that 50-year-old typewriter, walking out of Ray's house with it and taking it home.

'Hey, it's Elvira's boy, isn't it?' says Ray. 'The writer?'

Joaquín nods, lowering the gun a little. Ray lowers his hands.

'I get it, she told you about the typewriter. All you had to do was ask. Why'd you bring the gun?'

'You might have said no, then I'd never have seen it.'

He waves the gun, which is suddenly too heavy to hold still.

'What makes you think I'd say no?'

'You'd probably say yes, then forget about it, like you did with my manuscript.'

'Your manuscript? But I…'

Joaquín's eyes flick to the in-tray on Ray's desk.

'Oh.' Ray smiles. 'I rarely read *anything* I'm given right away. I have assistants to do that. *Please, don't take it personally.* Well, look. If that's what this is about, maybe…'

Joaquín bangs the gun hard on the desk, pushing the heel of his free hand against his forehead.

'Fuck. You fuck. You didn't even read it! Who do you think you are? It was four fucking years ago!'

He sights Ray with renewed purpose, the gun now as light as paper.

Whatever could have happened next is thwarted by the door flying open. Joaquín swings the gun round. Elvira storms in.

'Joaquín, you said ten…'

She stops when she sees the gun, which is now pointing at her. The next few seconds are a blur. Ray grabs the shotgun from the wall, cocks it and swings it towards Joaquín.

There are two shots, the second louder than the first.

One nicks into the wall above Elvira's head, sending out a little puffball of plaster. The second brings down half the ceiling. The falling mortar sounds like a sudden dry rainfall. Everything is shrouded in white debris.

Joaquín and Ray look at each other. There is a moment's static as they gauge they are unharmed, then they both look at Elvira. She's lying motionless in the doorway.

'Elvira!'

'Mama!'

They run to the door. Ray jumps over her into the hall, kneels and gently lifts her head onto his lap.

'Elvira, honey,' he coos, 'speak to me. Speak to me.'

Joaquín crouches at her side, his ear to her chest, then frantically kneads her hand.

'Mama – no – Mama?'

Elvira breathes in heavily, coughs and opens her eyes. Dazed, she stares up at Ray and then at Joaquín. She shakes her head and scrambles backwards, extricating herself from the hands of the men. Scuttling into the hall, she stands unsteadily, holding onto the wall for support. Her face is burning with anger.

'*¡Váyanse a la chingada, pendejos!*' she shouts, rubbing the back of her head. 'You two are fucking crazy.'

She runs up the hall, slamming the front door behind her.

Joaquín and Ray look at each other again. They are both covered head to toe in white dust. Only their gaping mouths and wide eyes provide any colour.

'She must've just fainted,' says Joaquín, blinking.

Ray laughs first, a small guffaw blossoming into an infectious, throaty chuckle.

'*¡Váyanse a la chingada, pendejos!*' he says, taking a handkerchief from his shirt pocket and wiping his face.

Joaquín smiles.

'*¡Váyanse a la chingada, pendejos!*' he repeats.

Soon they are giggling helplessly, their sides aching, tears streaking their powdered faces.

'Your mother is… feisty,' says Ray, getting to his feet, wiping his eyes and holding out his hand to Joaquín. 'I don't know about you, but I could use a drink.'

He steps back into the office and, after a brief glance at the front door, Joaquín follows. Ray pulls out the chair behind his desk.

'Here, sit down. Bourbon?'

Joaquín nods and sits.

The chair is made of dark wood and has a faded leather seat that squeaks as he swivels on the uneven feet. It's more comfortable than it looks.

'Did you just shoot at me with Hemingway's shotgun?'

Ray chinks ice into two tumblers.

'Well not the one he killed himself with, but his none the less. Like the chair? It was Steinbeck's.'

Joaquín almost upends the chair, then rubs his palms along the worn wooden arms.

'These glasses,' says Ray, handing one to his guest, 'belonged to Henry James and the bourbon was Raymond Carver's.'

'Ray, why do you have all this stuff?'

Ray sits opposite him at the desk and slugs his drink.

'You'll laugh if I tell you.'

'Try me.'

'You know who my father was, right?'

Joaquín nods. 'Who doesn't?'

'Well, he always talked about me as if I was going to do the same as he did and become some great American writer, churn out masterpieces with minimum effort, win a Pulitzer. It's incredibly rare you know, for a child of a genius to be one too. It almost never happens but I tried. I tried a million times to create something extraordinary and I just couldn't do it.'

He sighs.

'I'm a great publisher. I can spot genius a mile off but I can also tell when people don't have it and I – don't have it. Still, I didn't want to let old Fernando down so I thought if I had the things that belonged to great men, something of them might rub off on me. Maybe if I wrote sitting in Steinbeck's chair at Fitzgerald's desk with McCarthy's typewriter, I might just come up with something as great as they did. Maybe you thought the same.'

'And have you?'

'See for yourself.'

Joaquín looks down at the sheet of paper in the typewriter.

It was just like any old man's room

'What comes next?'

'Damned if I know,' says Ray, slugging his drink. 'That's as far as I've got and if I'm honest it's as far as I'm getting.'

He looks across at Joaquín as if seeing him for the first time.

'How about you decide? I dare you.'

'Really?'

'Sure, why not? Finish the sentence. And if I like it, you can carry on.'

Joaquín types. The keys stick, especially the space bar. Each decompression is an effort, each collection of letters in itself a hard-earned reward.

Ray walks round the desk and stands behind Joaquín watching the words appear on the page.

It was just like any old man's room; a gunshot wound in the ceiling and a bullet hole in the wall.

Ray looks at Joaquín, and nods, expectation on his face.

'I like it.' He smiles. 'Keep going until Mr McCarthy's typewriter tells you to stop.'

Joaquín looks down at the typewriter, stretches his fingers like a concert pianist and lets it guide them deftly over its keys.

THE END

Note: Cormac McCarthy's 1963 Olivetti manual typewriter was sold in auction at Christie's New York on 4 December 2009. Its reserve was $15,000, but it was bought by an anonymous bidder for $245,000. McCarthy told reporters that having written over 5 million words on his old Olivetti, the keys had started to stick and he had decided that it was time to get a new one. A friend bought him a replacement for $20. It is widely believed that the anonymous bidder was the actor Tom Hanks, who has a vast typewriter collection, but this has never been confirmed.

6

The Unstoppable Roar of the Universe

'Yes, we're fully accessible,' says David into the phone. I look up because, after the initial bumpkin 'Hullo', he has put on his country-squire accent that he uses to take restaurant bookings. 'We were modernised earlier this year,' he continues, 'all open plan, everything on the same level, not even a step into the...'

I watch David listening to the reply, a faint expression of concern crossing his features.

'Oh, I see.' He gives a throaty cough. 'Well, it's there if he needs it.'

He catches sight of me watching and shoos me back to work as he says, 'Not at all, it will be an honour.'

The kitchen already smells of lunchtime. Huge pots of meat and gravy broil on the stoves and steam puffs to the extractor fans. The pie dishes are ready to fill and fluffy puddings are rising in the ovens. 'As good food as you are likely to find this side of Southwold.' That's what *The Good Beer Guide* said about my work. Course, that was a year ago, before I went away. I get the feeling that since then my food, like its maker, has lost some of its enthusiasm.

I hear David hang up and rub his hands together, then a loud knock at the front door. He unbolts it and lets Elena and Orson in. Elena is as beautiful as ever, elfin, sunbeams glinting on her shiny golden hair as she springs inside. Orson looks like a big, dirty bear beside her. They're laughing, and I realise they've arrived at work together every day since I've been back, even when I stayed at hers. I'd come into work at eight as usual, leaving her to slumber, and she's arrived with Orson at ten. I try to put this coincidence out of my mind; they live near each other, they start work at the same time, they bump into each other on the way... Elena looks over at me and raises her hand, her smile faltering.

'Ah, glad you're here,' says David. 'I've something to tell you. You too, Toby.'

In the bar, the smell of sunlight on polish makes me feel unaccountably queasy. The coolness of Elena's skin as I kiss her cheek instantly calms me, and she lets me hold her hand, which is rare lately. Orson, standing at her other side, winks at me.

'Morning, Jamie Oliver,' he says with a smirk. He's always taking the piss. I can't stand him, so I'm glad that I won't have to put up with him much longer. He's got a job in a fancy restaurant. He'll just be washing pots but he keeps telling us he'll be running the place within weeks.

David stands in front of us doing the full ex-army bit, shoulders back and chest out, as if he's about to send us on a mission.

'Now then, I have just taken a very special booking. I just had a call from Stephen Hawking's assistant. The great man himself is coming to our little establishment for lunch. Table for four at midday, himself, his assistant and his medics.'

David is grinning like the Cheshire Cat.

Elena looks amazed, like somebody took the oxygen away.

Orson snorts.

'Woohoo! Stephen Hawking! Coming here. Wait a minute. Can he even eat?'

David frowns, the whiskers of his walrus moustache drooping.

'Of course he can eat, Orson.'

'How though? Like a baby? Won't mind that you overcook it then, will he, Tobes?'

Orson smacks me on the back so hard I have to step out of rank. I hate it when he does that. David sighs.

'This is precisely why I called you in for a briefing. I want you on your best behaviour. No staring. No jokes. Just good service. I want the professor to think the Ship is the best little pub in the universe. Understood?'

We all nod, trying not to laugh. David is such a buffoon sometimes. *The best little pub in the universe!*

'Right.' I almost expect him to salute. 'You know what to do.' He actually clicks his heels together. We are dismissed.

Elena lets go of my hand and snaps her hair into a ponytail. Orson does actually salute the retreating David and then he drapes his arm over my shoulder, his cheek close to mine so I can smell his morning breath.

'Man's a genius,' he whispers. 'Not setting much of an example to the kids though, is he? Sitting in front of his computer all day.'

Elena and I groan.

'Are you going to do this all day, Orson? Because it's really childish.'

'Have to say though, Tobes, it's a big responsibility, cooking for the great man and not just because he's probably eaten in the best restaurants in the world. I mean, what if he chokes? It's your food. You've cooked it. You'd be responsible for killing the greatest scientist of our times. It would certainly put this place on the map. It would be all over the papers. You'd be famous – or infamous at any rate.'

He ambles off to the dresser to start work on the tables.

I feel sick.

'Shit,' I mutter.

Elena is grinning.

'Don't let him get to you,' she says. 'It's all front. He's probably scared of dropping gravy in his lap.'

I look over at Orson, who's whistling and happily throwing knives and forks into their respective drawers.

I grimace. 'You think?'

'You'll be fine,' she says, touching my arm like she used to. My stomach does a little flip.

Elena and I have been together since I was in Year 10. She has been my one and only girlfriend. Sounds a bit wussy, doesn't it? At my age it should be a different girl every week, but Elena arrived from the city when I was 15 and that was it. Besides, it's a small village and all the other girls are a bit, obvious, you know. But Elena, Elena is different.

I started working at the Ship when I dropped out of school. David did it as a favour to my dad, helping out a regular with a no-hoper son, but he was surprised how good a worker I was and I quickly moved from pot boy to sous-chef. I liked it, cooking; liked watching delicious meals slowly build from raw ingredients. Michael, the Ship's original chef, wasn't too adventurous and in truth he was a bit of an alky, but he taught me the basics. I used to go home and watch every cookery programme on telly and borrow all the books from the library. I enjoyed experimenting – a pinch of saffron for colour, harissa with chicken, chocolate with chilli, sea salt in desserts – then I'd try it all out on Elena. The way she used to close her eyes and smile when she liked something. She had this way of saying 'Mmmm' and biting her lip. It made me feel as though anything was possible. She said I was wasted as sous-chef, that I should tell David I was better than Michael. In the end, I didn't have to. Michael turned up too pissed to cook one Sunday and I had to take over. David had more compliments about the food that day than ever before. Michael was out and I was in.

I would have been happy with that, working at the Ship, spending my time off with Elena. I don't need much, a bit of money, Elena and a few hours a day outdoors. That's why I love it here. You can sit on a deserted beach for hours and not see a soul. I often do that after work, just sit and watch the ocean rolling away over the horizon. It's not enough for Elena though. She's a year younger than me but she's ambitious. In a month's time she's going to university to study journalism. I'm both happy and sad about this; happy because she's so excited and I want her to do well and sad because I don't want things to change. Things have changed too much already.

It was Elena who made me apply to college. After a year at the Ship I was accepted with a scholarship to Marten's Catering School in London. The kitchens at Marten's were enormous, full of students and chefs shouting at us, flames and clattering pans. London was just as bad, overwhelming noise and traffic and people. I spent most of my time in my room in the halls of residence. The other students were nice and friendly but if you made enough excuses they stopped asking you to go to the pub. I was there for six months. I rang Elena every day. I thought it might help me to feel at home, but after a few weeks she told me to stop, said she was too busy studying for her exams and besides, I wouldn't settle if my head was in Suffolk. Not contacting her didn't help though. At the Ship I could go at my own pace, make what I wanted, but at Marten's… One day I burnt my hand really badly, ended up in hospital. I suppose I had a breakdown. For a few days in the hospital bed I thought I was still in the kitchen with all the noise and flames. They kept me in for a few more weeks.

It's funny the professor coming here. I tried to read his book last year to impress Elena; she's well into all that astronomy stuff. I only understood a couple of sentences in the whole book. From what I could make out, the universe is a frightening and violent place – big bangs and supernovas, imploding stars and black holes – unimaginable noise and fire. That's what the kitchens at Marten's were like – a universe in turmoil.

After my episode, the doctors gave me pills and sent me home. Marten's said they'd keep my place open but I know I'll never go back. I've decided to look for work in Norwich, so I can be with Elena. She'll have someone with her when she starts uni, won't have to go it alone. I can't wait to see the look on her face when I tell her.

I can tell when our famous guest wheels in because a hush descends over the pub as Elena shows him to the private dining room. I hear David shouting what a pleasure it is, as if the professor is deaf as well as everything else. The wheelchair whirs past, accompanied by two men carrying medical bags. Through the kitchen hatch I catch sight of its leather headrest and the small head lolling against it, wisps of mousy hair sticking up as if attracted by static electricity. Then I hear the voice.

Orson crashes through the door with plates for the washer.

'Poor sod,' he says, 'the voice is wild! Like a human sat nav.'

Elena comes in with the order. As she clips it up, I catch Orson looking her up and down.

'He's adorable,' she says. 'I swear he's flirting with me. David is treating him like an imbecile. It's so embarrassing.'

Orson comes over and drapes his beary arm around her shoulders.

'Really, Elena? He seems a bit shifty to me – the way he keeps looking over his shoulder.'

He booms at his own 'joke' and, to my surprise, Elena giggles too and leans into him, like it's the most natural thing in the world.

When they've gone with the food I leave it a beat, then follow into the pub. I can see David, Elena and Orson through the dining-room door, standing at the professor's table, chatting and laughing; they obscure him but the flat buzz of the mechanical voice drifts indecipherably towards me.

The professor's party lingers as the lunch crowd dies down. Orson brings in the last of the plates.

'God, he's funny. Says he's feeling refreshed today, pressed F5 when he got up.'

A little voice in my head says, *Just fuck off and die Orson*, but then his face goes all serious.

'Sad though, all those brains but completely reliant on others.' He grins. 'He wants to see you.'

Me? What did I do? Is it the bolognese?

I walk over to the dining room with some trepidation. Elena is now sitting with Hawking's party; she looks apple-cheeked and glowing.

'Ah, Toby,' says David. 'The professor would like to meet you.'

'Stephen,' says the metallic voice.

I nod in greeting and he smiles. He looks frail, both saggy and jutting. His bottom teeth stick up over his lips like a terrier's and his head has collapsed onto his right shoulder – but his eyes! There's so much intelligence in those eyes I can't stop looking at them. I can see the whole of time and space recognised and understood. I am lost in those eyes.

I realise everyone is waiting for me to speak, looking at me expectantly. The silence ticks by. It should be something good, something clever, a question that probes the nature of the universe. My mind goes blank.

'So,' I say, 'did you enjoy your lunch?'

Back in the kitchen, Orson and Elena are teasing me.

'Got to hand it to you, Tobes,' scoffs Orson. 'You must really love your work. I mean, given access to the most intelligent man on earth, the only thing you can think to ask him about is pasta.'

He's shuffling around behind Elena as he clears plates from the worktops, closer than he needs to be, the space between his front and her back infinitesimally small. She sees me noticing. She moves away from the sink and comes towards me, no longer smiling. She stops just far enough away to be able to say quietly enough for Orson not to hear, 'Toby. We need to talk.'

We walk home together after work, across the marshes to the radio transmitters that used to send signals into space in the Cold War. Their metal rungs stretch high into the cloudless blue, like ladders to the stars. She stops under one of the tall iron towers, looming silently above us, now obsolete. Pulling up a blade of grass from the clump at the bottom of the tower, Elena picks off the seeds at the end and opens her hand to watch them scatter on the wind.

'Thing is, Tobes,' she says without looking at me, 'I've been seeing someone else.'

I say nothing, just watch the seeds flutter away from her fingers and disappear into the swaying grasses that surround us.

'Did you hear me, Toby? It's finished.'

She looks me in the eye and the earth and the sky seem to fly off in different directions, leaving me suspended in entropy. I can hear her saying my name, getting increasingly angry when I don't respond. All I can do is stare silently up at the towers. Perhaps if I stand perfectly still like this, as quiet as the void, then everything will be all right. I won't add the sound of an imploding heart to the unbearable crescendo of time and space, and in my own small way, I'll bring a moment of much needed hush to the unstoppable roar of the universe.

7

Scarlett Fever

It was a girl who took Christian to see his first Scarlett Johansson movie. She was small and dark and not at all like the woman who was to become the most important person in his life, save for his mother. They had only spoken on the phone before, the date having been suggested by mutual friends who said they were perfect for each other. The girl (whose name he can't now remember) had said she wouldn't mind seeing a movie. With the aid of the local paper, they ruled out *The Lord of the Rings* sequel and *The Matrix Revolutions* and he said he'd rather be boiled alive than watch a Jude Law film.

'You pick,' he said, 'surprise me. Whatever you choose will tell me something about you.'

She texted him the time and place at lunchtime on the day they had arranged to meet. Wednesday, 28th of January 2004; the first day of the rest of his life.

He grinned as he strode up the hill to the cinema, excited by the snowflakes elegantly descending from an almost violet sky. The south was braced for heavy snow brought on by biting Arctic winds and Christian wondered if he might have a good enough excuse to be off work the next day and also, if the date went well enough, whether the girl might stay home with him, cocooned in his bed against the elements. *Baby, It's Cold Outside.* He whistled the tune as he walked, just one detail of the thousands he remembers from that evening. Some are mundane like what colour socks he had on (red with a Fred Perry insignia). What he'd had for dinner (being short of time, baked beans from the tin). That he'd bought new underwear especially, and how it had felt soft against his skin as he walked, the way that only first-wear fabric can. Some details are more cataclysmic, gleaned from the news he'd listened to as he'd got ready; the cannabis laws had been relaxed, to the celebration of some and the horror of others. In Newcastle, a drunken teenager had frozen to death in her front garden because she couldn't find her keys and wasn't dressed for the Arctic conditions (he'd decided to put on his thick wool pea coat). Twelve people had died of bird flu in Hong Kong and, though airports had been closed, it was predicted that it would inevitably reach the UK. *Best to live every day as if it's your last,* he'd thought as he moisturised his face with Clinique for Men. Christian remembers the whole evening in glorious technicolour, as he would if it had been the night he'd met his future wife or the mother of his children, only – it wasn't.

He wasn't disappointed when he spied his date in the bar at the Duke of York's; she was pretty with a *Pulp Fiction* bob and skinny legs encased in tight jeans and clumpy snow boots. Her lipstick was Marilyn Monroe red and her lips curled into a smile as he tapped her arm and asked her name. She was a foot shorter than him and there was an awkward banging of heads as he bent to kiss her on the cheek, but when she reacted with a breathy giggle it was all he could do not to clap his hands together in anticipation of the enjoyable night to come. He bought two large glasses of wine and an enormous bucket of popcorn, and she insisted on buying the cinema tickets. So, you see, she really did take him.

They sat in a love seat at the back, newly installed like the bar to revive the glories of cinemas past. Chatting amiably together through the trailers, they drank their wine quickly and gobbled the warm, salty popcorn, and he was aware of the white-hot contact of her thigh against his.

'I spent a year in Tokyo,' she whispered as the censor's certificate was projected. 'That's why I chose this film.'

Christian was just about to say he'd love to go there when the image that would stay with him for the rest of his adult life appeared on the screen. The film company's logo gave way to a darkened blur and then came a close-up of a bottom. It had a fuzzy, dream-like quality to it and seemed to linger for a lifetime, the mountainous curve of a hip lit softly from one side by a bedside lamp, the unmistakeable undulation of feminine flesh in repose, its dark, subtle valley visible through sheer, outsized knickers. The top leg stretched, altering the tension of the buttock muscle, then settled back into symmetry with the other, while bass-heavy music drifted in as if from a faraway party. Christian sat with a fistful of popcorn in sticky transition from box to mouth. He was aware of his date whispering something to him but he couldn't say what it was, nor did he care; he was too busy watching the bottom. The perfect peach of womanhood shifted again larger than life before his eyes and his breath stopped.

Bill Murray was immediately funny, gently mocking. His hangdog expression looming over the heads of his Japanese hosts drew chuckles from Christian's date but he himself could think of nothing but the now absent bottom

– that is until he saw her face. Christian remembers everything about the first moment he saw that face.

At the age of 24, Christian had never been in love before – lust certainly, but not love. He'd had 'relationships', including a couple that had lasted months rather than weeks, but he'd never been *in love* with anybody. He was a looker and he knew it – tall, rangy and handsome with dark eyes and cow eyelashes, his hair falling in fulsome curls and his face punctuated with heavy eyebrows that made him look as though he was perpetually planning something naughty, which he invariably was. He was a commercial artist but knew he was destined to be a pop-art superstar and he wondered if it was possible to render the perfection of the face he was now watching into minimal lineage.

That face. That face as it emerged through the blur of the Tokyo nightscape, through the distraction of pale, shapely legs bare to the hip. That face. With its lips like billowing cloud, its adorably pointy nose and deep-set eyes. That face was the most beautiful thing he had ever seen. When she turned full on to the camera, Christian felt as though she was looking directly at him and his mouth opened as if to take her in.

They tried to dress her down, to cover her up with frumpy clothes and minimal grooming, make her lips smaller, hide her eyes with muted lights, but to Christian this worked only to make her beauty more aching. She was sad and vulnerable and her goon of a husband was ignoring her. As she cried softly to herself in her third scene and Christian's heart melted, he moved his leg a little away from the girl sitting next to him. By the end of the film he wanted to slap Bill Murray. *What are you doing?* he said to himself. *How can you bear to let her go?* There was a decidedly un-English smattering of applause in the auditorium and a lot of tissue rustling. He watched the titles roll over the black screen for as long as he could, aware of his date beside him putting on her jacket and picking up her bag, but wondering if there might not be one last glimpse of the leading lady before everything went black – a little bonus like kids get at the end of animated features.

'Fancy a drink?' said the girl, and Christian knew he'd have to leave his love in the auditorium.

They went to a local pub because the cinema bar was full, their feet plunging into the two inches of snow that had settled while they'd been inside. At a fireside table they discussed the film.

'Did you like it?' she asked.

'Very much.'

'Bill Murray was excellent, wasn't he? So funny.'

'Yes, he was good. I thought *she* was amazing.'

His date took a loud gulp from her glass before adding, 'She's very beautiful.'

'She is, but it's more than that. I thought she was simply brilliant. It was heartbreaking how she had to go back to that pig of a husband and he went home to his nagging wife.'

His date pushed her short curtain of hair behind her ear; Christian thought it made her look a bit too rodent-like.

'But I didn't think that her husband was as bad as you make out. I mean, he's working. He's brought her to Tokyo and all she does is lounge about feeling sorry for herself. She doesn't do anything. She looks down on everyone and then this famous movie-star guy comes along and she's ready to drop everything.'

Christian bristled and downed half the contents of his glass.

'Well, I think you've missed the point entirely. It's not because he's a movie star. It's true love. Unrequited but true. They can't be together – they've got commitments and they'd end up hurting too many people. Besides, it wouldn't be the same anywhere else. It's definitely a *Casablanca* moment.'

His date looked blank.

'We'll always have Paris?'

Still nothing. He sighed.

'Never mind. Anyway, I think you're definitely wrong about the husband; he was clearly banging the bimbo actress they bump into in the lobby. He had no interest in Scarlett whatsoever.'

He smiled at being so quickly on first-name terms.

'Charlotte.'

'No, Scarlett, the actress, Scarlett Johansson.'

His date frowned and gulped her drink again.

'You have no evidence that he's sleeping with the blonde girl; you've just jumped to conclusions. He's into his wife. He faxes her a love letter at the end.'

'Oh, big deal! Apart from that he completely ignores her! She's walking around him in nothing but her underwear and there's not a flicker. Believe me, he's either gay or he's getting it elsewhere.'

The couple at the next table looked over at their raised voices and smiled at each other.

'And this outrage on her behalf has nothing to do with her being beautiful? I suspect, Christian, that if she didn't look like a model you wouldn't care nearly half as much as you seem to.'

She pointed a well-manicured finger at him as she said this, so he replied with suitable indignation.

'But did she? Look like a model? To me she looked more like a real woman. She's not thin, is she? She has a round bottom and big boobs. That's how real women should look.'

His date folded her arms in front of her and it was then he became acutely aware that she was as thin as a rail with a pancake chest. After this the minutes passed awkwardly and when they had finished their drinks, hastily and in virtual silence, they left to get home before the snow got any worse, and walked away from the pub in different directions.

That night, after making love to Scarlett Johansson, Christian slept deeply, engulfed in dreams and wearing only a self-satisfied smile. Outside, his world compacted beneath a snowfall so heavy it brought the country to a standstill for a week.

Christian has been in bed with Scarlett Johansson for 10 years. Today he, his girlfriend Scarlet and her best friend Angelica are sitting in a booth at his local pub. The mood is quiet; it's been a hard week. It's the eve of his 34th birthday and Christian is feeling his age. He is both taking stock of his life and trying to pretend he is 10 years younger. What has happened to our hero in the last decade? Well, he has his own company, a small graphics team providing commercial design coverage and, in his spare time, he draws a weekly comic strip for a national newspaper. 'Ruby Tuesday' features a blonde pneumatic actress in a white dress giving her views on events in football, media and politics from a decidedly male perspective. The huge cult following (many of them female) consider Ruby to be a deliciously ironic comment on modern chauvinism, but actually Christian means every word; to him, Ruby is simply a representation of his perfect woman. Of course, he would never say this out loud to anyone.

He has a beautiful apartment overlooking the marina, with a concierge. He met Scarlet five years ago. She's also an artist. They met online initially, on a comic book fan site. He was drawn to her name and her posts about Marvel. They quickly realised they both lived in Brighton and arranged to meet. She was about as close as you could get to Scarlett Johansson without moving to LA and risking an exclusion order. On that first date, he couldn't stop looking at her lips. The red hair was a bit of a distraction but her name confirmed that they were meant to be together.

For the first two years with Scarlet, Christian was extremely happy; he felt as though, finally, he was in love with someone who could love him back. Things aren't quite so good now. Since Scarlet moved in it's not how he imagined it would be. He's been distant. He knows it but he can't help it; dissatisfaction rumbles in his heart like air in a hungry belly.

Scarlet and Angelica are chattering and giggling next to him as if he isn't there. He finishes his drink and looks pointedly into the empty glass. He knows Angelica won't take the hint. He's never really thought much of her; his heart sank when he arrived at the pub to find her sitting next to Scarlet. She hogs Scarlet too much. They go way back, primary school or something, so they share too many in-jokes that make them squeal with laughter and make him feel like a spare part. He liked Angelica's boyfriend, Seth, though – a fellow artist and always to be relied on for good grass and pocket philosophy. Seth made him feel less of an outsider. Angelica's hot, obviously, Spanish-looking with long, wavy hair and big breasts. There's a touch of Penélope Cruz about her and, as the girls chirp away next to him, he wonders if he could orchestrate a threesome, like in *Vicky Cristina Barcelona*. Scarlet would be Scarlett, obviously, and he and Angelica could be the painter and his wife. Scarlet has a platinum wig in the wardrobe; she wears it to play dress-up, or at least she used to. He smiles to himself; they might be into it – it is his birthday, after all. It would be better than a pair of socks. He laughs out loud. Scarlet and Angelica stop their chattering and look at him.

'What's so funny?'

'Nothing, I was just thinking about something.'

'You're grinning like a sociopath,' says Scarlet. 'It's creepy. Want another?'

Scarlet shimmies past Angelica to the bar. He can't quite place the expression on Angelica's face as she watches her go – wolfish perhaps? They sit in silence for a while until he thinks of something to say.

'So, how's Seth?'

'We split up, Christian, about three months ago. Didn't Scar mention it?'

'Oh, that's a pity. He was a nice guy.'

'He was a total loser. It's the best thing that ever happened to me. He was holding me back. Now I'm with Victoria I've finally found the real me.'

'Victoria?'

'Yes, Victoria. My life partner.'

'Victoria, as in a girl?'

Angelica rolls her eyes as Scarlet comes back with the drinks.

'What's wrong?' says Scarlet.

'Nothing,' says Christian. 'Angelica was just telling me about the developments in her love life.'

He drinks his beer and wonders how he could mention the *Vicky Cristina Barcelona* thing.

'I don't think your friend likes me much.' Christian pours himself a coffee and sits at the breakfast bar. Scarlet pours a cup for herself and sits opposite him. He's still more than a bit drunk, his body unsteady, his speech slurred.

'She does. She just thinks your Scarlett Johansson obsession is getting a bit out of hand.'

She takes a tiny sip from her drink as if it's contaminated.

'She thinks you should see a doctor to get a referral to a hypnotherapist or something. She says you're a fantasist and it's interfering with your real life – and with mine.'

Christian splutters into his coffee, spilling some onto the marble.

'And you,' he says, trying not to laugh, 'what do you think?'

But Scarlet isn't smiling.

'Actually, it might be worth a shot. It is becoming a bit of a bore.'

He puts down his cup.

'For goodness sake, Scar. It's perfectly normal behaviour. I've got a couple of posters and copies of her movies on download, so what?'

She raises her eyebrows.

'You know what I think?' he says. 'I think that Angelica has an obsession with you and that's why she's causing trouble between us.'

'Don't be ridiculous. You've never thought that before. You didn't even know Angelica was gay until tonight. I have known her since we were five.'

'So? She's still a dyke, isn't she? However recently she's decided on it. What's to stop her fancying someone she's known for twenty years?'

Scarlet puts her face in her hands as if she is weeping, inhales deeply and looks up at him.

'You are very fanciable, you know?' He smiles. 'Why not a girl? Like in *Vicky Cristina Barcelona*.'

Scarlet doesn't say anything for a while, just narrows her eyes and sips her coffee and he thinks their confrontation might be over (get a hypnotherapist indeed!), but then out of the blue she says, 'I have fantasies too, you know. I have a recurring dream about Jack White. He lives here with us and he sings to me and strums his guitar and he's handsome and rock starry…'

'There you go, then; perfectly normal.'

'No. I haven't finished yet, there's more. After a while it gets boring. I mean, he's nice and everything and hot, obviously, but he keeps borrowing my hair straighteners and my eyeliner, he is constantly demanding cups of tea and when he says "sugar" in that growly Midwestern drawl, I don't know if he's trying to charm me or if he wants some for his tea.'

'Well, I can see how that would be annoying. They're all the same those rock stars. And besides, he should probably lay off the sugar – he's getting a bit porky these days…'

'Christian! Let me finish, please, that's not why I'm telling you this.'

'Oh, okay, go ahead.'

'You see, although I dream about Jack White, I also dream about you.'

She bites her lip and looks him in the eye.

'What I want to know, Christian – what I need to know – is when you're not dreaming about Scarlett Johansson, do you ever dream about me?'

She's got him there; he really doesn't know what to say. He never dreams about his girlfriend. Why would he? She's always there so he doesn't need her in his head when he's asleep as well. The way she's looking at him though, all expectant and nervous, makes him wonder if he should lie to her. Tell her what she wants to hear, even if it isn't true. He strums his fingers on the table.

'And don't lie to me,' she says, 'because I'll know.'

They stare at each other for a long time. Christian thinks that if she looks away first he might not have to answer her question, but as the seconds become minutes he realises that he doesn't have a choice. She wants to know and she's not going anywhere until she finds out. He shakes his head quickly and looks into his half-empty coffee cup…

Scarlet doesn't say anything. She gets up from her chair and walks into the bedroom, closing the door behind her. She's away for ages. He assumes she's gone to bed, that maybe she'll be in a better mood tomorrow; it is his birthday, after all. He sits down on the sofa with a beer and puts *Lost in Translation* on his laptop; it always comforts him when he's feeling down. The soporific effects of the final beer kick in as Bill and Scarlett meet in the bar and Christian relaxes against the sofa cushions. It'll all be okay tomorrow.

In *Vicky Cristina Barcelona* Scarlett Johansson instinctively knows when it's time to leave the painter and his wife and his Scarlet must have a bit of that instinct too, because a little while later the bedroom door crashes open and she drags an enormous suitcase through it.

Christian is startled. He watches as his girlfriend struggles with the bag, at first not realising what is happening. Then she goes for her coat and he understands all too well. He pauses the movie and puts down his laptop.

'Scar, what do you think you're doing?'

She wriggles into her coat.

'I'm leaving you,' she says, checking her reflection in the mirror. Her voice is so calm he doesn't register what she has just said; the discrepancy between words and tone is too great for his addled senses.

He gets to his feet, banging his shin on the coffee table and letting out a small cry of pain as he moves towards her. He limps to the door just as she's about to go through, holding onto it so the gap is too small for her to leave by.

'Don't be silly, Scar; it's one in the morning. Where are you going to go?'

She looks him full in the face.

'I'll stay with Angelica tonight, then I'll sort something out.'

'Fucking hell, Scar, all this because of a few stupid dreams? I don't need to dream about you, do I? You're always here.'

'I wanted to have your baby,' she says. 'What was I thinking? I can't have a child with you; you're too much of one yourself. Open the door.'

'Scar?'

'Don't call me Scar. It's Scarlet. I'm Scarlet,' she hisses. 'Understand?'

She looks away from him, out through the gap in the door and says, 'I'll be back for the rest of my stuff next week when you're at work. I'll leave the key on the coffee table.'

He goes to touch her but she takes the opportunity of his loosened grip to push the case through the door and pull it as quickly as she can down the corridor.

'Scar,' he calls half-heartedly, his enthusiasm for making her stay receding with her presence until his voice is no more than a whisper. 'Scar...'

When she's disappeared into the swish of the lift doors he goes back into the flat and sits on the sofa.

Fuck her. His thoughts ramble like a street-corner alky. *It's perfectly normal to have fantasies. In fact, women spend a whole lot of time trying to play off men's fantasies. She used to make herself look more like Scarlett Johansson to please me: bleached hair, pouty lips, prancing around in big knickers just to turn me on. She can't then turn on me for it. Ruby will have something to say about this in her next column. It's all that bloody Angelica's fault, I bet. We were fine before she stuck her nose in. Fucking Angelica – who changes their sexual preferences like socks? It's my fucking birthday tomorrow. I am 34 years old. I need a fucking drink.*

He stumbles to the kitchen and takes down the bottle of whisky from the top cupboard. Suntory Hibiki, the type that Bill Murray drinks in *Lost in Translation*. Scarlet bought it on import for his last birthday. It must have cost her a fortune and it wasn't even his main present. He pours and necks one glass, then another, shaking his head like a wet dog as the dry liquid burns his gullet. He takes the bottle and glass over to the sofa and flicks on the TV, channel-hopping for a few seconds before transferring the movie and settling back down to watch. The whisky mingles with the tranquilliser proportions of booze he's already had and he can't focus on the screen. He knows every word off by heart now so he doesn't really need to see it clearly, but somehow he can't settle. The sounds and images swirl in front of him until the disorientation brings nausea. Leaving the movie playing, he takes his whisky into the bedroom. He stands inside the door with Scarlett Johansson's ethereal voice seeping in from the living room. A few of Scarlet's things are scattered around the room – a pair of sheer tights on the back of the chair, a silk scarf on the floor, a dirty T-shirt on the bed. He can smell the perfume he bought her – Dolce & Gabbana – and notices she has left the bottle on the dressing table. Next to it is a pile of boxes beautifully wrapped in masculine tartan paper and secured with thick red ribbons. His name shines in glossy black on the white envelope propped up against them. Christian walks past them to the life-size framed poster of the only woman he really loves. When he hung it he made sure to get it at the right height so that Scarlett's eyes were a little below his own, as they would be if she was really standing there in his bedroom. He puts down his drink.

'How are you today, baby?' he says, blinking the tears from his eyes. He tries to hold her, shifting his arms up and down her frame with chicken-wing elbows and wrists at right angles. In the end he lays his cheek against the cold glass. There, alone in the bedroom he used to share with Scarlet, he struggles with all his might to hold onto Scarlett Johansson, but she just won't fit into his arms.

8

Tea and Frankenstein

The postcard in the window says, 'Waitress Wanted – Apply Within'. It's raining like the flood and as Anna stops to read the card, Daniel strides on ahead completely unaware she isn't beside him. She's been past the place a million times before but never once gone inside. She can't afford tea out anyway, unless it's gnat's pee in a paper cup from the university vending machine.

The leaded windows are steamed up on the inside. She makes a tunnel with her hands against the glass. She can see shapes but it's all a bit indistinct, wisps of chequered tablecloths and gleaming teacups, abstracts of coats and bags hung over chairs, the swish of a white apron. A raindrop breaks free from the general wetness of her hair and works its way down her spine like an icy finger. She looks up the road to see if Daniel is coming back for her but in the bustle of backs and faces there's no sign of him. She wonders if she should run after him and tell him what she's doing, but she doesn't want him to talk her out of it, and he would, she's sure of that. As she goes to the door, the wrought-iron sign above swings in the wind, creaking on its frame. She looks up.

The Tudor Tea Rooms

The little bell tings as the door shuts; people look up momentarily from the industry of eating cakes and stirring drinks. Dry warmth blasts from an electric heater by the door, evaporating moisture from the wet coats on the hat stand. Bessie Smith sings softly from an ancient speaker up high in the corner. There are parlour palms and horse brasses and dark wooden beams. Every table is taken, cutlery chinks against china and the low hum of conversation fills the room. The customers are mainly elderly; their beige clothes merge together around the bright red-and-white tablecloths. The room smells of lavender and buttered toast, and Anna feels an instant warmth in her soul.

A woman in a black dress, white maid's hat and white frilled pinny stops, hands full with a piled-high tray of used plates and cups.

'Be at least ten minutes for a table,' she says breathlessly.

'I've come about the job,' says Anna.

The woman looks her up and down, making her acutely aware of how she looks; the combination of cropped blonde hair, fishnet tights, heavy boots and dark lips.

'Going to a Cure concert?' Daniel had said when she came downstairs this morning.

Daniel hates red lipstick, though she was wearing it the night they met, and he didn't seem to mind it then. That night he'd rescued her from the attentions of a drunken rugby-player type just by holding out his hand and saying, 'There you are.' That night when his mouth was smeared scarlet from her kisses, he sat on his bed and touched her lips with his fingertips as if they'd been painted by angels.

'Can we order?' a man at a nearby table asks crossly.

The woman sighs and smiles at Anna.

'In that case, dearie, take a seat and I'll be with you in a minute. Yes, sir, what can I get you?'

She nods to the table in the window, tucked behind a wooden pillar. An old man in a tweed suit is sitting at it and opposite him is the only empty seat in the house.

'You don't mind, do you, Peter?'

'Not at all,' says the man with a voice of clipped perfection.

Anna pulls the wooden chair from the table, sitting down and quickly wriggling out of her sodden jacket. The man gazes at her with a kind expression. She feels a jolt of recognition.

'Devil of a day, isn't it?' he says with a smile.

His voice is beautiful – the clear, deep ring of a 1950s radio announcer; the sort of voice you never tire of listening to.

'Isn't it,' she says, adopting a slightly posher accent than her usual Burnley.

She rubs her hand over her hair, sending stray water droplets onto the tablecloth.

'Oh, I'm terribly sorry.'

The old man hands her a damask napkin.

'Here, use this.'

She thanks him, pats at her head and takes the opportunity to study his face to try and place him. It's thin, almost equinely angular; the bones beneath autumn-leaf skin as sharp as daggers. His hair, dove grey and still lush, recedes from a point in the middle of his liver-spotted forehead. He watches her watching. A smile lifts the corners of pencil-line lips and is repeated in his bird-like eyes. The eyes themselves have yellow-stained whites spread over with tiny red veins, but the irises are as blue as a June day and sparkle like sunlight on water.

The tea urn blasts a cloud of steam from the counter and Anna jumps. Her companion laughs, showing tiny white teeth and multiplying the deep creases around his eyes. There's a laboratory gurgle of running water. The image of a wet stone wall flickers through Anna's mind, torches flaming on a downward-leading staircase, an underground chamber, bubbling flasks, test tubes, scalpels, giant electricity conductors zigzagging a crackle of neon light, a body under a sheet, a grey, gnarled hand falling, its fingers twitching.

He raises his eyebrows.

'Oh! You're...' She stutters.

'Yes, I suppose I am.'

She blushes.

'I was staring, wasn't I?'

'Yes, I'm afraid you were.'

'I'm sorry,' she gushes. 'It's not often you get to meet a... a legend.'

'Oh Lord,' he says, extracting a cigarette from the packet of Rothmans on the table, 'not that. Legend makes me sound about nine hundred years old.'

She's flustered and rattles off words with machine-gun speed.

'Oh, I didn't mean that. It's just – well I'm a bit of a fan. Me and my dad used to watch the Hammer films when I was a kid. It's what first got me interested in films. I'm doing film studies at the university.'

There had been rumours that he lived in the town, that you could see him riding his bike around the prom; one of the seniors even claimed to have had tea with him at his seafront home, but Anna hadn't dreamt she'd ever be sitting here like this.

'I've just written an essay on Hammer,' she adds.

'Really?' he says kindly. 'Being studied in colleges now, are we? Well that is something.'

He taps his cigarette and lights it with a squeaky brass lighter and the greasy tang of gasoline tickles her nostrils, followed by acrid nicotine. She breathes in deeply through her nose and glances at the three stubs already buried in the ashtray.

'Would you like one?' he asks, offering her the pack.

She would – but Daniel doesn't like women who smoke, even though he smokes himself. He says it's either common or aristocratic, and that she's neither. She gave up to please him but occasionally she lapses. She took a cigarette she was offered at a party a few weeks ago. Daniel came into the room while she was smoking it, took it from her hand and put it out. They didn't talk about it at the time but he sulked for days afterwards.

'No, thank you,' she says, looking longingly at the pack.

'Trying to give up, eh?'

'Something like that.'

'Well good for you. Too late for me now. I must have been smoking for fifty years – but I'm not dead yet.'

He makes the sign of the cross and raises his eyes to heaven. Anna laughs.

'Would you like tea? There's plenty left in the pot.'

She nods and he pours some into the empty cup set at her place.

'There's a scone too. Mary always gives me two, but really I can only ever manage one.'

She looks at the plate he's proffering. The scone is big and fat, oozing with cream and blood-red jam. She can't remember the last time she ate a cake. Daniel only likes skinny girls so she's on a perpetual diet. If he were here he would say, *Are you sure you want that?* Her stomach grumbles loudly.

'Sounds like you need it.'

'Go on, then. Thank you so much,' she says, taking the plate from him. She bites into the soft, buttery flesh of the scone. It crumbles on her tongue, the perfect combination of sugar and fat.

'Mmm,' she says, sucking icing sugar from her lips. 'It really is a pleasure to meet you.'

He beams at her, his face young with pride.

'It's always a pleasure to meet fans – especially young ones. I'm amazed people still watch the things.'

'Oh, but they're wonderful. So colourful and menacing, and quite risqué for the times, weren't they? Censor busters – that's what I did my essay on: "Unchecked Urges – Buried Sexuality in Classic Hammer Horror".'

'Goodness, did you really? Well, I'd be delighted to talk to you about your work. You can find me in here most lunchtimes – but look out, here comes Mary. I think you're about to have your interview.'

She looks around the room and realises that, while they've been talking, the lunchtime rush has ended and the woman with the white apron is making her way to their table.

He puts out his cigarette, stands and takes his coat from the hatstand. He secures bicycle clips on his trousers and puts on his hat. He actually wears a deerstalker, just like Sherlock Holmes. He kisses the woman in the apron on the cheek.

'Bye, Mary. I won't be in tomorrow. I'm going to see Chris for a few days.'

'All right, Peter.' She smiles. 'See you next week. Mind how you go.'

He squeezes Anna's shoulder and she looks up into his whirlpool eyes.

'I hope you get the job,' he says. 'We all have to start somewhere. I worked in a Lyons Corner House myself about half a century ago.'

He nods farewell and walks quickly through the door, the little bell signalling his absence.

Anna looks up at Mary, whose face is red from the exertion of the non-stop lunch shift. She smiles fondly as she watches Peter through the window, gives a little wave, then looks down at Anna.

'Does he mean Christopher Lee?' asks Anna.

Mary sits down in the recently vacated seat.

'I expect so, dear – they're very close. Now,' she says, taking a pen and notepad from her apron pocket, 'you do know it's part-time don't you? All day Saturday and Sunday, and Friday afternoons, twelve to…'

'What are you doing here?'

Daniel is standing by the table looking down at her, bedraggled and rain-soaked, his eyes flaring.

'I've looked in every shop on the high street for you.'

Anna can feel her face burning, torn between the need to please him and the growing realisation that she never will.

'Well?'

She looks hesitantly at Mary sitting opposite her, pen poised, her face the picture of distaste. She looks at Daniel again, her heartbeat rushing to a crescendo, and this time she sees him as Mary does.

'Not now,' she says. 'I'm having an interview.'

'A what?' he scoffs.

'An interview.'

'You're joking, right? Why would you want to work in here?'

Mary straightens her back and folds her arms.

Anna thinks about Peter, about the napkin, the tea and the scone, his hand on her shoulder, his encouraging words and benevolent eyes. Since she met Daniel, she's been losing herself piece by piece. If she stays with him, she might lose herself altogether. She'll be nothing more than his creation – her body under a sheet, fingers twitching.

She looks him in the eyes.

'I'm busy now, so I'll see you later, at your house.'

He blinks, his expression a deflating balloon.

'But...'

Anna turns back to Mary with an unshackled smile. 'So, Saturday, Sunday, and Friday afternoons – it sounds perfect.'

The tea urn blasts a cloud of steam from the counter and the water bubbles.

9

What Me an' Pa Saw in the Meadow

'What is it?' I whisper.

Me an' Pa spent the morning fishin' in the Diamond Bank river an' we are on our way home. We jus' walked through the Primavera Forest, with its thick, feathery trees, which is how come we didn' see it sooner.

As we turn into the blue meadow, there it is standing on the path a little way uphill. It stops us dead in our tracks an' we stand on the edge of the grass starin' at the thing blockin' the route home. At almost quarter-day, with the sun nearin' its most ultraviolet, I think I must be hallucinatin', but Pa holds up his hand, fingers splayed, in a silent hush.

From its vantage point on the path, the thing lifts its head an' looks at us with big black eyes as deep as space. Its jaw, which is grindin' from side to side, stops an' falls open, showin' ridged yellow teeth an' crushed blue grass. Aqua saliva an' pieces of grass dribble to the ground. My mouth is dry with fear. My heart beatin' so fast I can hear it outside of my ndy. Those teeth look like somethin' from the horrors. I imagine those chompers bitin' into me, crushin' my cells an' veins, an' me dyin' right here from blood loss an' infection – that's if it doesn't just gobble me an' Pa up right now, bones an' all. I silently cuss Pa for makin' me come all the way out here, so far from civilisation, with only Dawkin's neons skitterin' the skies for company.

Pa likes to go fishin' at end week. We live right on sprawl's edge. It's the only place we can afford, an' it ain't the nicest part of town, but it means we can be outsprawl quicker than most folks. We go fishin' early day, before sunrise an' the cloudless sets in, an' then come back in time for lunch so as not to be out in the tip heat, but today we stayed longer at the river cos Pa was sure he'd get a bite, said the fish would be easier to catch as the river warmed up.

Course, we never actually do get a bite. Fish aren't made to be caught. Fishin's suppose' to be jus' for fun, but Pa always says, 'Ya never know.' An' there was this one guy down New Miami way, who landed a quawn fish as long as his arm. It was all over the news stream for days. He was real famous. Baxter

Dartmouth III was his name. You couldn't close your eyes without seein' his smilin' face as he hugged that big, ugly fish. Some said it was a throwback fish an' that's how he caught it, but they did tests on it an' it was legit an' all. They let him keep it too, on account of him being the first human to catch a fish in over 60 years. Now they use that photo to advertise fishin' lines. Dartmouths they're called an' everyone's buyin' them; everyone thinks they can catch the next one, an even bigger one. Not that we can afford a Dartmouth. We jus' got TaiAm wire an' a 3-D rod. Mind, they have nothin' but water down in New Miami so it must've bin easier for Baxter Dartmouth III to catch that fish than it would be for us to get one so far into the dry lands. The Diamond Bank river is more of a stream really, but Pa says, 'If he can do it we can. We just gotta keep tryin'.' An' it is true that if we did happen to catch one (hopefully an even bigger one) we wouldn't have to worry about credit no more (an' Ma does worry about credit). If we did catch one we'd be famous like Baxter Dartmouth III. We could move insprawl. It would have to be a pretty impressive fish, though, now that Baxter has set a precedent, an' that's why Pa says we should try an' catch somethin' really rare, somethin' no one's laid eyes on for a very long time.

The best fishin' grounds round about, the ones with the really rare fish, those ones are way outsprawl. That's how come me an' Pa are out here in the blue meadows on a rest day, as far from the sprawl an' the security pods as you can be without a vehicle. There's no stream cameras out here. Pa says walkin' is good for you – says in the old days when he was a kid everybody walked everywhere. Says it's better for your cells than the hover plates. An' I do like to walk out here with Pa, away from the sprawl, even though it is usually almost too hot to think. But Ma frets. 'Be careful,' she says. 'Anythin' could happen.' An' today she's right.

The thing snorts an' stamps one of its four feet an' I nearly jump from my skin. Its feet have two pointy, dust-covered toes that look as hard as titanium. Its legs seem too thin to hold up its wide barrel body. It looks like it could crush us with that body – just land on us an' roll the life right out of us. Maybe it's a robot? They have things like that on the funny streams: robots from outer space! Or maybe it's somethin' to do with the military? I edge behind Pa an' cling to his arm, peerin' round his body. I'm sure that at any minute the thing will attack us an' I wonder what I should do if it does. If it knocks Pa flat, should I run, or would that be worse? Would it come after me an' charge me down? But it just sneezes, bends its head into the blue grass, rips up a hunk of it an' sets about chewin' again.

'Well I'll be,' says Pa.

He motions for me to sit an' I find a big ol' diamond rock next to the meadow but I don't take my eyes offa the thing, not for a second. Pa sits next to me an' his face is all crinkled up an' smiley like it is when the Perseids blaze. I still keep the thing in sight, but Pa's expression is makin' me feel less shaky. If he ain't scared, I shouldn't be either.

'What is it, Pa?' I ask.

He scratches his head.

'I saw one years ago when I was just an infant, couldn't have been no more than five. It was on display in the town cube. Looked just like this one. I remember it clear as day, constantly chewin' at grass.' He looks at me an' winks. 'The grass was green back then, son, not blue like now.'

Pa has mentioned this green grass thing before but I don't know as I believe him. I know they had green grass in Germanica but I never seen any pictures of it here in the CUSA, an' Pa's only a hundred so I don't see how he canna' seen it.

'It's called a K-OW.'

'A k-ow?'

Rhymes with POW, I think to myself. I can feel my eyes get real wide despite the sun.

'Is it dangerous?'

Pa laughs.

'No, son, it's not dangerous. Well that is, the individual k-ow ain't dangerous. See years ago, before the Disaster, there was k-ows in every field. You couldn't go anywhere outside the sprawls without seeing a k-ow. Millions of 'em, big black-an'-white lumps in every meadow, all chewin' away at that green, green grass.'

'What were they for, Pa?'

'Farming, son. You could get meat an' milk from 'em an' somethin' like Theal for shoes an' clothes; it was made from the skin.'

'How's that, Pa? Didn't they have the vats back then?'

I have just completed Food Techno Level 8 so I know all about the utero vats an' manusustenance.

'No, son, food wasn't cultured then, came straight from the animal. No cloning either. The milk came from that dangly bit underneath an' it wasn't flavoured like now. To get the meat they had to terminate the k-ow an' cut it up. We have one of Grandpa's history files about it in the archive – Cattle Farming an' Butchery for Begin—'

He sees my face an' stops talkin'. I feel well an' truly nauseous – terminated an' cut up! Milk from inside an animal! Pa takes an atomiser from his backpack an' I squirt it twice onto my tongue.

'You look like your cell glucose is down,' he says. 'You should eat somethin'.'

He takes one of Ma's shrink-wraps from the bag an' hands it to me.

'What is it?'

'Meat an' algae bread.'

I bite into it an' immediately feel like I'm back home in our kitchen surrounded by smells from our food creator, an' the horror of cuttin' up the k-ow doesn't seem so bad. Ma creates the best meat an' algae bread I ever tasted. She knows jus' what compounds to add an' when, an' the whole thing comes out jus' perfect. Whenever an' wherever I eat Ma's meat an' algae bread, I always feel like I jus' got a kiss on the forehead from her.

I swallow an' take another bite, feeling calmer by the milli-flic.

'So why did people want to eat the k-ows?' I ask with my mouth half full.

'Well they say the meat was delicious. The most unbelievable taste. Grandpa was always talkin' about how good it was, how juicy an' soft. Melted in your mouth, he said, like the best meat times a graham. He said when it was cooking you could smell it for miles round an' the dogs used to whine with anticipation it smelt so fine. He made it sound so good I always wished I coulda tasted it – just once. By all accounts the world went mad for k-ow meat; people demanded more an' more. But this was before fat gobblers an' targeted exercise pills an' it was really bad for you. Clogged up your heart; made it so it couldn't beat proper. People only lived to around eighty years old then. Imagine that! Just eighty years old. But that wasn't all. K-ows ate fields full of grass every day an' well, that much veggimat causes gas – y'know, in the belly.'

He makes an ass-fart sound with his lips an' I can't help but laugh. Pa laughs too; there is just somethin' so funny about ass-farts no matter what age you are. Probably because we're nervous about the k-ow, we laugh until our sides ache an' I need another spray from the atomiser. Pa wipes his eyes an' carries on. He likes talkin' 'bout the past. Sometimes he sounds like our Urban Mythology facilitator Partner Price. But she says we shouldn't believe everythin' we hear from our families, that folks like to make things up, especially about the times before the Disaster. But when Pa talks he's just so convincin' I don't know what to think.

'They didn't have pills for breakin' up veggimat then an' that many k-ows all ass-fartin' at once made the world smell an' the ozone thinner. Some said the k-ows was responsible for the Disaster an' they made it illegal to keep one unless it was in a laboratory with a licence. We were lucky they stopped it when they did, otherwise we wouldn't have the pink sky an' clean air we have now.'

I look at the beast chewin' the blue grass in front of us an' feel kinda sorry for it.

'Where'd it come from?'

Pa shrugs.

'I streamed they have to keep one or two full clones in the factories for source cells. It must be one of those. There's that Meat Link bio-dome close by – it musta escaped from there. Higgs Boson knows how!'

Just then the k-ow stops chewin', looks directly at us an' makes a loud an' low noise the like of which I haven't even heard on the streams.

MEEEUUUNGGHH!

Then it falls down with a thud, frightnin' a cloud of neons from the trees so they all scream for help as they fly away.

Me an' Pa look at each other an' then he goes over to where it lies. He takes his scanner from his pocket an' holds it above the k-ow. After a minute it beeps the safe message. Pa crouches an' puts his hand on the k-ow's body, then looks back at me an' shakes his head.

'It's all right,' he says. 'It's terminated. Probably the heat. There's no contamination. I think they need as much water as grass an' there's not much water out here; musta dehydrated. Come see.'

He gestures with his free hand.

I'm scared, but I don't want Pa to know I am, so I walk over to it. The sun is as high as can be an' the grass is still. I look down at the k-ow, black an' white like solstice clouds, an' stretch my fingers out to touch it. It's still warm, an' as soft as Nap, but it's not breathin' an' its eyes are shut. It looks so sad lyin' there – terminated. I ain't never seen anythin' terminated in real life before.

'What should we do?' I ask. 'Should we get help?'

Pa takes his hat off an' wipes the back of his neck with it.

'I don't think so, son. Security might not believe we just found it. Traffickin' full clones is a serious offence, a hundred years or more in correction. With no security stream out here to prove we didn't take it, I don't think we should risk reportin' it.'

He's right, without stream proof they'd think the worst. You hear about it all the time; the authorities never take the word of ordinary folk. There's always people on the streams gettin' charged with citizenship violations. Sent away to the Correction State for years at a time. Most of 'em don't look like criminals but I guess they mus' be if they're on the streams; but it's certainly not the sort of fame Baxter Dartmouth III got when he caught his fish, an' it's not the sort of fame we was after when we set off this pre-dawn either. Even if the guards didn't charge us for stealing a clone, there'd be months of surveillance an' when you're under surveillance everybody watches you: the guards, family, neighbours, even people you don't know! An' besides, Ma would hate it; she likes to keep our business ours.

'Are we jus' goin' to leave it then?' I ask. 'Pretend we didn' see it?'

'Well now that seems a bit disrespectful, dontcha think? Such a wonder deserves better than jus' bein' left to decay.'

I'm confused. We're not gonna report it an' we're not gonna leave it.

'What are we gonna do with it then, Pa?'

He grins an' stands up.

'Cattle Farming an' Butchery for Beginners,' he says. 'First, we go get the solar jeep.'

10

Jackson Was Good

The man in the suit holds out his hand. What is he, a bank manager or something? He stands at the door holding it open and grins at Bill.

'Hello, Bill,' he says. 'I'm Mr Patrick. I'm a doctor.'

Bill goes for a handshake but realises he's holding a walking stick. He looks down at it, wondering where he got it from and why he needs it. It must be to do with the fight – a busted knee or something.

'Shall I take your stick, Bill?'

It's that girl again, right behind him. Pretty little thing. She's been hanging around him for days. Not that he's complaining – big blue eyes and tits like beach balls. She's trying to hide it all under that plain blue dress but she can't cover up the movie-star curves. He looks at her smiling face. She's not wearing any make-up. Funny that – girls usually like to wear make-up; a bit of red lipstick and eyeliner would set off her blonde hair. Improve on nature's gifts. Like his Eileen, always made up, always dressed to please him. That's why there's only her, nobody else ever looks as good. Where is Eileen, anyway? He hasn't seen her since the fight. She's probably with the kids.

The girl keeps smiling at him and takes the stick out of his hand.

'Here, sit down, Bill.'

It's a right palaver to get into the chair. He must have taken more of a beating than he thought. It doesn't help that there's a desk in the way. They must be in the boss's office. Bill's legs are stiff and a dull pain radiates over his back. The girl guides him sideways until he's standing in front of the chair, then she leans over him, her hands under his armpits, and those magnificent breasts rub against his face as she lowers him down into the seat. He smiles up at her. He's having evil thoughts – and him a married man.

She crouches so she's level with him and squeezes his hand.

'You okay, Bill? I'll be right outside. Mr Patrick just wants to ask you a few questions.'

He looks at her big blue eyes, like sapphires – like Eileen's.

'All right, darlin'. Anything you say. What was your name again?'

'Cherry.'

'Blimey O'Reilly – what a name. All right, Cherry.'

She gives his hand a pat. He watches her go, turning his head slowly as far as the pain in his shoulder will allow. What a wiggle, even in her old-lady shoes; imagine her in heels. She smiles at him again and shuts the door quietly.

'Bye, Cheryl,' he says.

Bill faces front, glad to release his shoulder from the effort of turning his head – Jackson must've really laid into him before he went down. He looks around the room. It doesn't look like the boss's office. There's a bookshelf full of books on the far wall, a couple of filing cabinets and blinds at the window. There's a big plant too and pictures on the wall – creepy they are, diagrams of brains and skulls. Bill turns his attention to the man in the suit.

He's not as pretty as Cheryl and he's smiling like an idiot. Face all covered in freckles; they reach right up over his bald patch. Little piggy eyes and white lashes. No oil painting, that's for sure. Bill smiles back. His mother taught him to always return a smile. 'Be nice,' she used to say. 'It won't cost you a thing.'

The man in the suit sits down on a big black chair behind the desk. Bill watches him intently as he picks up a pen and scribbles on some sort of form with terrible scrawly handwriting. Bill leans forward to get a better look but it's impossible to see what he's writing; it's like a spider jumped in some ink and then tap-danced across the page. When he's finished he looks across at Bill and smiles again, but it's a fake smile, one that's painted on.

'Well, Bill, I'd like to ask you a few questions if I may. It's not a test so don't worry.'

'Is it about the fight? Jackson – is he all right?'

'No, Bill, it's not about the fight – just a few easy questions.'

Bill shrugs.

'Could you tell me your name?'

'Well you just called me Bill so I'm guessing you know it already.'

Scribble.

'Surname?'

'Johnson.'

Bill narrows his eyes.

'Am I under arrest or something? It was a fair fight. Jackson knew what he was doing.'

The man in the white coat smiles his fake smile again.

'No, no. Like I said, it's not about the fight – just a few questions. Now, what day is it?'

'Thursday.'

'And the month?'

'July.'

'The season?'

'Well, last year July was in the summer – same the year before that – so I'm guessing it's the same this year.'

Scribble.

'And the year?'

'Um, the year?'

'Yes, Bill, the year.'

There's a camera flash. A punch landed across a jaw. A poster for the fight at White City.

'1959, of course,' says Bill and looks away towards the sound of rain against the window.

The man in the suit looks away from Bill and writes down some numbers.

'So, can you tell me where you are?'

'Actually, I was hoping you could tell me.'

'Hmmm – how about the country?'

'The country?'

'Yes – what country are we in?'

This guy's a prize idiot.

'England.'

'The county?'

'Err… London.'

'Town?'

'City.'

'Sorry?'

'City of London – it's a city *and* a county. The capital city. Don't you know where you are?'

'Yes, Bill. I know where we are.'

Bill smiles indulgently.

'Do you know the name of this hospital?'

'Hospital?' Bill sounds alarmed. He looks around the room again, at the books and the medical diagrams. This bloke said he was a doctor. Funny sort of doctor without a white coat.

'I see, says Bill. I'm in hospital, am I? Jackson must've hit me harder than I thought. Knocked him out in the fifth, you know – put up a good fight though. He's all right, isn't he?'

'I'm sure he is. Do you know the name of the hospital?'

Silence. Bill shakes his head.

'No. I must've been out of it when they brought me in. Is that why my leg hurts? Did I land on my knee again? It's not been right since that bout up in Newcastle. Didn't do so well up there. Made up for it with Jackson though – what a fight!'

Scribble.

'Do you know what floor we're on?'

Bill sniffs and looks at his hand. The tattoo of a flying bird that used to soar brightly on the back of it is almost entirely covered in a green-and-purple tinge that blurs the edges of its open wings. Bill rubs at it and winces.

'My hand's in a bit of a state, isn't it? What a bruise. Still a bucket of ice will take that right down.'

'Bill? What floor are we on?'

'Look, I didn't even know I was in hospital until you just said, so I'm not going to have a clue about the floor am I? Do you box, Mr...?'

'Patrick. No, Bill – I don't box.'

Bill looks him up and down; he's a bit thin but he could soon bulk up.

'You should take it up. It's the best job in the world.'

The man in the suit smiles his fake smile again but he looks Bill in the eye this time; everyone's interested in boxing.

'There's nothing like it. Keeps you fit, keeps you sharp. Nothing gets past me. Welterweight I am, like Sugar Ray; it's the best category – light enough to spring around the ring but heavy enough to do some serious damage. Dazes you a bit, a good match. Can take a couple of days to get over it. When you've got the right opponent it's like a fucking ballet. You dance with each other. He meets every move, anticipates everything you've got and then, just when you think there's no way to get him, you see it – the opening, the weakness – and BAM! He's down. Jackson, he was good, but I put him down in the fifth – he never got up again.'

Bill punches his right hand into his left – it hurts, from his knuckles to his elbow. He winces.

'You all right, Bill?'

He nods but it takes a minute for the pain to go. He opens and closes his fingers a few times, flinging off the numbness. He must've cracked something when he laid Jackson out.

'Now, Bill. Can you name the three things on the table for me?'

Bill leans forward to look and covers his top lip with his bottom lip and twitches his nose. His lips smack as he parts them, his teeth feel weird, maybe he lost a couple – in the fight.

'Which three?' he says.

'Sorry?'

Prize moron.

'Four. There are four things on the table. An apple, a penny, a watch and a stack of paper. Which three do you want me to name?'

The man in the white coat puts down his pen and smiles properly for the first time.

'You know, Bill, you are quite right – there are four things on the table. I wasn't counting the paper.'

'Do I get an extra point for that?'

The man in the suit laughs.

'No, Bill, no extra points. Try not to think of it as a test.'

'If you say so – but the way I see it, if you're asking me questions and you want answers, then it's a test.'

Scribble.

'What are the three, sorry four things that were on the table?'

Bill looks down; there's only the paper left. He waggles his finger at the man in the suit.

'You're trying to trick me. Paper. Apple. Penny. Clock.'

'Again.'

'Apple. Penny. Clock.'

'One last time.'

This time Bill grinds the words through closed lips.

'Paper. Penny. Watch.'

Scribble.

'Now, Bill. Do you know who the prime minister is?'

'Oh, man. The questions you ask. My son knows the answer to that one and he's only five.'

'I know it seems odd but it would really help me if you could just answer the questions no matter how silly they seem.'

'I know what this is – Jackson laid on a few head punches, didn't he? You're checking for brain damage.'

He taps his head with his finger, making a hollow knocking sound.

'Nothing wrong with my brain, Doc – it can just take a couple of days to get over a fight, that's all.'

'The prime minister?'

Bill stretches his hand. The bird's wings spread with the bruise.

'It's that dancer fella, isn't it? Never could stand him. Should've stuck to dancing – done us all a favour.'

The man in the suit scratches his bald patch.

'Dancer?'

Bill smiles.

'I'm pulling your leg – I know it's Tony Blair. I like to pretend I think it's Lionel Blair. Winds the missus up. She likes that Tony Blair – bit smarmy if you ask me.'

He gets a flash of a dream he keeps having; an old lady watching the news on TV. She's talking to him about the news, about Tony Blair, but he can't hear what she's saying. He doesn't know who she is, although her face is familiar. It's not his mother. At first he thought it was her but she was dead before anyone had even heard of Tony Blair. It's there at the back of his mind somewhere but right now he can't get to it.

'You with us, Bill?'

'Sorry?'

'I asked you if you could spell WORLD backwards.'

Bill's eyes ache.

'You did? Why on earth would I want to do that? Had enough trouble at school spelling things frontwards – now you want me to spell them backwards.'

'Can you?'

Bill scratches his nose with his thumbnail. It hits the bridge of his glasses and he takes them off and looks at them, holding them up to the light as if he's never seen them before. He coughs and looks around the room. It's all blurry, like after a fight when the blood seeps into your eyes – must be why he's got them; Jackson cut his eye.

'Bill – can you spell world backwards?'

Bill hangs his glasses over his ears. Things are much clearer now.

'I don't want to. Where's that girl? She's much more fun than you.'

'Nurse Jones will be here soon, to take you back to the ward. Just a couple more questions. Can you repeat the following? "No ifs, ands or buts."'

Silence.

'Bill?'

'Yes?'

'Can you repeat it?'

'It?'

'Yes – "No ifs, ands or buts."'

'Oh sorry, guv – was waiting for you to say something I had to repeat. "No ifs, ands or buts", is it?'

'Yes, Bill – that's it. "No ifs, ands or buts."'

Bill has a funny thought. 'No tits, hands or bums,' he says.

The man in the suit smiles again – another proper smile. He looks down at the form and scribbles on it.

'Now, can you take a piece of paper from the table, fold it in half and put it on the floor?'

Bill picks up a sheet of paper. His hand shakes, the paper flaps like a frightened bird and escapes his fingers, swooping to the floor behind his chair. Bill rubs his hand.

'Must've smacked him hard when he went down. Think I've broken a few bones. Need a bucket of ice. Maybe that lovely girl could get me one.'

'Do you want to try it again?'

'Well, how important is it to you to have a folded piece of paper? Me, I'm not bothered at all.'

The man in the suit pushes another piece of paper and a pencil across the table towards Bill.

'Can you read this and do what it says?'

Bill looks at the paper, squints and then closes his eyes.

'Good. Now the next bit?'

A loud snore fills the room.

Silence.

'Bill?'

Snore. Silence.

'Bill?'

Bill opens one eye and grins.

'I'm pulling your leg, guv.'

He picks up the pencil with his right hand. It shakes violently but he holds it steady with his left hand at the wrist and scrawls on the paper, then pushes it back to the man in the white coat. The man smiles and turns the paper round to see what Bill has done.

Bill has written A SENTENCE.

He laughs.

'Good. Now, Bill – can you copy this shape?'

'Actually, guv, my hand's a bit sore. Must've been when I floored Jackson. Need a bucket of ice – that'll set me right.'

'All right, Bill – I think that's enough for today. I'll get Nurse Jones to take you back to the ward. Your son is waiting for you there.'

'Billy? Don't be daft, guv. Billy's at school. He's a good kid, little Billy – a fantastic right hook, just like his old man. Clever, mind – he'll be doing his eleven-plus this year. Teachers say he'll probably get into the grammar school. Takes after his mother that way…'

Bill trails off and he stares at the blinds on the window. The rain has cleared and the early evening sun is filtering through the slats. It looks like somewhere he once knew – somewhere he can't quite place.

The man in the suit goes to the door.

'Nurse Jones – could you take Bill back to the ward now?'

She comes in with a wheelchair. *Damn, is that for me? Am I an invalid now?* Still, he can think of worse things than being pushed around by a beautiful girl and he's tired – very tired.

'I need a bucket of ice for my hand,' he says to her. 'He was no match for my right hook, went down in the fifth. Is he all right?'

Mr Patrick holds the wheelchair steady as Nurse Jones lowers Bill into it. The old man thumps down onto the seat like a bag of bones. He looks down at Bill's feet as Nurse Jones crouches and lifts them onto the footrests one at a time. In the gap between the tartan slippers and Bill's pyjamas, Mr Patrick notices how white the feet are; translucent skin stretched over wrinkled mountain ranges of blue veins. Bill asks if his wife will be waiting for him where they're going. Nurse Jones coos and smiles reassurances to him. She tucks a blanket over his knees. The brakes click off and the seat squeaks under Bill's dressing gown.

Mr Patrick holds open the door so Nurse Jones can ease the chair through it. He offers his hand again and says, 'It was a pleasure to meet you, Bill.'

He looks down at the old man's face; his eyes are glassy. There is no comprehension. Then suddenly, Bill focuses; he smiles a broad, ageless smile and grabs the doctor's hand – a good strong grip. The bird tattoo flexes under the anaesthetic bruise.

'Thank you,' says Bill, 'thank you.'

Mr Patrick feels a lump in his throat. It's been a while since anyone thanked him; in this job he doesn't get to give good news.

The old man lets go of his hand and closes his eyes. He's gone again. A small tear smears under each lid. Little tufts of wiry white hair stick out from behind ears that seem too big for his head. His mouth has rested into a thin, curved line, a rickety bridge on the road map of his face.

Mr Patrick nods to Nurse Jones, who smiles sadly. They like Bill, the nurses; he's heard them talk about him in the canteen. The nice old bloke who used to be a boxer, so cute, so smiley – a real gent. Mr Patrick wonders if that's enough for a man like Bill in the end. Does he even care?

He hears the wheels of the chair roll over the lino as he closes the door. Through the glass he hears Nurse Jones ask Bill what he wants for lunch and the words treacle tart and the old man's laugh, fractured, as it echoes down the corridor.

Bill Johnson is the last patient of the day. Mr Patrick is tired. He just has to write this one up and he can go home. It's not a good idea to test patients this late in the day but they need a quick assessment so that they can place Mr Johnson in a home. The hospital needs his bed. He came in after a fall two weeks ago and had a hip replacement but he didn't recover well after the surgery. Bill has been living alone since his wife died eight years ago. Two sons – both living hundreds of miles away. He's probably been showing signs of dementia for years with no one to see it. Families deny it's happening; they only visit for a couple of days every six months and just put it down to Dad getting old, forgetting, talking about the past. It's not that people don't care – they just don't want to be reminded. It could be them one day. Maybe the fall accelerated it. Maybe the fall was caused by it. Who knows? He won't be going back home again, that's for sure.

Alone in the quiet room, Mr Patrick sits back down at the table and rubs his eyes. He looks over Bill's test, reading through the responses. It's not Alzheimer's – there's too much residual wit. His responses are too clever, too connected. Vascular dementia maybe, something to do with the boxing or an extreme reaction to anaesthesia? Mr Patrick scribbles recommendations for an MRI scan in the oblong box at the end of the test. He's been a dementia specialist for 30 years. He's 60 this year, close to retirement himself, five, six more years at best. He's learned to distance himself from tragedy. Sometimes though the job gets to him. Sometimes, when he can see what a patient used to be, when he gets a glimpse of a former vitality, still there but buried beneath the disease. In these cases he's reminded of his powerlessness; he knows there's nothing much he can do to keep the spark safe and is all too aware that it will soon disappear, like paint on a brush dipped in water. That's when it gets to him. Sometimes this job is nothing more than an act of diagnosis.

He thinks about his own father, in his eighties now. He hasn't spoken to him in weeks. He should give him a call, take some time off and drive over to see him. They could go fishing like they used to, spend some time together, just the two of them.

When he was about eight years old, his dad took him to Wembley to see a boxing match. He's never forgotten it. His dad worked for the *Mirror*; he didn't usually take him to assignments but this was different – this was a once-in-a-lifetime opportunity. He was the envy of all his friends; everyone was obsessed by boxing back then. There was a new boxer from America. He was unbelievable. All the kids wanted to be him and he was coming to England to fight a Brit. The American was going to win; he was unbeaten in the States in 14 fights, but everyone was rooting for Henry Cooper: the brave opponent – the underdog. 'Our 'Enery.' And maybe – just maybe.

The American got into the ring wearing a crown and a fur-trimmed cape, pretending to be royal, waving to the crowd like the queen did. The noise was immense. People booed and cheered and laughed. The fight wasn't the foregone conclusion it was meant to be. The crowd roared as 'Enery laid into the American, who jumped and danced around the ring like a butterfly, pounding at him with his huge gloved fists. BAM BAM BAM! Like Bill said – *a fucking ballet*. Then it came, in the fourth round – a left hook that sent the American reeling against the ropes, glassy-eyed with shock. The crowd leapt to their feet. The stadium fell silent. Time literally froze. The American wavered inches from the floor, his arms hooked on the ropes, tantalisingly close to sitting down, to being out when the bell rang. And then it would surely ring before he got up. It was only seconds away.

But by some miracle the American pulled himself up just in time. The bell sounded for the end of the round – three tinny rings with no other noise to muffle them. The dream was gone. The American went on to win easily in the fifth round. He cut Cooper's eye with an early punch and that was that. But when it was over the crowd went wild for Cooper; after all, not many Brits can say they almost knocked out Ali.

Dr Patrick picks up his pen and, with a sigh, he writes '17' in the box at the bottom of the test.

SEVERE COGNITIVE DYSFUNCTION.

And then, as an afterthought, he writes in the margin:

J
A
C
K
S
O
N
W
A
S
G
O
O
D
B
U
T
H
E
W
E
N
T
D
O
W
N
T
H
E
5th

11

Fifteen Minutes

It hasn't been so good with Marianne lately. When they first met she told him that ever since she was a little girl bandaging up her dolls she'd wanted to be a doctor, but now that she is one, she's as grumpy as hell. She's tired, he gets it, long hours and intense situations, but even when she's been off for a couple of days she doesn't have any time for him. Okay, so his job is nowhere near as important as hers but it's a good job. Sometimes when he's working at his drawing board she looks at him like he's trash that needs to be taken out but she's too tired to do it.

A few days ago she told him she didn't want to be a doctor anymore – now she wants to be a mother and she wants him to be a father. In her mind it's all settled. She'll have the kid and go back to work part-time, maybe something in family medicine, and he works from home so it will be easy for him to do half of the childcare. She's had enough of the front line. They should get married too; it's a proven fact that the children of married parents do better in school. A low-key wedding though; they don't need to waste money. She'd only have to bring home enough a month to pay off her school fees as he earns enough to keep them going over the next few years. It will be tight. There won't be lavish holidays or new apartments, but if he loves her he'll agree. He does love her, but... There was no row or anything. He just told her he needed time to think, that it was a big step but that he'd give it his full consideration. It was like a business proposition.

They were supposed to go to his parents' house for the weekend but Marianne volunteered to cover at the ER. That was another thing – she *volunteered*. She'd rather be knee-deep in stabbings and drug overdoses than spend Thanksgiving with her future husband, the father of her future child.

He decided to work too. He had illustrations to do for a picture book on the demise of the American buffalo. By Sunday he had inked and washed so many buffalo horns, the beasts were invading his dreams. Waves of the great herd migrations crashed through his sleep until he was surrounded and dragged under, left to the mercy of a million trampling hooves. He woke screaming just as the sky was obscured by dust and bovine breath and his body began to bruise.

He hated this fucking job, wanted to be rid of it by Christmas in the hope that the next assignment would be something that actually ignited his imagination. But this stuff with Marianne had distracted him and he was behind schedule. It was always the same these days. He was lucky, he knew that. He had an in with a successful children's book publisher. He was being paid to paint. Many of his college friends would be prepared to kill for a job like his but, while it was better than waiting tables, it just wasn't what he'd pictured himself doing when he'd graduated, full of ambition, nine years earlier. He was being paid to paint what someone else wanted him to paint. He was going through the motions and often he found himself sitting before his drawing board staring at blank paper for hours.

He called his mom and told her he couldn't make the weekend. Her voice changed in tone, her disappointment palpable, but she said she understood. He didn't think about the food she'd bought in or the decorations she would have made. His dad came on the phone and told him how proud they were of him and asked him to make the trip at Christmas – for his mother's sake.

Richard hadn't seen a soul all weekend, just locked himself up tight in his own little graphics factory drawing buffalo till the herd came home.

Interior – A New York bar Thanksgiving weekend.

Characters – RANDY and TRENT (a couple) and their sad-sack friend RICHARD. RANDY is mid-flow with his Thanksgiving story.

RANDY: It's an eight-hour drive to Aunt Elizabet's; we set off on Wednesday night so we'd actually be there in time for Thanksgiving dinner the next day.

TRENT: You know how he hates to fly. (*Trent interrupts, gently touching Randy's arm. Richard's eyes follow his action.*) Next time, I'm flying and he can take the bus.

RANDY: Trent is *the* worst navigator, so inevitably we get lost, end up in some God-awful backwater in laid-off steel country, and we're low on gas because *somebody* didn't fill up when he had the chance. We see this sign for a truck stop up ahead, there's a diner attached and they're open all night. When we pull into the parking lot we're getting a bit nervous. You know how it can be in Hicksville and he has on his violet cashmere and Star-Spangled Banner pants.

(*Trent grins and nods like a puppy.*)

RANDY: There are two, maybe three trucks parked up, all of them jalopies. I know it's 2014 and things are better than they ever were but you can't be sure, right?

TRENT: I knew it would be okay but Randy insisted on texting you his funeral song from the parking lot before going in. He's such a drama queen.

RICHARD: The 5am text! *I just don't know what to do with myself.*

RANDY: Thank you for your reply by the way – it was characteristically charming.

RICHARD: You can always count on me.

TRENT: We go inside and oh my God it's 1959 in there! Like a themed diner only it isn't themed, it's just never been updated. It's all faded red vinyl and broken neon. There's a couple of ancient truck drivers sleeping over their coffee and Johnny Cash is playing from a genuine Wurlitzer. For all Randy's worry about getting beaten up, no one pays us any attention.

RANDY: 'Guess Things Happen That Way'! That was the song that was playing. One of my daddy's favourites. The waitress is in a pink coverall, bobby socks and sneakers, little hat on her head, fully made up with hoopy earrings and bright red hair, but she's 150 years old if she's a day. She's scooting around the counter with a coffee pot. 'Mornin',' she says, which technically I suppose it was.

TRENT: We take a seat by the window. There's an equally old cowboy type reading the paper at the next table, plaid shirt, a Stetson sitting beside him. Gun on the table. 'How do,' he says and he winks at us like he's Sam Shepard's grandpoppy. At this point I'm trying not to laugh. I can't risk looking at Randy. This guy's face tells me he was probably around for the great flood. If things turn nasty even Randy could take him, but no one so much as glances our way, they're that old. The waitress comes over with the menus. You could tell she used to be a real beauty, the bone structure's all there, the make-up is perfect, but she has so many wrinkles she makes Liza look like Jennifer Lawrence.

RANDY: (*With a breathy feminine accent and Vivien Leigh hand gestures*) Would you boys like coffee?

TRENT: Gwyneth Paltrow here asks her if they have any green tea and when that's a negative he asks for decaf with soya milk. She winks at the cowboy and says, 'You boys ain't from round here, are ya? How about black?' and leaves us to the menu.

RANDY: The old guy comes over and sits next to Trent. 'Are y'all from New York?' he asks. There's more gravel in his voice than on Aunt Elizabet's path. 'Cherry there lived in New York for a while, til' I made her see sense.' Then he tells us the most amazing story. You have just got to hear it.

TRENT: (*Excited*) It was the best thing about the whole weekend.

RANDY: The cowboy introduces himself. His name is Roy and I notice how clean he is, his shirt is pressed and his long white hair and Buffalo Bill beard are all combed and shiny. He has a gold tooth and a matching twinkle in his eye. You can tell he still works out – his arms are sinew – and he's lean and sits a head taller than us at the table so he must be well over six feet. He leans back in the booth and starts to tell his story.

(*Randy adopts an old cowboy accent.*)

It was way back. I was 18 an' Cherry was just 17. We were still in Pittsburgh then; we didn't move out here until years later. I'd asked her to marry me, got her pa's permission an' everything.

TRENT: (*Adoringly*) You know how Randy loves his accents.

RANDY: (*Continuing in Roy's accent*) As I was saying, Cherry was unbelievably beautiful – still is, a course – but imagine her then, all fresh an' new. Me an' her pa have it all worked out but Cherry has different ideas. She loves me an' she wants to marry me but first she wants to go to New York an' study to be an actress. It's her dream. She has a cousin there called Ida who says she can stay with her so she can audition for this acting school she's applied to. I'm disappointed a course but she always was a talent, school plays an' local theatre productions, always the star of the show. I used to be so proud of her up there on the stage with all the boys mooning after her. I was the one she snuggled up to afterwards. What can I say? I wanted her to be happy, so we got engaged an' I let her go to New York wearing my ring.

RICHARD: Wait, what year is this?

RANDY: Forty-eight. Forty-nine, thereabouts, Roy said.

TRENT: I scribbled '83' on a napkin and showed it to Randy and do you know what he did then? He called Cherry over and ordered blueberry pancakes.

RANDY: (*Laughs*) I was tired. I thought that's what you wanted. Number 83, I thought he meant. I mean, how could people that old still be working an all-night diner?

TRENT: After ten years you would think he'd remember I was wheat intolerant. So, Cherry goes off to New York to become an actress and then Roy's story gets really interesting.

RANDY: (*In Roy's accent*) So after a couple of months she sends me a long, long letter, Roy says. She's staying in a dorm with her cousin Ida. She failed the audition for the acting school; they thought she was too wholesome or somin'. She's got a job as a waitress but Ida has introduced her to some Italian guy who says he can get her a job singing in his friend's nightclub. Now Cherry was very young an' she always thought the best of people, which is a fine quality to have, but it can also get you into all kinds of trouble. I had an idea of what sorta place this Italian guy was talking about so I went straight to the soda fountain to call the number Cherry had given me for the dormitory. I just had this really bad feeling that she was gonna get into somin' she'd regret just so she can sing in front of an audience. At this point I'd just started working in steel town an' the night before I had lost most of my week's wages in a poker game with my new colleagues. I didn't have the money for a bus ticket to New York an' that's what I really wanted to do, hop on a bus an' bring her back home. I call the dorm several times an' eventually one of the girls goes an' wakes Cherry up. It's 10am on a Saturday morning an' she's still in bed! This is something Cherry would never usually do, so I know she musta been out late the night before. I'm going outta my mind. Anyway, she's real grumpy. Tells me to mind my own business. Says she can look after herself an' then I run out of money an' the line goes dead. I'm shouting her name an' I'm angry now cos I just used my last quarter in the payphone, so I bang down the receiver real hard an' cuss out loud. I notice this dorky young man sitting at the counter an' he's looking over at me an' smirking. By now I'm in a real bad mood an' I've a hangover to match from the poker game, so I walk over to the counter an' order a coffee, use my last 5 cents to buy time to think of what I can do next. The kid looks down at the counter like he doesn't want to make eye contact but I can see he's writing somin' down so I stand next to him an' look at what he's doing. He's not writing at all, he's drawing on the napkin. It's only a few strokes with a pen but I can clearly see that it's a picture of me on the telephone.

'Hey,' I say, picking up the napkin. The kid kinda shrinks away like I'm gonna hit him or somin' an' I might have given the mood I'm in, but the drawing is a real good likeness. 'This is really good,' I say an' I see him relax. I set the napkin back down an' sit on the stool beside him to take a swig of coffee.

'Girl trouble?' says the kid. He's got this tiny, reedy voice an' I can hardly hear him but for some reason, I don't know if it's cos he's got this little-boy, wide-eyed face or what, I start to tell him all about Cherry an' New York an' the poker game. He hangs on every word, an' every so often he'll say somin' like gosh or golly gee, like he's Shirley Temple or somin'. When I'm finished he says, 'I know a way you can make the fare to New York in an hour. You'll be done in time to catch the lunchtime bus and all you have to do is stand still.'

Well, I'm intrigued now but suspicious, y'know? I don't want to do anything illegal. It turns out he's an art student an' he wants to sketch me for his exams, says he's doing a series on ordinary working people an' needs a cowboy like me for 'symmetry'. That's what he says, 'symmetry'. Well, what harm can it do? He's got a studio in his mother's house so we finish up an' leave. He even pays for my coffee. The girl at the counter looks at me real funny as we go like she wants to tell me somin'.

'Bye, Andy,' she says. That was his name, Andy.

TRENT: At this point, grandpa cowboy gives us a massive grin and stretches back in his seat, stringing out the tale – masterful. The pancakes come and I decide to risk the wheat allergy. They're delicious. I've never tasted better pancakes than that, fluffy like pillows and swimming in syrup and berries, neither of us can resist. Cherry fusses around us with napkins and refills. She kisses Roy on the cheek and is off before he draws her into the conversation again. He watches her go like she's teenage ass.

RANDY: So as Roy was saying…

That summer was one of those asphalt-melting summers, when the whole world felt like it was being baked in an oven an' the dogs slept in the shade til' sundown. Even the traffic was tired. Andy told me his studio was just around the corner but outside the diner he went all quiet an' edgy like we was in a really rough neighbourhood an' we was gonna get robbed. He shuffled along hardly lifting his feet off the floor. He was so pale his skin shone in the sun an' he hid his eyes under big black sunglasses that nearly covered his face. I tried to keep the conversation going but he just smiled softly an' mopped the sweat from his forehead with a big white handkerchief. It was a very long short walk. I was glad when we got to his house. It was a yellow-brick building with three storeys an' it was neat enough, but you could see the windows were in need of repair an' the front yard was overgrown.

'Here we are,' he says. 'The old homestead.'

He fishes for his keys in his pockets an' even though his eyes are covered I can tell he's looking me up an' down like he's measuring me up for a coffin or somin'. It makes me feel real uneasy.

'Is your mother home?' I ask.

He shakes his head an' holds open the door so I have to squeeze past him to get in.

'Ain't nobody here but us chickens,' he says.

TRENT: A few more people are coming in the diner by now and Cherry's rushing around, clearly in need of help, but Roy just carries on with his story.

RANDY: Anyway… (*Then in Roy's voice*) Inside it's cool an' dark. He leads me into a living room; the curtains are still drawn an' there's a funny smell, disinfectant mixed with earth – it's not pleasant. There are crucifixes an' religious icons on every wall an' family photos on every surface. I pick one up. It's a picture of a toddler, all dressed up in a coat an' hat. Even that young the face is unmistakably Andy's. He's sitting on the lap of a plain-looking woman in a hat an' glasses that must be his mother, an' a slightly older kid, that must be his brother, is standing next to him.

There's a kitchen at the back an' Andy opens the refrigerator an' takes out a beer an' throws it over to me. I only just catch it an' he laughs at me, all playful like a kid, an' sort of skips back out into the corridor an' unlocks the door on the other side of the hall. Now that room is something else. It's painted white an' it has no curtains so the sun streams through enormous windows an' I have to shield my eyes after the dark of the living room. There are paintings everywhere, on the floor, propped against the wall, lying on the sofa. It smells of oil an' turpentine. The floor is covered with a fly sheet an' there are hand-drawn sketches in rolls an' stuck to just about everything. They are all of people an' they're real good, like the one he done of me in the diner – just a few lines on the page to create a whole recognisable person. Apart from the couch, the only other furniture is a paint-splattered wooden chair an' an easel.

Andy tells me to go an' stand by the couch an' drink my beer. I feel a bit uncomfortable being there alone with him. I don't know why. He's got this funny way of looking, head turned to one side, a half smile on his face. Anyways, I do what he says, an' he puts a blank canvas onto the easel an' starts sketching me. He's working real intently, in total silence, an' the beer is almost finished. I'm getting a bit bored just standing there. 'Don't slouch,' he says an' then he asks me to take off my shirt.

''Scuse me?' I say, but he comes over to me, still smiling, an' tucks twenty dollars in my shirt pocket. 'Take it off,' he says. Twenty bucks is twenty bucks, right? So I take off my shirt an' Andy gives this little sigh, then sets about working again. After a while he puts down his pencil an' he says, 'How would you like to make another twenty?'

Forty dollars back then was two weeks' wages but I'm worried what he might want me to do for it. He's giving me the creeps but he just smiles again an' says, 'You won't have to do anything you don't feel comfortable with. Nothing you haven't done before in the high-school gym.'

Anyways, he wants me to take it all off. 'For art,' he says. When he asks me, my first instinct is to sock him in the jaw an' hightail it outta there, but it's forty bucks! I could go get Cherry an' put a deposit down on a place of our own an' there's dollar signs before my eyes an' visions of the showers after work an' skinny dipping in the waterhole. I mean, guys get naked together all the time, don't they? Why was this any different? I ask him to get me another beer an' when he comes back he finds me in my birthday suit. He just blinks at me an' hands me the beer.

It takes him another hour to finish the sketches an' then he says, 'I'm done,' an' sits down on the sofa. He watches me get dressed, looks at every inch of me real slowly an' I can feel my skin crawl. Just as I'm wondering about the money he produces a couple of folded bills from his sleeve like a magician. I walk over to him an' try to take it but he holds it tight for a second an' then he runs his finger over the top of my hand an' closes his eyes. He doesn't say goodbye or anything, just lets go of the money an' I hightail it outta there as fast as I can an' run downtown to the bus station. I'm in New York by dinnertime an' I catch Cherry as she's leaving the dorm, all done up for a night singing in the club. At first she doesn't want to come with me but I take her to a fancy restaurant an' I tell her how much I love her an' by dawn we're back in Pittsburgh an' a month later we're wed with our first son on the way an' she's never looked back.

TRENT: At this point Cherry leans over and fills up our coffees.

RANDY: 'Ain't that right, Cherry?' says Roy. 'Uh-huh,' says Cherry with a smile. But it's a sad smile, a wistful smile, like she's back in New York in 1948, getting ready to take to the stage and sing her little heart out. The door opens and she hurries away to greet her customers, the only audience she has. (*He sighs dramatically.*)

RICHARD: That's the saddest thing I ever heard.

RANDY: Wait, it gets better. So Roy tells us about their early married life and his excitement at becoming a father and then he tells us about how they're ready to move into their first apartment and how he's borrowed a pick-up from one of his friends and he's driving from Cherry's parents' house to the new place with their belongings.

(*Randy continues in Roy's voice.*)

I come up to a stop sign an' then I see the diner where I met Andy. Somin' makes me park up an' go inside. Haven't been past the place for months, an' though he was creepy I figure I owe Andy a thank you for making it possible for me an' Cherry to be together. I go in, half expecting him to be sitting at the counter sketching customers, but the place is empty, 'cept for the same waitress as was there before. I order a coffee an' as she pours she looks at me real quizzical like an' then she says, 'Are you Roy?' Anyways, turns out Andy has moved to New York but he's left somin' for me at the diner in case I come in again. She runs out back an' brings a square bundle wrapped in a paint-stained piece of cloth. Inside there's two paintings. Not like the sketches he done, these must've taken hours. They're of me in all my glory; you can't see my face but you can tell because I've got my hat on. I can feel myself going red as the waitress watches me looking. She tells me they were in an exhibition in City Hall but they had to be taken down because people thought they were 'obscene'. She said that it didn't do Andy any harm though because he sold everything else he had on show an' made enough money to go to New York an' be a proper artist. She said someone wanted to buy these too but he insisted they kept them in the diner to give to me in case I came in again.

He went to New York to pursue his dream an' he must've thought I helped him somehow which is why he left me paintings he could've sold. He did all right for himself too because the next I hear of him he's on the TV talking about some pictures he's done of Campbell's Soup cans.

RICHARD: (*Almost choking on his drink*) No fucking way.

RANDY: Way. Roy goes out back and gets one of the paintings to show us; says the other one is on loan to the Carnegie Museum of Art. The painting is amazing. I wouldn't say you could tell who did it but it's got something all right. Here, see for yourself. (*Takes out phone and shows it to Richard.*)

(*Fade.*)

For the rest of the evening, Richard thinks of nothing but the painting on Randy's phone. Even in photo form it is exceptional, so fluid it looks like it's moving. The lines of the cowboy's body flow but his hat is static; the colour is blocked but natural, except where it is cartoonish, the little human details – hair, muscle – are picked out in charcoal paint, simultaneously precise and softened. It is a work of genius, an almost holy artefact. Richard has Randy send him a copy and stares at it all through dinner, tapping the phone into life when the colour times out to grey. When he gets back to his apartment he sits in the living room sipping a beer and enlarges the image incrementally until it is too pixelated to see. He shows it to Marianne when she comes home in the small hours, tired from her shift in ER. She glances at it and sips her wine as Richard retells Randy's story.

'Very nice,' she says when he has finished and hands him back the phone.

Then she yawns and puts down her glass. 'I'm going to hit the hay. I'm back on duty at ten. Did you think any more about our conversation?'

Richard hasn't, not really, his mind has been occupied with pictures of buffalo and cowboys. He opens his mouth to say as much but Marianne stops him.

'Actually, don't tell me now,' she says crisply. 'I'm too tired. We'll talk about it tomorrow.' She exits the room.

'Goodnight, then,' whispers Richard to nobody.

He doesn't go to bed. He hears Marianne use the bathroom then shut their bedroom door. He stares at the cowboy painting until his eyes hurt. Dawn paints light shafts through the windows, brightening the night colours of the apartment. Richard puts down his phone. He rotates the table lamp so that it shines starkly on his drawing board and the illustration he's done for the last page of *Goodbye Buffalo*. With his right hand he grips the top of the page, pauses for a moment and then pulls sharply, ripping it right down the middle. The two halves hang on the drawing board like opening theatre curtains. He goes over to his art case and unzips it, then takes out the 46 A2 buffalo illustrations and lays them on the table. He holds each one up in turn, examines it briefly, and then rips it in half, discarding the pieces into fanned piles on the floor. When he gets to the last one, he rips it into four, and a gigantic grin crosses his face. He grabs some running shoes from the closet, hooks his iPhone to his sweatshirt and puts in his earphones. While he's tying his laces he whistles along to the music he has chosen, 'So Long, Marianne' by Leonard Cohen. He pulls on a woolly hat and jogs out of the door. He has plans. He's going to run around the whole park, stop in at Madison for blueberry pancakes and then he's going straight to Lee's Art Shop because he's just remembered that they have a canvas sale on.

12

Shipwrecked

'Shit. I'm wrecked.'

Those were the last words spoken by Jelly Raven as he fell through a vortex of psychedelic swirls, sweat and inflated heartbeats, and concussed himself on the Venetian marble sink of the penthouse bathroom. Over the last four years he'd often felt tossed on the turbulent seas of superstardom but before this blow to his ego he'd always been waving, not drowning. Now, buffeted by the whirlpool of drugs, booze and adulation that had become his normality, he had a moment of clarity just brief enough to utter those words before he went under. He lay on the tiles out cold, hangers-on oblivious in the next room, and subconsciously woke on the bleached sand of an archetypal desert island. Birds sang melodies to the waves; the sun warmed his back and fresh air cleansed his senses. There was everything he needed there: fresh water, coconut palms, even a shelter complete with a swinging hammock and tethered goat. It looked at him and bleated and Jelly crossed breadcrumb sand to the hammock and lay back with his eyes shut. He was woken by a coconut thudding like a fist into his chest and the smell of vomit as he was lifted unceremoniously onto a stretcher and bundled into an ambulance. The last thing he remembered before blacking out again was the flash of a camera.

'Sign,' his manager, Starkey, had said. 'It's either sign and do the twelve weeks or the company drops you. They're not happy. You bailed on a tour with a month left to run and the press had a field day with that photo of you in the ambulance. The company has a responsibility to keep it clean – it's not as if you're a real rock star, is it? You know the public expect more from their *Supernova* stars.'

'It's not my fault I won some shit TV talent competition by a mile,' Jelly had snapped back. 'You should be grateful I went stratospheric.'

'If only I'd kept a tighter hold on you,' Starkey said, shaking his head.

They both knew that Jelly had taken his first few pills just to stay awake through his demanding schedule and then he'd taken everything he could get his hands on to fill the void. The normal human rhythms of activity and sleep were all chemically induced, and after four years of bestselling albums, stadium tours, TV shows, a movie soundtrack, even a US No. 1, Jelly hit the iceberg – head first.

He met Melody on his first morning at Lake View when he went in search of coffee in the dining room.

The catering lady had looked at his red eyes and mismatched clothes with undisguised contempt.

'We only serve tea here,' she said, and turned away with a tray of half-eaten fruit salads.

'The green tea,' said a girl sitting in a leather armchair too big for her slight frame, 'is stuffed with caffeine – they haven't noticed yet.'

Melody was all jutting bones, saucer eyes and sleek blonde hair. Her voice was 1950s cut glass with a smoky undertow.

He made himself a cup of green tea with two tea bags and sat down opposite her.

'Jelly,' he said.

'Yes,' Melody replied. 'I know who you are.'

'C'mon you two, the meeting started ten minutes ago.' Miles, Jelly's case-worker, had come to find the stragglers.

Jelly followed Miles down the corridor, Melody lagging behind, walking so close to the wall she had her back against it. Every so often Jelly looked over his shoulder at her and smiled. She stared blankly ahead. Progress was slow. When they finally made it into the therapy room, everyone else was sitting down expectantly in a circle.

Jelly walked past the circle and poured himself and Melody a cup of green tea from the bounty table at the back of the room. When he turned round he saw that Miles was glaring at him and tapping his pencil on his clipboard.

'We are running a bit late, James,' he said through gritted teeth.

Jelly handed the tea to Melody and took the only seat available, which was next to Miles. The other captives were the usual NA misfits: a man in his sixties with a Brylcreemed quiff and gold jewellery, a glamorous woman a few years younger, all perma-tan, bleached hair and pink lips, a bloke in jeans and a T-shirt who looked like he was missing his suit and the office and a wispy, hippy-looking girl with red eyes and a permanently runny nose. Jelly could have told Miles their stories without them saying a word.

'Jelly,' he said. 'The name's Jelly.'

'Really?' said Miles. He flicked the pages on his clipboard until he found the right one, then tapped it with his pencil. That pencil was like his own personal symbol of authority.

'It says James here. James David Black.' He fixed Jelly with an even stare. 'No one is a rock star at Lake View, James. Everyone, this is James. It's his first time, so remember the golden rules. James – maybe we could start with you? Why are you here?'

'Believe me, I am asking myself that very question.'

'You know, James, you are free to leave any time you want. Now maybe you could answer me this question. What do Jimi Hendrix, Amy Winehouse and Kurt Cobain have in common?'

God, the 27 Club, thought Jelly. *A bit of an unoriginal opener.*

Jelly shrugged, affecting ignorance. 'They all owned white lighters?' Then, with some enthusiasm, 'I know, I know – they all have a little bit of genius about them?'

'No, James,' said Miles. 'They don't have anything about them. They're all dead.' He pressed his hands together like a guru and looked Jelly directly in the eye. 'Do you want to die, James?'

Jelly almost laughed. Almost.

'Get straight in there, Miles; don't spare the new boy.'

'I believe your heart stopped on the way to the hospital, did it not?'

'I bet your parents are real hippy-dippy, summer-of-love types, aren't they?' countered Jelly. 'Off their faces throughout your whole childhood. Missed all the school assemblies and football matches. Christ, you were probably home-schooled. I bet that's why you do this job, isn't it? Some sort of inverted act of rebellion?'

Miles was unnervingly calm, but a few of the others started shuffling uncomfortably on their chairs.

'We're not here to talk about me, James.'

'I'm right though, aren't I?'

Miles took off his glasses and cleaned them on his T-shirt.

'Okay, if you really want to know, my parents were exactly as you say. They were also both addicts. They died of an overdose in 1979. I was ten. I found them together in the garden when I came home from school. They'd been dead several hours. There was no suicide note, so I can only assume it was an accident.'

Everyone looked at Miles with wide eyes. He went on.

'They were both thirty-six years old. That may seem old to you now, James, but believe me it isn't – just ask Melody.'

'Thanks, Miles,' said Melody. 'Just when I'd started to feel sorry for you.'

'As I said before, Melody – this isn't about me.'

'No offence, Miles,' Jelly butted in, 'your parents dying is sad and everything but they weren't in the same league as Jimi Hendrix, were they?'

There was an audible intake of breath from the other inmates but he continued.

'What do the Rolling Stones, the Chili Peppers and Liam Gallagher have in common?'

Miles frowned – just slightly – and shook his head. Jelly smiled.

'They're all shit now they're clean.'

Meetings carried on in the same vein, twice a day for the next few weeks. Jelly wouldn't back down; insisted that as soon as he was out he'd be back on it, that it enhanced his creativity and he couldn't do without it. Miles responded with frustratingly pertinent facts that blew Jelly out of the water every time and he knew precisely when to play the death card. Melody always stuck up for Jelly and they developed a friendship of sorts.

One evening, as he was walking around the garden, he heard a gagging sound coming from inside a weeping willow next to the greenhouse and then a voice. 'Oh my,' it said. 'Oh my, oh my.'

Jelly parted the branches and peered inside. The tree formed a tent-like hiding place. There was Melody against the trunk, sitting cross-legged in the dirt, a can of wood varnish upturned beside her and a spaced-out smile on her lips. Jelly knelt down and shuffled in beside her. The air had an overwhelming tang of paint thinner. Jelly could tell Melody had been there for some time.

'Jelly,' she said, reaching up to him in a hug. 'I'm terribly sorry but I've finished it all.' Her pupils were wide and her nose was red. She laughed, slightly manically.

'Daddy's going to kill me. Said he'd disinherit me if I didn't play ball this time.'

She tightened her grip on Jelly and stared wildly into his eyes, her voice desperate.

'What will I do, Jelly? Without Daddy's money. How am I going to live?'

He looked down at her, her eyes filling with tears, her face pale and vulnerable and, at that moment, heart-stoppingly beautiful.

'It'll be all right, Melody,' he said and bent to kiss her. She tasted of chemicals and expensive moisturiser. He tried to drum up some enthusiasm, probing with his tongue, laying her back onto the soil. He put his hand up her dress, pressed his body against hers, but he'd known from the moment their lips met that he felt nothing. After what seemed like an eternity of fumbling and rubbing he'd still failed to rise to the occasion, his penis a limp curl in his boxers. Jelly broke away and sat up, then hunched over with his face in his hands. This had never happened to him before. He was 21. He was almost permanently hard, and it wasn't that Melody was old enough to be his mother (just) – she was stunning and, despite the drugs, in amazing shape. Could it be his enforced sobriety? He'd not sung or played a note since arriving at Lake View. All the songs he had written in his head over the last year had disappeared. Now his libido had gone too. *Fuck Miles*, he thought. *And fuck the company*. After all, there wasn't much chance of fucking anything else while he was stuck here. He groaned and crawled out of the tree, leaving Melody shaking the can of wood varnish. He made his way to the dining room and drank four cups of green tea, each one stronger than the last.

One day, about a month into his imprisonment, Jelly rose at dawn and went for a run. He used to run at school but he hadn't done any exercise outside of nightclubs or bedrooms for years. He figured that he might get a buzz from an increased heart rate and endorphin release and, besides, he was sick of pacing the dark-panelled rooms of the house avoiding its even darker-panelled inhabitants. He ran in a spiral from the front door, rounding the lawn a few times before branching out into the trees. The brochure said the house sat in 300 acres of woodland and Jelly was soon submerged in a dense forest; he zigzagged through the trees at speed, only stopping when his heart threatened to burst through his chest. He bent forward and grasped his knees, gasping and blinking sweat from his eyes, then straightened, wishing he'd brought a cigarette from Melody's stash. As he did so, he spied something glinting through the trees. At first he couldn't make out what it was – thought it might be the reflection of an adjacent building – but then he remembered the brochure's description of 'complete tranquillity and isolation' and knew instantly what it must be. He walked slowly towards it, twigs crunching underfoot until he found himself standing before 15 feet of criss-crossed metal topped with barbed wire.

'I can leave anytime, eh, Miles?' he said aloud.

Jelly walked along the perimeter, a stitch kneading at his side, the rings on his fingers jangling along the fence, until he reached the lake. Still, dark water stretched away in a semicircle, dotted with lily pads and bordered by tall reeds. There was a DANGER DEEP WATER sign and an orange lifebelt on the shore. Jelly could see that the fence only covered about half of the lake's perimeter and that the opposite bank was as free as the wind.

That evening he heard a commotion on the lawn and, looking out of his window, saw three security guards trying to catch two topless women who were screaming and holding a 'We Love Jelly Raven' banner between them. This small flash of his previous life wriggled its way under his skin and though he pulled his curtains shut and lay still under his duvet listening to his iPod, he could still hear the girls screaming his name. He needed to get back, wanted to break free. What did the company know, anyway? He could do it without them, start again, do what he wanted, really succeed this time. No short cuts. No faking. He might only have six years left, but in that time he could conquer the world and have a ball doing it. Need crawled over his skin and balled in his stomach. He made up his mind.

He waited until after midnight, when the house was asleep, and tiptoed down the stairs to the front door. He pushed, but it didn't budge. He pushed again, then, realising that of course it was locked, he began beating at it with his fists, frantic, screaming, 'Let me out, let me out.' Bleary-eyed inmates gathered at the top of the stairs. Two security guards and the night warden bundled him into the office.

'Why not sleep on it?' the warden kept saying. 'Miles will be back in the morning, then we can let you go.' Jelly sobbed and pleaded for hours, reduced to a cowering heap of snot and raw eyeballs. In the end he realised he wasn't going anywhere; he was stranded, shipwrecked without a raft. He'd have to wait it out until Miles arrived in the morning; try to discharge himself. He still had rights, didn't he? He hadn't signed those away too. Deep down though, Jelly knew that Starkey would be with Miles, a company lawyer, perhaps, more documents to autograph. He saw his future mapped out for him. Endless years of contract, recording terrible cover versions, badly written originals, stadium shows, maybe even a cheesy movie as he moved soberly further and further away from his true self. Was everything lost? He asked to go to his room and the warden agreed, providing he went straight there.

'Do you want me to take you?' he asked.

'I'm not a child,' said Jelly. The warden's face told him different.

He made his way into the dining room, moving his hands along the walls like a blind man without a stick, nausea rippling his empty stomach. His hopes for the pleasant buzz of triple-bag green tea were quickly devastated. There wasn't any. He pulled all the individually wrapped bags from their decorative wooden boxes, checking each one before tossing it to the floor. Camomile was as hardcore as it got.

'No!' he cried out in anguish.

'Are you ready, then?' asked a husky voice from the armchair.

It was Melody, dressed like a jewel thief, primed for escape.

They legged it through the kitchen window, triggering the security lights as they crossed the lawn, laughing like children as they stumbled into the cover of the trees. The wood was damp and earthy, full of water drops and pungent ferns. Creatures rustled away from them unseen. Jelly's chest felt like it would burst, his breath fogged in front of him with every step. The lake was nearer than he remembered – a chequerboard of rippling dark and light where the surface reflected the moonlight. As they neared it, he faltered. Melody kicked off her shoes and glided up to her waist through the reeds, as fluid as the shimmering water. Jelly froze, suddenly taken back to the humiliation of holding onto the side of the pool during school swimming lessons, quickly followed by the nausea-inducing memory of being thrown into Tooting Common pond by some of the boys from his class. They laughed as he went under, their sounds fading under the volume of murky water, until one of them realised and dived in to save him. He remembered waking up to the kiss of life, a crowd and an ambulance, and the boy standing by, his clothes sodden.

'I can't swim,' he shouted.

Melody looked back at him.

'Are you serious?'

He stood poker straight with fear and nodded.

She turned, emerging from the water, dragging reeds and ripples with her. She was a mermaid, a nymph, Aphrodite riding her giant clam shell. His mouth fell open. She crossed the distance between them, light as a deer, and took his hand. Her fingers were icy.

'I'll hold your hand the whole way,' she said calmly. 'Besides, how deep can it be? That sign is just there to frighten us.'

Her voice was like honey in whisky.

Torchlight flashed through the trees behind them, catching on the lake. Jelly wondered what Miles's remit was, what the company had given him permission to do. Lock him up? Sedate him? Brainwash him? All he knew was that he had to escape. If he stayed, he would forever be the property of the company.

'Okay,' he said, and Melody led him into the water.

It was cold, but halfway across it was still only waist deep. Jelly began to relax. He could walk through waist-deep water. Melody was right; the sign was just there to scare them, after all. Through the trees Jelly could see the pinprick lights of the next town. From there he could phone a friend from the old days, from the simple times before he was famous, reverse the charges. He realised he didn't exactly know where he was. The journey to Lake View had been in a car with blacked-out windows. It was somewhere in Norfolk, going by the accents of the staff. He imagined himself finding a country pub with a real fire and a friendly landlord whose wife recognised him off the telly. He could wait there for the friend to drive over with money and his passport, eat a home-cooked meal and then go on from there – Europe, America, the Far East.

Melody grinned and let go of his hand. 'I'm swimming the rest,' she said and dived seal-like beneath the surface.

Jelly was alone and surrounded by water. Tonight he had overcome his biggest fear, a fear so all-consuming he kept it hidden most of the time. Now freedom was just a short walk away. He was buzzing. He was a god. He could do anything.

Melody surfaced as torchlight wrinkled back across the lake. Jelly heard someone shout his name and turned to see Miles splash into the reeds. He smiled and gave a jolly wave to the startled therapist, turned back to Melody and stepped after her. It took a second for him to realise there was nothing solid underfoot, but by then he'd committed his other leg to an unstoppable forward motion. His feet sought anchor but found only instability. Paddling wildly, he fell face first into deep, mercurial liquid. Muddy water flooded his senses, stinging his nose and clogging his throat. He threw his arms up into the air, this time drowning not waving. Melody and Miles both saw him go under and swam quickly towards him from opposite sides of the bank.

Blood flooded Jelly's brain.

Man, what a rush, he thought. *I wonder who will get to me first, Melody or Miles?* Then a terrifying possibility crossed his mind. *Oh… maybe neither?*

As he blacked out, Jelly knew that whatever happened next, James would be saved.

13

A Cake in the Rain

The Old Lady was already dying on my first visit. I wasn't a kid but I'd never seen anything like her. She looked like a melting wedding cake. There was a song my sister liked at the time, by Donna Summer, 'MacArthur Park', with its ridiculously catchy and incomprehensible cake-in-the-rain chorus. It had been in the charts all winter but it was our summer song. We used to dance around the kitchen to it whenever it came on the radio, singing the crescendo into hairbrushes as my dad tried to read *The Times*. Those words made absolutely no sense to me at all until I saw the Old Lady standing in the sea, the waves lapping at her legs. Then, with the sun baking the pebbles and the taste of salt on my lips, they started to mean something.

We'd gone on a day trip. My sister Kim, then 18, had managed to persuade her boyfriend, Frankie, to drive a group of her friends and me to the coast in his old Morris Minor van. They were all hippy types, flowing dresses, flares and long hair, funky cigarettes and patchouli joss sticks. I was 14 and they treated me like a pet – talked to me in coochy-coo voices and actually patted me on the head from time to time. Kim and Frankie sat in the front, with six of us so crammed in the back that every time we went round a corner we all slid giggling to our knees. In the end I sat on the floor in the middle, trying not to look at Kim's best friend, Sandra, and a skinny boy with acne snogging slurpily. It was hard not to stare. It wasn't that I wanted a skinny boy with acne to be kissing me, it was more of a morbid fascination, like when you drive past a car accident or watch a spider eat an insect wriggling on its web.

Frankie liked to drive one-handed, his left arm draped over Kim's shoulder. He was older than her; she'd told me he was 29. He was her tutor at college and once he'd been interviewed for a BBC documentary about Andy Warhol. I'd never met anyone who had been on television before. I thought Kim being Frankie's girlfriend was the height of sophistication. A couple of years before we'd still been hanging out in the park and walking home from school together. Now she was an adult. She'd had sex with a grown man. Not that I knew what that really meant. I mean, I'd done biology at school, copied diagrams of reproductive organs from dusty textbooks, learnt the official version by rote for exams and obviously I'd read the 'Dear Claire' column. But I'd only ever kissed one boy (playing spin the bottle at a party) and I'd kept my lips pressed shut the whole time.

Kim had warned me not to tell Mum and Dad that Frankie was taking us to Brighton because they didn't know she was seeing him. She said they wouldn't understand because of the age difference. I'd been tempted to tell, just to see the fireworks, but then I wouldn't have got a day out by the sea and I was so bored of my little home town that a whole day on the south coast sounded like a trip to paradise.

I could see why Kim was into Frankie. He had long, dark curls framing deep blue eyes and a square jaw. He wore short, faded T-shirts that gave you a glimpse of smooth brown stomach and showed off muscular arms, and around his neck was a shark's-tooth necklace sitting like a pearl on his breastbone. He was the type of bloke you dreamt about losing it to; not one of the spotty kids from school with their fluctuating voices and tide marks on their shirt collars, but someone who would know how to do it properly, like in the 'True Life' stories in *Jackie*.

I'd seen a lot of him in the weeks before Brighton. I suppose I was my sister's alibi. Whenever I needed anything from town – a haircut, school shoes, swimming lessons – she'd offer to take me and then Frankie would meet us and she'd leave me for an hour or so, settling me in the Wimpy with a milkshake. I often wondered why she needed me at all but I suppose it was easier that way, fewer questions from Mum and Dad. They'd want to know who she was seeing and when they could meet him, and they could never do that, because Frankie was not only much older than Kim – he was also married. Kim thought I didn't know but I'd seen him with his wife in the market, pushing a baby in a pram. I watched them from a distance, hiding beside multi-coloured mountains of pick 'n' mix. I chewed on a Black Jack as she chatted brightly to him while he fussed over the kid. She looked like Kim but rounder and I remember wondering if she was pregnant again.

We fell out of the van onto sun-sticky tarmac near the front, a cloud of grey smoke lingering by the door as we filed out. Frankie had his arm around my sister's shoulder, his long fingers dangling near her breast. My eyes lingered on them for a minute, then I looked up and saw myself reflected twice in Frankie's mirrored sunglasses. Sharp bile stung the back of my throat. The weed and the van's motion had got the better of me. I closed my eyes and breathed deeply until the queasiness eased, then I tugged at Kim's arm.

'Kim. I feel sick.'

She sighed and rolled her eyes.

'You'll be all right, Marie. Don't be such a baby.'

'Oh, poor Marie,' cooed Sandra, flapping at my face with an old-fashioned lace fan she'd told us she'd bought in the market for 20 pence.

A group of young punks walked towards us drinking cans of lager. They looked like the ones the papers warned you about, with their ripped clothes, black make-up and big boots, their hair stuck up in neon hedgehog spikes. One of the girls had a safety pin through her cheek that fastened at the corner of her mouth.

'Out of the way, Sixties,' she hissed and her friends laughed and tossed their cans at our feet.

I was beginning to wish I hadn't come.

The boy with acne moved after the punks but Frankie shook his head and looked away towards the front.

The closer we got to the beach, the happier I felt. The sea air blew away the fug. I felt grown up, out for the day without Mum and Dad. I'd worn my new jeans with embroidered flowers on the pockets and a *Grease* T-shirt. I ran ahead, out of the side streets, into the crowds on the main promenade, and that's when I saw her. She pulled me up short and I stood still in the way of the onward movement of passers-by. Eventually, I walked slowly across the road at the lights, keeping my eyes on her the whole time. She was huge, listing above the sea like a ghostly hologram. I leant over the peppermint-coloured railings and stared at her.

Blue skies stretched cloudless above the beach below, which was crammed with sunseekers sitting shoulder to shoulder on coloured towels, defending their ice creams and chips from seagulls as big as dogs. She loomed over them all. Birds clung to her spiky metal undersides, casting black juddering shadows onto the rippling water, or swooped around her roofs and lampposts, cawing wildly. Her walkways were deserted, her windows dark mirrors reflecting only the churning waves. She was desolate when all around her was fun in the sun. I shivered.

Kim joined me.

'That's the West Pier,' she said. 'The Grand Old Lady. Beautiful, isn't she? She's the real reason I wanted to come back here, to sketch her for my portfolio.'

I remember Kim's graduation exhibition, the work that came out of our little day trip. Her paintings had all been pretty before but that exhibition was filled with stark black lines, broken and endlessly repeated, demonic birds diving over red sunset waters. Those pictures had scared me. Reminded me, I suppose. I had hardly been able to look at them.

'There's no one on it,' I whispered.

'It's closed, silly. Too dangerous for people to walk on, too expensive to fix.'

Frankie ran in front of us on the beach, shirtless, followed by the boy with acne.

'Fancy a dip?' he shouted, picking his way precariously through the sunbathers.

I looked at Kim.

'There's nowhere to change, is there?'

She smiled, climbed over the railings and jumped to the pebbles below, then she pulled her dress over her head, dropped it beside her and walked to the sea wearing just her knickers. The other girls in the group dumped their stuff on a nearby groyne; a couple of them had worn bikinis under their clothes but Sandra went in topless too. They splashed each other and called for me to join them, a pod of magical, smiling mermaids, fully formed and naturally beautiful. I walked towards the tide but I was 14 and without a swimsuit. When my toes reached the foam I stood and shook my head.

'C'mon Marie, live a little!' shouted Kim. I scowled at her, this wasn't fun.

She whispered something in Frankie's ear and he grinned and strode out of the sea towards me. Before I knew what was happening he had lifted me up, carried me squirming to the water and dumped me head first into the waves. It was thrilling and excruciating. The water rushed down my throat and I couldn't breathe. I managed to find anchor with my knees and lift my head above the surface. Coughing violently, I ejected the water out through my nose and mouth, my chest gripped with pain and my throat burning. Blinded by the sea's vicious salt, I slid on the pebbles as I tried to stand. I could hear them all laughing at me. When I found my feet, I stropped up the beach away from them all and sat on the groyne alone, brushing the tears from my eyes. I looked over at them. Sandra mouthed, 'Are you okay?' but showed no signs of making sure that I was. Kim stuck her tongue out, curled her arms around Frankie and kissed him deeply. I looked away from them towards the West Pier, both drawn and repelled by the Old Lady's shadows.

After a while, Frankie and Kim came back. They stood dripping and bare-chested in front of me. I could see people staring – men mainly, smirking and whispering over their cans of beer. Kim looked irritated.

'You should take your jeans off and dry them in the sun,' she snapped.

'I don't want to.'

'You're such a baby, Marie; no one's interested in looking at you. You'll get a rash if you don't take them off and I'll get in trouble for not looking after you. And you know that's the truth.'

We stared at each other. This is what we did. What we'd always done. Frankie bit his lip, as if trying not to laugh.

'Fine,' I said and wriggled from my jeans, flinging them onto the barnacled concrete. My legs were white and bony. I never got them out in public unless it was for PE and then I covered most of their length with thick socks that came up over my knees. I pulled my T-shirt down as far as it would go.

Kim and Frankie sat down either side of me. Kim stretched her tanned, shapely legs out in front of her and kicked at the pebbles with painted toes, the sun catching on the gold of a delicate anklet I hadn't seen before.

When Kim and I fell out it always took ages to thaw. We both sulked for England and neither gave in. She was in a disproportionately bad mood with me and I certainly wasn't having a good time. I was the one who'd been dumped in the sea, for God's sake. What did she have to be angry about? We sat silent and fuming for an eternity as Frankie tapped his fingers on the groyne; suddenly Kim stood up and put her dress back on. She shook out her long blonde hair, now dulled by the sea, sending dark drips down the daisies on her yellow maxi-dress.

'I'm going to look at the pier,' she said. 'Want to come?'

It was a peace offering but the pier freaked me out. She was a wicked fairy castle in the clouds; one foot over the threshold and you'd be trapped for life. I didn't want to go anywhere near her. I pulled a face.

The rest of the party were still swimming. Frankie said he wanted to sun-bathe, which annoyed Kim even more. She made a face like she was sucking a lemon.

'Suit yourselves,' she said, shouldering her bag and gliding away with impossible elegance across the stones.

I watched her go, feeling self-conscious next to Frankie on the groyne, wishing I'd gone too. But the pier really did scare me. She looked dangerous, unsafe, like she could fall down with the slightest change of the wind and bury us alive in debris. I felt sick again.

As if he'd read my mind, Frankie offered me some gum.

'Thanks,' I croaked, my throat excessively dry from swallowing so much seawater.

'You're really uptight, aren't you?' he said, grinning, his voice deep and resonant. It was the first time he'd addressed me directly since he shook my hand and said hello on the day we were introduced.

'You should chill out, pretty baby.'

'I'm 14,' I answered, more to myself than to him.

'Exactly, you should be carefree. Besides, in some Eastern cultures girls are married off by the age of 11. I bet they're not so uptight. Here,' he said and moved swiftly so that he was sitting behind me with his legs on either side of mine. I noticed how the hairs made dark swirls over his thighs. I could hardly breathe. He began to massage my shoulders, his fingertips hard on my skin. I could feel the colour rising in my cheeks, across my chest, a funny tightness in my groin.

'Relax,' he cooed, leaning into my ear.

My shoulders tensed but I fought to relax them, hoping that if I could, he'd stop and leave me alone. The sun beat down on the top of my head and the breeze blew goosebumps up my arms. I kept my eyes on the pier and on Kim pacing around underneath her, taking photographs of the bulging, broken buildings that loomed like squeezed toothpaste over the beach below.

Frankie stopped massaging my shoulders.

'There,' he said. 'That's better.'

I let myself breathe out. Kim put her hand on one of the struts and shook it. I wanted to warn her, to shout out across the crowds for her to stop, but I couldn't find my voice and then Frankie placed his hand on my thigh as near to the top as it could be, bent his head and kissed the back of my neck.

I sat up in surprise, eyes wide. At that very moment Kim turned her head and looked in our direction. I was frozen, unable to move or speak. I should have wriggled away, shouted for Sandra and the mermaids, called upon the boy with acne, the men drinking beer, anyone, but I couldn't do anything except look at Kim.

I saw her let go of the pillar and I half expected the pier to crash into the sea, killing my sister and hundreds of day trippers as she fell. The waves broke against her remains and Kim began walking slowly towards us, her dress and her hair billowing in the wind. Frankie didn't see her coming. It was as if he had created an impenetrable bubble that shielded us from the outside world; he couldn't see out and so he assumed nobody could see in. Kim looked like she could see inside but didn't quite believe it, so dawdled on the way back to us as if to make sure she was right. When I thought about it over the years that followed, running it on a loop through my mind, I wondered if part of the thrill for him was the possibility of getting caught. Frankie stuck his thumb up under my knickers, into a place I rarely dared to touch myself. He was making a snuffling noise into my neck and moving his thumb up and down. I kept my eyes on Kim, walking faster now, breaking into a run as fast as the tears streaming down my face. When she reached us, she grabbed me by the arm and pulled me up. Frankie's thumb nail scratched the inside of my thigh, bringing a droplet of blood to the surface. 'You bastard,' Kim shouted and slapped him hard across the face – an explosion – and everyone nearby, including our friends in the sea, turned at the sound of it. She strode away, leaving me alone on the pebbles.

Frankie actually laughed.

'Kim,' he called after her. 'Ah, Kim, c'mon. What do you think was happening?'

I looked him in the face and he stopped talking, a puzzled look crossing his features. I turned and hurried after my sister.

She was going so fast I nearly lost her. My flip-flops kept coming off and my vision was blurred from tears that wouldn't stop. I kept shouting her name, aware of people staring at me, whispering to each other. No one asked me if I was okay. I find that odd to this day. Eventually, at the top of the road to the train station, she stopped and turned to me. Her face was like granite. She didn't say anything but took a cardigan from her bag and tied it around my waist. Only then did I realise I'd left my jeans at the beach – on the groyne next to Frankie.

'Stop crying,' she said. 'It's done now.'

She held my hand and walked me to the cafeteria in the station, bought me a strawberry milkshake and went to phone Dad from a payphone. I tried to drink the milkshake but I didn't like the taste; the first sip left a coating in my mouth, so I pushed it away. Kim came back 10 minutes later. She looked at the full glass in front of me and told me Dad was on his way, said she'd made up an excuse about falling out with the girl who'd driven us down.

'He'll be an hour or so. I'll get us some chips.'

I'd stopped crying properly by the time she came back with the chips. They were freshly cooked and covered in grainy salt and we ate them while they were still hot, blowing them cold as we chewed.

Neither of us mentioned that day again.

It was different afterwards. Kim avoided me for the rest of the summer. She locked herself in her room to work on her portfolio. We sat together for meals but she barely spoke or looked at me. She left for university in September and only came home for holidays and Christmas. It wasn't that we didn't get on when our paths crossed; it was more like the icing had melted on our relationship: there was a solid family bond underneath but there were no frivolities on top, no pink swirls or sugar sprinkles. In 1985 she went on a trip to America and met Mack, a man who lived on the edge of the tundra and cut down trees for a living. She never came back. I think she's happy.

Frankie's not doing so well. He moved to London before the new term began. I overheard Kim talking to Sandra about it on the telephone. He made a career for himself as the go-to art expert on television; a thinking woman's favourite – young, good-looking, clever. Later, he became a national treasure, always on TV. At one point he even painted the queen's portrait. It hung in the National Portrait Gallery for years. I'd always switch off immediately if I accidentally came across him on television, turn the page of any Sunday supplements he was in, pretend I hadn't seen. He dropped out of sight in the 1990s but he was back a few weeks ago. The first story on the news. This time I watched. Now a hunched, balding man in his late sixties, he stood outside a police station with fear in his eyes as the camera bulbs flashed and reporters shouted through the official statement read by his son. Eight women have come forward; a couple of them were interviewed with their faces in shadow. I was the first, it seems. The trial run.

It makes perfect sense now – the cake in the rain – over 35 years later. I'm looking at the West Pier again, a million miles from that sizzling day in 1979. The Grand Old Lady is still dying. Storm-ravaged and skeletal, major bones drop from her hourly and disappear beneath insurmountable waves. They say she'll go today. A few more people have braved the beach, the wind like chloroform over our faces. We stand together and apart, smiling through memories at a wake.

Maybe when she's finally gone, that day will go too. Maybe I'll be able to forget. The wind is buffeting her, the waves smacking her frame relentlessly. If she falls, I'll ring Kim and tell her I was here for the end. She's juddering, her ironwork whistling a mournful lament for times past, but deep down I know it's not her time yet. Her foundations are solid. She could carry on for years.

14

The Tenderness of Constraint

The tighter the corset, the more virtuous the woman.

The room is silent. Firelight flickers over the brass bedstead, dancing in Alicia's eyes, blurring her vision. Geoffrey stands tall behind her, his fingers moving over the half-opened ribbons of the corset. He pushes gently into the small of her back with his left hand to gain leverage on the silk for pulling it back through the eyes. The ribbon unravels and the corset loosens by degrees. He's having trouble but you wouldn't know it. Ever the professional, he doesn't falter; his speech remains seductively perfect but the next little shove is harder. It unbalances her and she has to reposition her feet to stop herself toppling forward.

Push. Pull.

Embedded in the silk, the whale bones seem to groan with each push and sigh in relief as the corset gapes open another notch. The air is fuzzy, tangible. Her heart gallops and her eyes dart from side to side; goosebumps prickle her exposed skin. Geoffrey's words are cloaked in fog, so she tries to picture his face. By now she knows it as well as her own; they've spent so much time together preparing for this moment. It wasn't easy to get to this point. There were so many obstacles in her way, it took a lot of dedication. His portrait inhabits her vision as his breathing fills her ears. She can see razor cheekbones under moonlit skin, his green eyes as laconic as sleep itself, the playful flop of black hair and the thin, slightly cruel lips prone to curl suddenly into voluptuous sunshine. She sighs. He is breathtaking. She feels a swell of pride that she is the one standing here being undressed by him. There was so much competition for this honour but she knew what she wanted and she fought hard to get it. Oh yes, all the girls swoon for Geoffrey, wish he was theirs, cuddle their pillows at night and dream of him pulling open their corsets with such virtuosity.

He's gay, of course. Bent as the proverbial. Got a smashing boyfriend called

Sven. She loves them both – but not like that. Why then, this flustered trembling, this inability to concentrate, this tightness in chest and crotch?

He's at the base of her spine now – one final push. She swallows, closes her eyes and tries to keep a level head. A bead of sweat meanders down her throat, pooling between her breasts. The corset falls away and Geoffrey turns her and kisses her like a wet haddock.

'Cut!' The shout rings out across the set.

The lights go up and there's a round of applause from the assembled crew. In a sea of smiling faces someone whoops.

Geoffrey releases her, then jumps up and down on his tippy toes clapping his hands.

'Daaahling – you were fabulous!' All trace of the script's callous aristocrat has been instantly replaced by dance-class camp. She marvels at his acting ability and at the fact that none of the press have caught on. The papers are full of pictures of him on the arms of glamorous young actresses. No doubt she'll be one of them when the movie comes out. She once asked him if it bothered him.

'You do what you've got to do,' he said.

'But don't you mind? Pretending to be someone you're not?'

He laughed at her.

'Alicia, darling, we're actors!'

Adam, the director, drapes a silk robe around her shoulders. She looks into his eyes, flinty and full of awe.

'Alicia,' he whispers, 'that was astonishing.'

She is suddenly unbearably hot. Her cheeks burn and the room swirls into a vortex, taking Adam and Geoffrey down with it. Everything is consumed by rushing blackness.

In her trailer, Alicia hooks up her Victoria's Secret silk push-up and anoints her ribs with body butter to ease the tenderness of constraint. The shoot medic has given her the all-clear. Probably, he said, too many hours in a tight corset and too little food. She'd asked the wardrobe girl to tie it as tight as she could. They'd pushed and pulled for an hour, squeezing Alicia into original stays until her ribs squeaked with pain and her waist was a mere 18 inches.

She'd researched exhaustively before she'd even got the audition. It was the most sought-after female role for decades. Career establishing. Starring opposite Geoffrey Wolfson in a tale of sex, opium and murder, with more than a hint of royal scandal. Every actress from 15 to 50 coveted the part. But Alicia wanted it more than any of them. Her agent pulled some strings and Alicia prepared for the audition by immersing herself in the proclivities of the Victorian bedroom. She sought out a fashion historian from Oxford University who informed her that corsetry was the key to understanding the role of the Victorian murderess. She gave her a book called *The Pleasure of Restraint*, which argued that far from indicating moral virtue, the over-tightening of corsets enabled the Victorian upper classes to enjoy sex more – to relish in the effort and anticipation of being undone. Alicia wore a corset to the audition. Adam watched her openmouthed and she knew she had the part. Afterwards, on the Tube, the corset had dug into her ribs and she had to stand all the way home.

There's a knock on the door and Adam walks into the trailer without waiting for an invitation.

'Are you okay?' he asks.

She looks at him closely. He's in his late thirties, slightly balding and paunchy, not what you would call a catch. In a certain light he reminds her of Shrek, but without the charisma. Ordinarily, she wouldn't even notice him in the room, but in the world that Alicia has chosen for herself, Adam is the next big thing. After this shoot he's Hollywood bound. If she wants to go with him she should take him as her lover. The only trouble is she doesn't know if she can stomach it. He has a mean streak. On the day of the polo scene, he made her stand for hours in the rain waiting for the perfect light, then blamed her for the loss of the day, proclaiming to the crew that she had the acting ability of a flounder. Then there's the BO. Alicia wants him to give her the lead in his next project, a big-budget sci-fi romance, but first she'll have to get through the sex without him knowing how repulsed she is. She'll think of something; she is an actor, after all.

A smile replaces her frown.

'I'm fine, Adam. Honestly. I just couldn't eat in that outfit.'

Adam smiles. 'At least let me take you out to dinner – to apologise for the corset torture.'

Result. 'That would be lovely, Adam.' She laughs, lightly as if she's still in character. 'Give me ten minutes.'

The big-shot director's face lights up and he strides from the trailer with a straight back and a purposeful smile.

Alicia's smile drops. She looks at herself in the mirror, her face and body starkly illuminated by the frame of naked light bulbs.

'What are you doing?' she asks herself. 'You're not that good an actor.'

Behind her, the discarded corset catches her eye, hanging over the back of a chair, as flat as a turbot, pink ribbons trailing.

Alicia pulls on a T-shirt, then grabs the corset, rolls it up as tightly as it will go and shoves it quickly into her overnight bag. She hopes wardrobe haven't left yet. It won't need to be as tight as before, just tight enough.

15

Glitterarty

'Let go,' he said. 'Sodding well let go. How dare they? It's that ignoramus who poses as an arts editor. Wears glasses when he doesn't need to. Wouldn't know art if it came up and bit him on his skinny-jean-covered bottom. Arsehole.'

Roland was apoplectic with rage. It was early, just past six, but Roland had eschewed food in favour of a liquid starter. He was most of the way through a bottle of Nuits-Saint-Georges 2011 Pinot Noir and he was slurring loudly. I did my best to look shocked at his news but it wasn't exactly a big surprise; he had been on the verge of extinction for at least a decade. He'd hung onto his weekly review column because he and the newly retired arts editor went way back. I think they may have been present when Caxton tried out his printing press.

Roland Campion had been doling out the same establishment nonsense for years. He liked his art to look like the thing it represented. Conceptual art was to him an abomination – 'Covering a sports stadium in Lego and tin foil is not art; it's a Hamleys' shopping basket. And as for that Banksy hooligan, I wouldn't know where to begin.'

Unsurprisingly, Roland had made a lot of enemies over the years. He listed his age as 72, but he'd been pissing artists off since the 1950s. His column was full of vitriol and personal jibes and he was a terrible snob, utterly obsessed with class and education. He was a liability for the paper, for the galleries, for everyone in the art business and that, ladies and gentlemen, was why I loved him. I was going to miss his fearless persecution of the in-crowd – those enfants terribles turned establishment, the ones who became everything they professed to hate the minute a billionaire collector waved his chequebook in their faces. Roland called them out, highlighted their hypocrisy and the role of luck in their fame. He pointed out lack of originality, out-and-out theft and unwarranted arrogance. He wasn't always right, but he brought a dissenting voice to the table of sycophants and in that he was alone. I was guilty too; everybody but Roland sucked up to the emperors and complimented them on their new clothes, even when there was nothing to see.

I had ordered the calamari appetiser and I studied Roland's face as he leant over the table and stabbed at it with his fork, clashing silver prongs against the oversized white plate in an attempt to capture an elusive rubbery ring. He had strange skin; it was paper-thin and covered in liver spots, but it had very few wrinkles. As the calamari eluded him his face turned redder and redder, and I imagined I saw cartoon steam coming from his ears.

'Waiter,' he said. 'WAITER.'

He was ignored by the supermodel rich kids posing as serving staff; none would go near him – they knew better than that. Roland treated waiting staff with nearly as much contempt as conceptual artists. Restaurateurs put up with his appalling behaviour because they sometimes got a mention in his column and then, inevitably, a review in the paper. Roland's endorsement, good or bad, was excellent for business.

'Oh, this really is intolerable,' he proclaimed. 'You can't eat this. You'll need a hearty meal before subjecting yourself to this mad-scientist debacle.' A Just William gleam lit up his face. 'I'm going to the kitchens.'

'No, Roland, not again…'

But Roland had already lifted my plate from in front of me. He marched past the open-mouthed diners and waiting staff and disappeared through the double doors into the kitchens.

I sipped my water, smiling apologetically at the bemused stares and whispers from the other diners, as Roland's curses drifted across the restaurant. There was a loud crash and then he appeared at the table again. He sat down with a big smile on his face and, humming a light tune, he tucked his napkin into his shirt with a flourish.

'I must say I rather enjoyed that, making those rodents scurry around back there. You will get a new, perfectly cooked plate of calamari immediately and I have procured another bottle of this beauteous tipple. Are you sure you won't change your mind?'

I shook my head. The last time Roland and I got drunk before a private view he was arrested and I ended up in A&E. Luckily, Damian dropped the charges and my arm was only bruised.

'So Roland, what do you make of this Elvis canary thing?'

'Utter bollocks, I should imagine. I fail to see how cloning a budgie from a hair bought on some disreputable website can be considered art.'

'Elvis Presley's hair.'

'Really, Marty. You are so naïve. It is a big con. The vendor of the hair is the real artist, getting two hundred dollars out of that untalented sap for hairbrush excrement.'

'Oh, Roland. You don't know he's talentless. It's his debut. He might be absolutely brilliant. And the hair comes with an authentication certificate, I believe – from the granddaughter of Elvis's housekeeper.'

'There's a guy works down the chip shop swears he's Elvis. Granddaughter of the housekeeper indeed, what nonsense.'

'Imagine it, though, Roland. Suppose it is Elvis's hair and the canary can sing more beautifully than any canary has ever sung before.'

He looked at me with disdain.

'Good God! Are you all right, dear chap? You sound like a love-struck schoolgirl.'

I blushed. Roland was spot on but there was a good reason. Davina. A girl like no other. Davina. The most perfect woman on this or any planet. The sound of her name was a Renoir brushstroke across my soul. That morning, just before she had left my apartment (after a rather heavenly night before), Davina had professed her love. 'Oh, Marty,' she'd said as I poured her coffee. 'I do love you.'

Davina was the PR girl at the gallery we were going to after dinner. She'd approached me to ask if I would do a feature about one of her artists for a coffee-table magazine I sometimes write for. Of course, I agreed immediately; she was so beguiling. I'd never been in love before. I used to laugh at the fools who claimed love at first sight but that was exactly how it had happened for me. I'm not a manly man; a lot of people probably think I'm gay (everybody did at school). I have only ever been interested in art, in the perfecting of humanity. Few women (and even fewer men) are perfect. Davina was everything I wanted: beauty, brains, a body like a fully limbed Venus de Milo and a laugh like a nightingale's song. She had ambition too; she was already collecting – any small pieces she could afford and donations from the artists on show at the gallery. She has sweet-talked original art out of most of them, unknowns and big names alike. All have been seduced by her but none was as lucky as I because she loved me. She told me so that very morning.

I was dimly aware of Roland telling me that nothing had excited him since 1977 and was broken from my trance by him clicking his fingers in my face.

'You with me, Marty?'

He looked at me with some curiosity.

I was about to confide in him, to tell him how happy I was. Roland was like a father to me; God knows he understood me much more than my own ever did. Contrary to his reputation, he'd been nothing but generous when I'd started on the scene. He seemed to view me less as a rival, more as an apprentice, making sure to introduce me to his contacts and fill me in on who was important and who wasn't worth bothering with, who to trust and who to treat with scepticism. We had become close over the years. I wanted his approval on most things but, as I opened my mouth to tell him about Davina, the chef himself approached our table carrying an enormous plate of sizzling calamari and laid it down in front of me.

'Enjoy,' he said.

I suddenly lost my appetite, wary of the tight smile he gave as he turned away.

Roland was almost too drunk to walk. He leant against the taxi we had taken to St James's and breathed yogically through his nose with his eyes shut. I had a bad feeling about the evening to come.

'Pay the man, Marty,' he said without opening his eyes. 'There's a good chap.'

Roland never paid for anything. Like the queen, he didn't carry money; he signed for everything and then passed on the bill. I wondered how he would cope without his expense account behind him. His friends would see him right, I supposed, but most of them were dead now and he was what they used to call a confirmed bachelor, with no family and no obvious lover. I pictured him in his Covent Garden flat with only his cat for company and a feeling of desolation passed over me. Then I remembered that when I had visited him there (as he recovered from one of his frequent bouts of pneumonia) I had been aghast at the number of original paintings he owned. World-class art hung all over his pensioner's beige walls. Roland was art-rich; he could keep his cat in foie gras if he chose to. I tried to imagine which piece he would sell first – the O'Keeffe, the Bacon, the Hockney? Then I realised he wouldn't sell any of them, not unless he was beyond desperate.

Roland leant heavily on my arm as we walked up the steps of the Georgian mansion housing the gallery. The inside had been completely gutted and now contained a huge ground-floor exhibition space painted in eye-splitting white and three mezzanines linked by neon Plexiglas stairs. The room was stuffed full of the great and the good. Black and red clothing predominated, though there were the usual eccentrics in Harris tweed and flowing, virginal white. Voices combined in a low hum as Elvis crooned about Hawaiian maidens.

Davina was sitting at the chrome reception desk, a vase of positively pornographic anthuriums nodding their stamens in her direction. I sighed deeply; even flowers were seduced by her beauty. She was wearing a figure-hugging black dress and glowed like an artist's muse. The sight of her rendered me speechless. Roland stumbled up to her.

'I say,' he said, 'do we sign away our souls here or are you an exhibit?'

She smiled warmly at him and came around the desk to kiss him on both cheeks.

'Why, Mr Campion, it is a real pleasure to meet you. I'm such a fan.'

She linked her arm through his.

'Let's get you some champagne, shall we – and the best spot in the house?'

She led him into the gallery, winking at me over her shoulder as I followed.

After safely depositing Roland by the bar, a flute of Dom Pérignon and a catalogue in his hands, she squeezed my arm and told me she'd catch me after the show. I watched her return to her desk and so, I noticed, did several of the artists in attendance. 'Hey, no looking,' I wanted to shout. 'She loves only me.'

Roland surveyed the room, his gaze met by hostile stares from those who had felt the poison of his pen over the years. I turned my attention to the catalogue. The cover was marbled black with 'Life after Death' written in funereal gold. The inside was the same blinding white as the gallery, printed with pictures of animals in various stages of life and death, photographs of foetuses and organs growing in vitro. Each animal was named after someone famous. The mouse was called *Diana*, the mink *Marilyn* and the globus monkey *Michael*.

'Oh Lord, they're all here,' slurred Roland. 'Even mad Tracey of Margit. I hope she doesn't get her vadge out; it must be as wrinkled as a pug's nose by now.'

Having heard Roland's voice, the infamous artist smiled and raised her glass in our direction, then turned away. I wondered if Roland knew how many careers he'd helped by trying to kill them. His indignation had often drawn attention to artists who might otherwise have languished in obscurity. Roland pulled a face. 'Let us away and peruse!'

The art was sparsely distributed. In all there were five exhibits. There was a table with a row of six test tubes filled with blue liquid and icky cellular masses entitled 'The Public'. Beside this were two bubbling specimen jars perched on pedestals, each containing a suspended white mouse, alternately labelled 'Princess One' and 'Princess None'. The mink was stuffed and was being walked by a life-size fibreglass Marilyn Monroe (circa *Some Like It Hot*), holding it by a diamond-encrusted collar and lead. 'Neverland' featured a taxidermy monkey with a melted face and a crystal-covered leather glove.

Roland frowned. 'Why do they always stick them in test tubes? Is the exhibition sponsored by SmithKline Beecham?'

I watched Davina work the room, greeting the guests as she had Roland, filling glasses with champagne and taking photographs, making each person she encountered feel like a VIP. She was amazing.

'Christ, it's the emperor and his tailor,' said Roland. 'As naked as the day he was born.'

'Roland!' The gallery owner grasped Roland's hand and nearly shook his arm off. 'Soooo glad you could make it. A little bird told me you were seeking employment.'

Roland kept his smile fixed.

'I have decided to retire, dear chap. This show will be the last I review. I had to see if you'd found somebody better than that cockney barra boy for us, didn't I?'

This was the last straw for the cockney barra boy who, from his position just behind his benefactor, had clearly heard Roland's last dig. Roland had been baiting him for years and no amount of success or wealth would make up for the disdain with which London's most famous art critic treated him. In the back of his mind the cockney barra boy must have wondered if Roland was right about his lack of talent. He pushed past the gallery owner, took a step towards Roland with his right fist balled and a snarl on his face and grabbed him by the collar. Roland lost his footing; his champagne flute crashed to the ground and silenced the room. Everybody turned to look at us. On the other side of the room a camera flash went off.

'Steady on,' I said and placed my hand on the artist's arm. His face was contorted with hate but even he must have seen the absurdity of a man in his fifties punching a pensioner at an art show, because he loosened his grip and stumbled away into the crowd.

'I am soooo very sorry, Roland,' said the emperor. 'Let me get you some more champagne.' He clicked his fingers. 'Davina!'

'Are you okay, Roland?' I asked.

He nodded, grinning. 'Of course, dear boy. It just proves how right I am.'

But as Davina presented him with a freshly filled glass I noticed that his hand was shaking.

Attending to Roland with sympathy in her eyes, my love looked so beautiful that I wanted to kiss her there and then.

'Davina,' I whispered, taking her elbow, 'when can we be alone?'

'Not now, Martin. I'm working.'

I watched her go. She walked straight over to the barra boy and there was a snarling exchange before he stomped away from her towards the emperor's office. Davina stood alone for a moment and then followed.

The emperor introduced us to the artist. He was a quiet-spoken young man with a Dutch accent. You wouldn't have guessed he was the artist; he looked more like a man of the cloth – ethereally pale with an almost visible aura of calm.

'I absolutely love your column,' he told Roland, flashing bright blue eyes that ensured the cynical old art critic was instantly smitten. 'You are never wrong.'

Roland giggled like a June bride.

'Oh pish, dear boy,' he said, leading him away by the arm. 'Now do tell me about this Marilyn piece. I met her once, you know.'

The emperor's office door had been closed for some time with both Davina and the barra boy inside. I couldn't bear the thought of her in there with that brute. Roland really was right about him. I made my way through the crowd, coming to a stop outside the door. I pressed my ear against it to see if I could hear anything, any sign that he was taking it out on my angel. If so, I would be in there like a shot, defending beauty against the beast. But the office was quiet. I should have left it at that. I knew Davina would be furious if I interrupted her while she was working but I wanted to protect her and besides, the emperor was about to introduce the artist. She should be there to get her face in all the press photographs; she deserved it.

I knocked 'Davina?' There was no answer so I turned the handle and pushed open the door.

Oh, the sight that I beheld! Davina was pinned to the desk, her dress hiked up over her waist and one shoe lying on the floor. The barra boy was bent over her, his arms firmly holding her down, his jeans and ridiculous spotty boxers around his ankles, his white (and equally spotty) arse pumping vigorously. Davina was struggling beneath him and trying to speak but he had covered her mouth with his own. It was disgusting. He didn't deserve to be in the same room as Davina and here he was defiling her. I rushed at him with a scream and pulled him away, surprising myself with the strength of the punch I levelled at his jaw. As he fell sideways onto the floor the side of his head struck one of the emperor's display cabinets and made a sickening thud. A thin red line of blood trickled its way down his face and dripped scarlet onto his white shirt collar. It was a striking image. For a moment I thought I'd killed him. He was down but his eyes were open. He groaned and put a hand up to the wound. I turned to Davina but she was already standing, smoothing down her skirt. She was furious – I presumed at her attacker, until I realised I was the cause of her anger.

'What the fuck are you doing, Martin?' she hissed and moved over to the barra boy, placing a hand on his shoulder and whispering in his ear. He nodded and patted her knee. They both turned and looked up at me, obviously eager for me to leave.

'But…'

I was dumbfounded. She loved me. Only me. She'd told me just hours before. There must have been some mistake. She couldn't have wanted this Neanderthal's attentions, could she?

'You love me,' I said.

She looked at me like the pathetic worm that I was.

'Get out, Martin,' she said. Then, when I moved toward her, 'Just – GO.'

Red-faced, I pushed past the small, whispering crowd outside the office door and made my way back to Roland. The emperor and his new protégé were on a raised area at the back of the main gallery. Next to them, on a white plinth, was the domed shape of a birdcage covered in red silk.

Roland looked at me and frowned.

'Are you quite all right, dear chap? You look like you're having a heart attack.'

I took the champagne from his hand and downed it in one.

There wasn't time to explain as the room had hushed for the emperor to make his introductions. I didn't hear what he was saying because Davina had joined him onstage, as poised and fragrant as ever. He said something about the greatest art event in living memory and then gestured theatrically with his hands.

'Behold the Elvis Canary!'

Applause filled the room and Davina whipped the red silk off the birdcage.

The bird was a tiny yellow blob in an ornate golden cage. It was still at first, dazed by the noise from the crowd, experiencing what must have been a bewildering artificial dawn, but then, as the room hushed again, it began to shuffle along its perch, cocking its head from side to side. It peered at us through jet button eyes, stark in sunshine feathers. There was a small black tuft on its head, like a quiff, but it was difficult to tell from a distance if this was genetics or artistry. Suddenly, it began to sing. There was a gasp from the audience. A few shrill cheeps and whistles built quickly into a car-alarm cacophony of unrelated notes before transforming into a xylophonic scale of beauty, melody after melody falling in a waterfall of sound around our ears. At least that's how it seemed at first. But then it went on too long, far too long, and the beautiful birdsong reverted in our ears to what it truly was – a random Jackson Pollock splattering of notes. Nobody had the presence of mind to step in and stop it and, after a couple of minutes (that seemed to last an eternity), the glitterarty started to shuffle their feet and whisper to each other. I don't know what we had all expected but it certainly wasn't the singing of an ordinary canary. Davina rather self-consciously covered the cage again and the warbling stopped. There was a smattering of applause and the emperor and the artist left the stage wearing the fixed grins of the crestfallen. Another promising career smothered before it had even taken its first flight.

I turned to Roland, expecting some contemptuous told-you-so remark, and was shocked to see his face wet with tears. They ran unstoppably down his cheeks, tiny drips making dark stains on the collar of his lilac shirt.

'Roland,' I gasped, 'you're crying.'

He took a handkerchief from his pocket and wiped his eyes, giving his nose an elephantine blow.

'It was genius,' he said, a croak of awe in his voice.

'Er, it was a canary.'

'Really, Marty – what did you expect? Did you think it would swing its hips and sing "Blue Suede Shoes"? No, we were all so wrapped up in what it could have sounded like that we forgot what it would sound like. When I heard it sing I knew what he was up to immediately. You can't improve on nature, dear boy – it is a thing of intangible beauty. That boy is a genius and I shall be sure to tell everyone so in my final column. In fact, I'm going home to write it now.'

He turned and walked steadily away with no hint of the drunkenness he had exhibited earlier.

The mood in the room was sombre. The emperor, the artist, the barra boy and Davina made their way to the office. I put my hand on Davina's arm as she passed but she yanked it away. The office door was closed to me again.

I thought of something Roland had quoted to me once. I can't remember who said it originally: 'An artist's job is to show people what was always there but they have never noticed.'

I hadn't agreed with him at the time. I had argued that art was all about the new, the original, the surprising, but I don't think I knew what he meant until he left me in that room full of people, alone. I would miss him.

16

Sleeping in a Coffin

He can hear them downstairs. Even his oversized headphones and epic Vangelis don't drown them out. Usually they leave him alone, his meathead brother and slapper girlfriend, Chaveen, or whatever her name is. Usually they go and drink cider in the park with the other deadbeats. Usually Saturday afternoons are safe. Usually – but not today. Today they're having their own little private party downstairs, cackling and yelling and playing shite R&B. From here it sounds like somebody's machine-gunning cats.

He's supposed to be revising but instead he picks up the copy of *Cahiers du Cinéma* he bought on eBay. Belmondo on the cover – aspirational cool, even with *that* nose. He tries to make out the words of wisdom and wishes he paid more attention in French, but French lessons never lived up to their euphemistic promise. He picks up a pencil and instructs the orchestra in his head to up the longing as 'Rachel's Song' blasts desire through his cerebral cortex. He has both hands raised and his eyes closed when he realises his bedroom door has opened. *Prick*, he thinks and turns in fury to spit bile at his brother.

'My room – fuck off!'

Momentarily disarmed. This honey is standing with her back to the closed door, one hand on the handle, caressing the metal with long, pale fingers tipped with pillar-box red. She's thin, a blonde, but not bottle. Her skin has an unnaturally orange gleam but she's wearing black at least, tight jeans, low-slung on coat-hanger hips, and a strappy vest that covers her small breasts but exposes her belly button. And those eyes…

'Hello.' Through a white-toothed, cherry-lipped smile.

Thrown off balance, his chair wheels spin and the headphones pop their connection, filling the room with smoky brassiness.

'What *are* you listening to?' she smirks.

He spins his chair back to the desk and turns down the sound, then clears his throat.

'Can I help you, sugar?'

'Sugar?' She raises a perfectly drawn eyebrow. 'Is it from a film – sounds like it's from a film? Almost classical, y'know what I mean?'

'*Blade Runner.*' He frowns. 'The film.'

'Never heard of it. Has it come out yet?'

'Who are you and what do you want?'

'They're snogging each other's faces off downstairs. Denny's friend Baz was meant to be here for me but he's a no-show. Can't say as I'm devastated. Thought I'd come up and say hello.'

He takes off his redundant headphones.

'Sorry, but do I know you?'

'I'm in Denny's year. Don't you recognise me?'

He shakes his head.

'We see each other every day – try and imagine a white shirt and a school tie.'

'Sorry, sugar. I'm still not getting it.'

Eyebrows raised.

'Well, that's… flattering.'

'Sorry, dollface. I'm only observant when I need to be.'

She looks at him like he's escaped from an asylum and starts to walk around his room.

'So, this is your room – I wondered what it would be like.'

'You've thought about my room?' He can't keep the surprise from his voice.

'Well, you know you're a bit of a mystery. Haven't you noticed people looking at you at school? It's all that walking around scowling, the sunglasses, the trilby. Some of the girls think it's cute – that you're our very own R-Patz. When I knew I was coming here I told them I'd see if you slept in a coffin.'

At the mention of sleep his eyes move to his unmade bed. It's clean, at least. His mum changed it yesterday – his favourite candy-stripe covers. The cupcake looks at it too.

'No coffin. What's your name, sweetheart?'

She smirks. 'Why are you talking like that? You've been talking like that since I came in, like you can't move your top lip. Do you need some Zovirax or something?'

He coughs and sits fully upright. She laughs – a heartbreaking little-girl laugh.

'Amber,' she says, holding out her hand. 'My name is Amber.'

He takes her fingers lightly in his own; it feels like his hand is burning. He lets go quickly.

'Amber,' he repeats. 'The past distilled.'

She gives him a quizzical look.

'Denny's right – you are weird.'

She looks at his posters – *Breathless*, *Pulp Fiction*, *The Big Sleep* – and then at him. She paces his room, stops at the fireplace to pick up its occupants one by one: his replica Oscar, his vintage Ray-Bans, his classic Zippo. Her opinion of his belongings registers on the celluloid of her face.

He flips a Lite into his mouth.

'Match me,' he says, offering her the pack. 'Want one?'

She grimaces. 'Na, coffin nails my grandad calls 'em.'

But she flicks the Zippo into life and bends to light his cigarette. He holds her hand steady and looks into those eyes for the delicious intimacy of taking the flame. She looks away, towards the bookcase that takes up the whole of one wall.

'No actual coffin,' she says, wafting smoke from her face, 'but it looks like you've been buried in a library.'

She walks over to it and runs her forefinger along the cracked and faded spines of his dime-store novels.

'Have you read all these books?'

He exhales a huge plume of smoke.

'Most of them.'

He must remember to open his window or his mum'll do her nut.

She picks out a book and reads the back. *The Big Nowhere*.

'Sounds intense,' she says, putting it back. 'You need to get out more, Vampire Boy.'

'Don't you like books?'

'Not much.'

'You must like some – what's your favourite book?'

'I dunno. *Twilight*, I suppose.'

'*Twilight!*'

She flashes him the daggers.

'Okay then – *The Fault in Our Stars*. I liked that.'

He shakes his head.

'Sorry, baby, but I really can't decide which is worse, virgin-vampire romance or schmaltzy cancer tourism.'

She frowns and walks quickly towards him. For a moment he thinks she's going to punch him, but instead she leans over him in slow motion, one leg between his knees and her left hand on the arm of his chair – so close he has to lean back so she doesn't touch him. She points at the book he left closed on his desk. *The Great Gatsby*.

'I read that one. We did it in English last year. It's all right. All that money and all that "old sport" stuff – *a riot*.'

She moves away and he almost falls off his chair, recovering his composure with another cough. She stands near the door again, playing with the handle.

'Bet you like Gatsby best, don't you? Bet you think you're like him. Better than everybody else. Thing is R–Patz – Gatsby doesn't get the girl.'

With that she is gone, leaving the door wide open for him behind her.

17

A Spring Wedding

It's not as warm as they hoped it would be. The sun has declined to attend. After the endless weeks of speculation and weather predictions, it's merely muggy. But at least it's not raining – not yet, anyway. 'Be here by ten,' Lizzie had said yesterday on the phone, 'or you'll miss the dress.'

The conversation with my sister then pretty much went like this:

Me: 'As if I could avoid it. You've been planning this little celebration for weeks – no, months. Pictures of that dress are going to be in the news forever.'

She, dreamily: 'I wonder what it will be like. How long do you think the train will be?'

Me: 'Short – so she can do a runner and spare herself birthing all those buck-toothed, chinless children.'

I laughed at the future balcony scenes that played out in my head – rows of royal mini-mes sticking their monstrous teeth out over thin lips.

She, in her poshest accent: 'Don't be such a bitter old lezzer, Andrea. Everyone loves a royal wedding; it's a day of national pride.'

Not quite everyone.

Mum phoned later just to make sure I was definitely going. ('But don't come if you're going to sit there sniping at everything like you usually do,' she reprimanded in her natural cockney. 'It's supposed to be a nice day. You might think you're above it all now, but you're just like everybody else.')

Town is deserted. Marks & Spencer is shut, for God's sake. I miss the CLOSED sign handwritten in marker pen that they've taped to the glass with masking tape and push at the doors, but they just don't budge. It never occurred to me that Marks & Spencer would be shut. It is the end of civilisation as we know it. Down the empty street, Waitrose have no qualms about cashing in. The shop floor is heavenly; hardly a soul walking its shining aisles. Cool and quiet and air-conditioned. It seems like it's just me, an army of attentive, smiling staff and an old lady wearing a fur coat, pushing a Chihuahua around in the baby seat of a squeaky trolley. I want to lie down in the dairy aisle and breathe it all in, have a nap next to the Duchy Originals clotted cream... But it's 9.45 and I'm under strict orders, so I grab a Union-Jack-labelled bottle of Pimm's, some Essentials diet lemonade and venison pâté (not essential, but on special offer) and head for the tills.

Lizzie opens the door in her own wedding dress – a slightly stained Princess-Diana meringue – and full veil, which she lifts with a perfectly manicured hand to slug from a plastic glass of pink champagne. She's so excited she looks like she's gonna pop.

'Andrea, darling! You're just in time – Wills will be arriving any minute!'

Wills – as if she knows him personally. She air-kisses me, so as not to smudge her flawless make-up, makes the requisite *mwah mwah* noises and turns on her heels, nearly tripping over her train.

'Where's Melissa?' she asks over her shoulder.

'Said she'd rather poke her eyes out with sharp sticks.'

Lizzie turns and fixes me with a concerned look.

'You're not going to spoil it, are you? Just because it'll never happen to you?'

Then she grins, a new idea boiling in her party-organiser brain.

'Mind you, you can do that now, can't you? Do you know which one of you would wear the dress? Of course, Melissa has the better figure. She can borrow this if she likes?'

She swishes her skirt and turns back up the hall.

Inside, the lounge is ablaze with flags and bunting. A table against the wall is about to collapse under the weight of crustless sandwiches and fairy cakes topped in roses and rice-paper royals.

All the family's here. Aunty Sylvia and Mum sit on the sofa cradling gigantic handbags, each wearing the hat they bought for Lizzie's nuptials last June. A bored-looking Uncle Frank dressed in his best suit and Lizzie's partner, Ian, are clutching flags and sitting on tricolour beanbags. The twins are playing with plastic miniatures of the royal family on a bright, new, red, white and blue rug. A tiny Queenie and Phil, complete with crowns, wave at a bride in white with a tiara, sitting next to a prince in an elaborate horse-drawn coach; a horse guard, palace guard and a corgi stand by as printed crowds cheer from a cardboard viewing platform. Shops actually sell this shit.

Everyone looks up at me.

'Have you all gone mad?' I ask.

'Shut up, Lindsay Lohan,' says Ian. 'It's about to start.'

I've always hated Ian. We barely acknowledge each other's presence these days. He just can't cope with me having a girlfriend. He once told Lizzie he thought it was a waste of two 'reasonably attractive' women. And then there's the little matter of him jilting Lizzie at the altar. We all had to cope with the fallout from that one and he was well aware of what we all thought about him. If he wasn't the twins' father, he wouldn't be here at all.

'Hello, Andrea, love,' says Mum. 'No Melissa?'

'Champagne?' interrupts Lizzie before it can become a thing.

I nod and hand her my offering. She peers in the bag and takes out the pâté.

'Ooh, VENISON! Very fitting,' she trills.

The TV, which is also encircled in mini Union Jacks, shows the crowded streets outside Westminster Abbey – a mass of red, white and blue, hand-scrawled banners, police vans and horses. Eamonn Holmes's voice booms out across live pictures of smiling children squashed against metal barricades, telling us that the princes will be leaving 'any minute now'. The picture switches to the view outside Clarence House, then shakily back to the Abbey as Samantha Cameron, a vision in teal silk, strides elegantly along the red carpet with some bloke whose suit is two sizes too big.

'God – is that the prime minister?' I ask.

I take my champagne from Lizzie and down it in one.

'Yeah – he's done well for himself, hasn't he?' leers Ian.

'In your dreams,' I reply.

'And yours,' he snarls.

I stick out my tongue and wiggle it slowly up and down, while Uncle Frank splutters into his pint.

At 10.10, according to the clock at the bottom of the screen, Sky pans back to Clarence House, but there's no sign of anyone leaving to get into the Daimler parked outside. Eamonn says something about there being 'a short delay'.

The foreign royals start to arrive at the Abbey, including the King of Tonga and the Queen of Spain.

'I don't know why they have to invite all these foreigners,' says Aunty

Sylvia, wiping a stray bit of coronation chicken vol-au-vent from her bottom lip. 'They should just have English people there.'

Lizzie and I exchange smiles.

'Like you, you mean?' says Mum. 'Your invite must have got lost in the post.'

'Ssh,' says Sylvia, jabbing her sister in the ribs with a bony elbow.

'Ow,' says Mum and wriggles herself into some more sofa room.

'Like a pair of kids,' says Frank and reaches for a scone.

There's still nothing at Clarence House. Holmes is starting to get edgy. There's sweat on his forehead and he keeps repeating the short-delay explanation. Thank God Kay Burley has been startled by a horse – who knows what she'd be saying by now.

'William's chickening out,' says Ian with a grin.

'Not everyone is like you, Ian,' says Mum, tersely.

Minor royals arrive at the Abbey in minibuses, clambering out onto the pavement and rearranging their hats and coats.

At 10.20 Sky flicks to the exterior of the Goring Hotel, where Mrs Michael Middleton and Mr James Middleton are supposed to be getting into a car. Nothing.

Mum frowns. Aunty Sylvia takes a hankie from the jaws of her handbag and wafts it in front of her nose.

'What is it? What's going on?'

'Cupcake?' asks Lizzie, parading a plate of cream-piped confectionery in front of us.

I take one and bite into its swoony lightness.

In a studio overlooking the Thames, a panel of useless royal watchers sit twitching next to Eamonn, stuttering about cars breaking down and stomach bugs, last-minute nerves, what, what! I'm on my third glass of champagne and I'm really starting to enjoy myself.

The inbreds leave Buckingham Palace – Anne and Andrew, Edward and Sophie – but there is still no movement from either the Goring or Clarence House.

Princesses Eugenie and Beatrice get out of their car.

We all blink in disbelief at the hat.

'Good God. Look at that!' says Sylvia. 'That's not a good look, is it, Andrea? You know about fashion – is that good?'

'No, Aunty. It's not good. Genie (or is it Bea?) looks like Queen Amidala of Naboo.'

Sylvia nods in agreement, then asks Mum, 'Is that one of those African royals?'

Having consumed several cupcakes and a vat of cherry cola, my nephews, Albert and Evan, have moved on from recreating the happy event to Godzilla crashes the wedding, using a plastic T-Rex to smash the cavalcade and stamp on Prince Philip. Godzilla now has access to high explosives (presumably nicked from the Chelsea Barracks) and the whole party goes up in an ear-splitting boom of tiny flying figures.

'C'mon, boys,' says Lizzie, 'not so loud. Ian, can you tell them?'

Ian shrugs. 'They're just having fun, Liz. It's meant to be fun, isn't it?' he says and drains his beer, crushing the can in his hand. 'I'll take some of that champagne now.'

Lizzie sighs and hands him a plastic glass.

The real queen and consort drive towards Westminster Abbey, blue headlights flashing on the car, TV cameras zooming through the windows as they smile and wave at the crowd.

'Ew, yellow,' says Mum. 'She looks like an omelette.'

Eamonn holds his earpiece, his eyes flicking from side to side like a startled toad. He nods, tight-lipped. Everyone in the room stares at the TV. Very solemnly, Eamonn tells us that there is no sign of the prince or his intended; both have disappeared since last officially seen at breakfast. No foul play is suspected and everything possible is being done to locate the couple.

Mouths drop open.

'Told you he's chickened out,' says Ian, smugly.

Lizzie downs her champagne.

'Actually, Ian,' she says, looking him calmly in the eye, 'I don't think I want you here. I don't really know why you invited yourself in the first place – you don't believe in marriage, remember?'

Ian stands level with the mother of his children.

'I'm here for the boys,' he says. Lizzie narrows her eyes like she did when we were kids and were about to have an almighty row. Mum coughs. The rest of us look on in silence as Lizzie and Ian stare each other out. The TV provides the only commentary; Eamonn talks about 'more details as they come in'.

Finally, the queen arrives at Westminster Abbey. She frowns as an official whispers something in her ear, then she follows him inside without turning to acknowledge the cheering crowds.

Ian looks away first. He bends to kiss the heads of his now quiet children. On his way out he throws his plastic champagne flute onto the kitchen floor where it clatters desolately onto the lino. He slams the front door as he leaves. I gesture to Lizzie to sit beside me and give her a hug as she slumps down. I can feel the tight little heartbeat in her trembling body.

'Prick,' she says, drinking what's left of my pink fizz. 'I've tried, Andrea. I've tried for the boys, but I don't think I'll ever forgive him.'

The kids resume their B-movie version of events, louder than before, with more roaring and explosions.

Throughout the morning we watch the news unfold over vast amounts of Pimm's and cucumber sandwiches; we hear how the couple spoke on their mobiles just after breakfast, and then both went out 'to get some air' and never came back.

At 1.50 Sky flashes over to the Famous Blacksmiths Shop in Gretna Green, where a man with an almost indecipherable Scottish accent tells a reporter that he married a 'very happy and well-spoken young couple' less than two hours before. The groom wore a baseball cap throughout and they were dressed in jeans and T-shirts printed with a picture of the royal couple. Aunty Sylvia drops her cupcake into the mouth of her handbag. He finishes the interview by saying that the groom gave him an envelope when the ceremony was over, 'a little gift for his trouble', but told him not to open it until they were gone.

'I didnae put the names together until I opened it.'

'What was inside it, sir?' asks the Sky reporter.

The man holds a ring up for the camera. It's an enormous dark blue sapphire attended by a circle of shining diamonds.

'Is that Princess Diana's ring?' asks Mum. 'I don't understand.'

You can hear the cheers from miles around. The parties go on for hours. There is still singing outside as Lizzie and I snuggle down under a duvet with cheese on toast, like we did when we were kids, and watch it all again on *Newsnight*. Jeremy Paxman can barely conceal his delight. England swings like the Sixties.

In London, alone at last, an old lady kicks off her satin shoes and rubs her toes through shredded support tights. Her little dog carries her sheepskin slippers from beside her bed, and drops them at her feet. She sits at her dressing table and tickles the dog behind its ears. It sighs and drops its head to its paws. As she picks up her hairbrush, she notices the note, propped against a jewellery box. She slices open the thick envelope with a silver knife kept handy for just such an occasion, and thinks how few letters she gets these days. In it is a single sheet, crossed with her grandson's spidery scrawl:

Sorry Gran – talk when we get back, yeah?

18

You Run

You breathe in through your nose. A moment of stillness. The icy air stings your nostrils and throat; dragon breath curls on your exhale. You flap your arms and jump on your tiptoes to keep warm, taking care to hold your right arm behind your body, hoping the other kids won't notice it. You can't wear sleeves for cross-country, even in this temperature. You'll get too hot, slow down your progress – that's what Mr Armstrong said. You need to be as fast as you can be. Taunting from other athletes is part of a sportsman's life. Couldn't he have ignored the fact that you had your hoody on instead of making a big thing out of it? Drawing attention to you again. You're not a sportsman, are you? You're not even a sportswoman, sportsperson – you are a 14-year-old girl.

Luca smiles at you as everyone bundles around the starting line – most of the other kids in an unruly huddle, you alone on the edge. His dark curls rest softly on his shoulders. He has to keep pushing them out of his eyes, so Mr Armstrong makes a show of giving him a pink headband from the lost-property box, much to the amusement of the other students. Luca doesn't care. He laughs along with them, pouting and posing with his hands on his hips. It's so cute you can't help but beam back at him, reddening. He winks and you look away. Armstrong blows his whistle, shrill across the chatter of the crowd.

'Quiet!' he shouts. 'Line up properly.'

The blow comes hard to your shoulder. So hard it makes a thwack noise and knocks you off balance. Your arm tingles, pinpricks shivering along the wasted nerve endings to your fingertips.

'Sorry, Spaz.'

Becky Palmer. Her face inches from yours as you try to regain your equilibrium. You feel your cheeks burning.

She's one of the blonde, popular girls – the sort that wears loads of make-up and flirts, but is also clever, so is well liked by teachers. They don't notice the sly punches and hair-pullings, feet suddenly stuck out to trip you, whispered comments from groups of sniggering girls (Becky at their centre). But Becky

Palmer is not the only one. All of your classmates are wary of you. In London people had bigger worries than your dicky hand. It was small fry. But in this Northern hellhole not only are you the cripple, you are the wrong colour. It's quite astonishing how rare you are. No one wants to sit next to you. Perhaps they think it's catching. You eat your lunch alone. You stay in the library during break and walk to school, and back, solo and a few minutes out of sync with everyone else.

You flex your hand, determined not to cry. You wear a brace on your arm made of leather and foam. Velcro binds it tightly. Your fingertips are the only part exposed. The kids call you Wacko Jacko. It's a bit cleverer than Becky Palmer's preferred Spaz. It started with a music lesson about the history of MTV. A documentary in the dark. Michael Jackson's gloved hand raised like a totem. Someone shouted your name. The whole class laughed.

Beneath the glove your arm has half the muscle it should. The wrist is bent and the fingers claw inwards. The distal phalanx of the index finger permanently touches the tip of your thumb. This will never change. There is slightly more movement in the other three fingers, largely due to countless hours of stretching exercises. Day upon day of physio, during which you had to visualise your fingers moving and watch desolately as they did absolutely nothing. After many agonising months there would be the tiniest flicker, a spasm of flesh and sinew. These tortures were inflicted after every surgery, along with infrared lights, boiled wax baths, cortisone injections, primitive physio machines with tiny pulleys and weights.

Beneath your brace the skin is criss-crossed with long, shiny scars. Every time you thought you were finished, the doctors said they could make it better. There would be anaesthesia and cutting and recovery, all for no more than a microscopic loosening. You do everything with your left hand and your pinky finger, the one with the most movement. It's numb but it's the best you've got.

'Chelsea, are you okay?'

Luca has manoeuvred himself to the spot beside you. You draw breath, still winded by pain. It fades from your arm into new agony in your side. You can't speak, just nod. Why the interest, you wonder. Is it some new cruelty, another joke at your expense? You frown, bent double, hands on hips. Luca places his hand on your back.

'You're not,' he says. 'She hurt you. Sir!'

He shouts it, ensuring the whole class hears. His hand radiates warmth through your sports top. You hear Armstrong canter towards you; look up and catch Becky Palmer's face down the line, etched with pure hatred.

'What is it?' Mr Armstrong's irritation is palpable. They call him 118 because of the tracksuit, moustache and ceaseless jogging, from one foot to the other, even when he's standing still.

Luca tells him Becky bashed your arm. 'She did it on purpose,' he says. They look at Becky.

Your breath returns and you shake your head.

'An accident,' you wheeze. 'Okay now.'

Luca frowns.

'You sure?' says Armstrong. 'You can sit it out if you don't feel up to it.'

Sit it out? Like a cripple. Fuck that. You've been practising. You've nothing else to do. For years you sat it out and then for more years you came last. *Didn't she do well – considering?* Fuck that.

'No. I'm all right,' you say, loudly, emphatically, and straighten your spine, shaking out your thigh muscles, your good arm.

'Okay then,' says Armstrong, jogging away.

'Why'd you do that?' asks Luca. 'Let her get away with it?' He gobs on the ground. 'Becky Palmer is a prize bitch.'

That's why.

The whistle blows and you're off.

You don't go as fast as you can at first. That would be stupid. That would wear you out. The other girls and boys move away at speed. You are at the back with the fat kids and the girl who has tape round her glasses. Luca looks over his shoulder and shrugs as he speeds ahead, leaving you behind. Speed is not the key to cross-country. Pace is the key. You know this from experience, but Mr Armstrong gave the class this information in the preamble. 'Pace,' he said. 'It's all about pace.' No one was listening.

The town has hills, lots of them. After three months running up and down them, you get an idea about pace. After three months your feet move out of instinct, finding footholds by braille. You feel the change of one season to another in the wind on your face. You watch the land alter in subtle ways from the top of each different peak you master. More effort going up, feet finding rocks and flat, legs like a crab's, this way and that.

You only have your running. There are no friends to hang out with and the pressure to make the best of it at home is stifling; every day the silent pleading concern in your mum's eyes. She had to move here for work. An opportunity for a better life. More money and less rent. There's only her to support you.

Daddy is long gone. You've gone onwards and upwards over hill and vale, losing fat, gaining muscle, whippet calves, rippling thighs. When you run, nothing matters; just your feet on the ground and your rhythmic breath. You've started to recognise other runners, regulars on similar routes. People with the same lost look on their faces you know you have. You've got to the point where they nod to you as you pass. You nod back but you've never spoken to any of them. You don't have time for conversation; you need to focus on one thing only. You need the freedom of concentrating on the way your feet hit the ground.

You speed up, not by much, but enough to pass the slow kids and catch up with the traffic jam of the average. You pass them easily. You've run this route many times. A 3.5-mile circuit from school – along the river, onto the moor's edge, around the forge, over a couple of stiles and back down to the school fields. It's easy – gentle inclines – but not if you sprint it from the off. Some of Becky's gang are in the average set, their boobs too big for effective running; even at 13 and 14 the extra baggage slows them down. You are as skinny as your mum's custard. That's what your nan says. It helps to be thin, as if your bones are hollow and filled with air. The girls glare as you pass, red-faced, breathless, sweat melting their make-up. Some of the boys look annoyed at being unexpectedly overtaken, especially by you. Humiliation sullies their faces. You focus on moving forward, see only what's ahead. There you can see the backs of the fastest, the athletes, the girls and boys with natural ability. These are the ones who tend to win everything, the ones who get the ball, the friends, the grades. The privileged few.

Armstrong cycles by on his bike with his megaphone. He nearly falls off when he sees you. You up your speed to overtake him and sense him scrambling behind you to catch up. He passes and looks back at you.

'Well done, DaSilva.' His voice is nasal in the wind. 'Keep it up.'

He zooms past the front runners, some of whom are slowing, holding their sides. You allow yourself a smile. Half a mile to go. You can see Luca clearly. You focus on his bottom and it breaks your rhythm momentarily. You right yourself and pick up the pace, overtaking easily. As you do so, he looks at you in surprise. No one expects this, least of all Becky Palmer. She is the one you focus on now. Poor cow doesn't even see it coming. She thinks Armstrong's excitement, as she crosses back into the school field, is about her. Bike abandoned, wheels spinning, he's jumping up and down looking at his stopwatch, shouting, 'C'mon, c'mon, you can do it!'

As you sprint past her you hear an anguished cry. You cross the finish line and are sitting on the grass getting your breath back by the time she comes in fifth. Armstrong is beside himself with glee. He pats you on the back and shows you your time on the stopwatch. It's not even your best.

Your mum has no idea until the spring parents' evening. She thinks you are happier at school, and you are. The bullying has stopped since you trashed Becky. She steers clear, as if she doesn't want to be reminded that you, a spaz, can beat her. They still whisper about you, but you can handle it. You and Luca hold hands on the way to school and in the cafeteria. He kept bugging you after the race, asking you how you could run so fast. He'd appear by your side at the school gates, run to catch up with you between lessons and after a while you started to look out for him. One day he walked you home and on your doorstep he touched your face and kissed you goodbye. You beat Becky Palmer to that too.

In the hall on parents' evening, Armstrong leaps from his chair and shakes your mother's hand vigorously.

'Chelsea is amazing!' he gushes. 'I mean truly. Her time was off the scale for the cross-country. She beat the school record by miles.'

Your mum is dumbstruck. She's looking at him as if he's mental.

'I think with the right training Chelsea could win a medal,' he says. 'And I don't mean just at county or national level. I mean international.'

He's talking so loudly, parents and kids seeing other teachers turn to look at you. You think you might die of embarrassment.

'I'm thinking of the Paralympics. Rio 2016.'

You flinch at the word *Paralympics*.

Your mum takes you for pizza to celebrate. You eat dough balls as she concentrates on her wine.

'You never told me,' she says, 'that you were so good. I mean I knew you ran, but... the Paralympics!'

A tear finds its way from your eye. That word again. You throw down your napkin and march off to the toilets.

In the mirror you see a teenage girl in school uniform, taller than average, thinner, brown-skinned, a few spots breaking out on her cheeks, frizzy hair tied up in a ponytail. You rip off your arm brace and look at yourself again, this time concentrating on the lopsided imperfection of your limbs. *The Parafuckinglympics.*

You and your mum are quickly obsessed. She's been watching any athletics coverage she can find since Armstrong said you were good. You come in from your evening run and before you even have a chance to kick off your trainers she's dragged you into the lounge to see him being interviewed. You watch, breathless from your exertion, unable to speak. On the screen you see a man with no legs. You wouldn't know he had no legs but they show footage of the race he has just finished. He is so handsome. There is determination in his eyes. He runs on blades and has won countless medals in disabled competitions. Gold. Gold. Gold. Silver. Gold. Gold. Gold. He had wanted to represent his country in the 2008 Olympics. No Para – the real thing. Your frown smooths into surprise as the commentator's words repeat in your mind: *competing on the same level.* They didn't let him.

Winter turns to spring. Posters of him cover your bedroom wall. Luca doesn't like them; he sticks his tongue out at them and laughs. You buy any magazine that has a photograph of him, not just athletics titles but gossip mags too. Luca picks them up from your bed, flicks through them, studying a few of the pictures, then tosses them away in disgust. He is jealous. This makes you feel warm inside, as if there is molten honey in your tummy.

You are in training; every day except Sunday. Armstrong sees to it. You have medals now. You have a coach and a club and you have competed in your first fixtures and won every time. The other runners were not able-bodied; all had some form of affliction. Your times are good enough to qualify for County but you haven't been put forward yet. You'll persuade them though. *What's the point in beating cripples?* You blanch at your thoughts but you've never been good with confronting disability, you cross the road if you see someone in a wheelchair or with a guide dog; you come out in a cold sweat if you see someone signing. Difference makes you nervous, sometimes physically sick.

Your mum has a surprise for you. She tells you when you come back from your run. She's waiting for you at the door, must have stood at the window looking for you. Her smile is enormous. She tells you the news in a breathless rush. Your Uncle Danny, your cool uncle, the one who works for the BBC, has tickets for the Olympics. Not just tickets, but press tickets; seats at the front, an arm's length of the starting line. They are for 4 August, a sprint day. You will see him run.

You have to wait for the next train because of the crowds on the platform. People have whistles, some are singing, waving flags of Olympic rings and Union Jacks, the colours of all nations. The party atmosphere makes you smile. Uncle Danny sits beside you on the floor, your backs against the wall. He hands over the bottle of Olympic-labelled water. It's sweltering hot. The mix of blazing sun and huge crowds robs the air of oxygen and you feel light-headed and sweaty. You are so excited you can't eat and the smell of bacon from someone's McMuffin makes you swallow back bile.

Another train comes. The crowd swells forward, funnelling towards the doors. The door directly in front of you opens but no one gets in or out. You watch people turn away and join the crowds trying to get on-board at either end of the carriage. Danny talks about how hot it is and wonders aloud if you'll get on the next train. After a few seconds there is a clear space between you and the door and you see that it is blocked by a man on the train, a man in a wheelchair. He sits facing you, staring blankly ahead, as more people try to get in and move quickly away. You look up at him from your position on the floor. His jaw is clenched and you can tell he is absent from himself. He isn't a man in a wheelchair stopping people getting into a train carriage; he isn't even there. Then something, perhaps your stare, makes him look down at you and for a second, as the door shuts, he returns to his body and stares back. The train rumbles away, announcements echoing around the walls.

You blurt out suddenly, stopping Danny mid-flow: 'Did Dad leave cos of my arm?'

He makes a jerky movement with his shoulders.

'Chelsea. No. No, of course not,' shaking his head vigorously. 'How long have you thought that?'

'A while. For ever.'

'Look, he just wasn't a settle-down type of guy then. He was young. He didn't want a job and a home and a family.'

You sniff.

'He's got that now though, hasn't he? In America?'

Danny places his hand on your good arm and looks into your eyes.

'It had nothing to do with your arm, Chelsea. He was 21 and he didn't want to be tied down. Have you never asked him about it?'

'I don't really talk to him any more. He hasn't asked me back since last time. Nothing happened; we just didn't – gel. I'm the last thing he needs.'

'I'm sure he doesn't think that.'

You look at him defiantly. He knows as well as you that your father – his brother – has a very nice life without you. You have two little American half-sisters, kitten-cute toddlers, with big, dark eyes and shiny curls, as pure and perfect as any father could wish for.

'Did your mum tell you that was why he left?'

His face hardens but it's not your mum's fault. You came to the conclusion all by yourself.

You sigh. 'I don't mention Dad to Mum ever. We talked about it once a few years ago when the girls were born and she cried for a week.'

Danny squeezes your arm.

'Chelsea. He did not leave because of your arm.'

The train pulls in, there are fewer people waiting to get on. You'll be able to take this one. Danny stands and offers you his hand.

The Olympic Park reminds you of a science-fiction film, from the domes of the arenas to the looming laddered sculpture in the centre, twisting upwards into sky so flatly blue it hurts to look at it. Everything is new. Futuristic. The air smells of excitement and roasted peanuts. You glimpse the enormity of the stadium through the press entrance. Danny shows his authorisation to the security guards and you are inside. The space opens up before you like a cathedral, too big to take in: the roar of conversation, vuvuzelas, whistles, piped pop music, manicured lawns marked out into areas by white lines, the mats and sand for the jumpers, nets and gradients for the throwers and, all around it, the bright orange lanes of the running track.

Athletes practise sprint starts in their tracksuits, pixelated and projected onto gigantic screens at each end of the stadium. Danny shows you to your seat, a bank of photographers just in front of you, heads bent to their telephoto lenses. You have a plastic pass on a red, white and blue ribbon with the word GUEST written in large black print, Danny wears one with PRESS on it. He greets some of the other people on your row, high fives, introduces you, but you can't take in any names. You nod politely, smile and say hello, then go back to your programme, to the running order of races and events. You watch time flick past on the giant digital clock.

Contests pass in a whirl. You marvel at how so much can happen at once; the shot put, the discus, the high jump and long jump. You barely speak, your sounds confined to whoops on a rising scale, as you clap and cheer with 80,000 others.

You see him before anyone else; you are sure of it. Your eyes register his presence before the cheer of the crowd confirms it. Danny nudges you in the ribs. The object of your obsession bounces along the track as if he's cloud jumping – lean, muscular, smaller than you'd imagined, his eyes covered with wraparound sunglasses. You watch intently, trying to get the measure of him, to see how he is different from you. He squats at the starting block, rests the curled feet of his blades against its slope. You realise that for the last few seconds you didn't even think about the blades, that to you they were no different from your legs, calves, feet. This is the first time in your life you have not noticed an obvious disability.

He's off – a practice start – and the crowd goes wild. He stops a few yards down the tracks and raises his hand in greeting, the faces of his admirers reflected in his shades.

Someone throws a discus, flashed large on the monitor as it arcs impossibly and lands, a small tuft of earth kicked up in slow motion. Beyoncé warbles, lyrics muffled, 'If I Were a Boy'.

Suddenly, they line up. He is in lane five and when the American-accented announcer reads his name the resulting noise rushes around your ears, too loud to hear what comes after. Then a moment's silence… and the gun, harshly cracking the calm. You stand, jump up and down waving your arm. You shout 'C'mon, c'mon' with everyone around you, excitement building to a deafening crescendo. He's overtaken by everybody behind him, but then on the bend it looks like he might catch up, arms and legs an indistinct blur. Forty-five seconds later, back on the flat, and he's last over the finish line, eighth out of eight.

The winners are announced but you don't hear their names. There is no disappointment in the stadium. His previously impassive face comes alive in a smile, the glasses jettisoned. The other runners high five him, one or two hug, another (James from Grenada) takes off his number and swaps it with him, as if they were footballers in the cup final. They bump fists. His smile is all you can see.

You are down from your seat and standing next to the TV cameras before you know you have moved. The interviewer is from NBC, an ex-athlete you assume, towering and star-spangled. He strides over, balletic, the grin never dropping, perfect white teeth, emerald green eyes. You are so close you can hear his breathing between words, smell sweat and cologne. He answers the questions, thanks everyone for their support, and says his dream has come true, says it's mind-blowing and makes to move away. You thrust your programme in front of his face, pen held by the same hand. 'Please,' you say, squeal almost.

He smiles and nods, takes the pen from your hand, but he doesn't really look at you. The crowd is still calling his name and he looks up at them. A breath of cold air ruffles his vest, makes you shiver.

'What's your name?' he asks.

'Chelsea,' you whisper, your courage gone.

He scribbles on the cover *To Chelsea*, then pauses, pen poised, and looks directly at you. 'Do you run?' he asks.

'Cross-country.'

'Ah, I'm no good at that.'

He hands you back your pen and, as he does, you see that he notices your hand. For the briefest instant a look passes over his face. It's not that his smile drops – it's too quick for that – but there is a change. You recognise it; you are well practised in it, and it is so hidden that only another practitioner would spot it.

'Are you any good?' he asks.

'I usually win.'

He looks you right in the eye.

'Always keep running,' he says and turns quickly away to start the much-anticipated lap of honour.

'I saw you!' says your mum. She has come to the station to meet you. 'You were on the telly. I screamed when I saw you. Something for them kids to talk about, eh?'

She rattles off questions and hugs you like you are a toddler again.

'C'mon,' she says, 'pizza!'

You groan. 'Okay, but takeout – I'm shattered.'

Over dinner she asks you about your trip and she's so excited you tell her everything you remember. Almost everything; you don't tell her about that look. You watch yourself on the television. You don't recognise yourself.

'Danny called after he put you on the train. He told me what you said about your dad. Do you want to ask me anything?'

You slurp your Diet Coke and think about that look.

'No,' you say, 'fuck him.'

'Chelsea!' says your mum. 'Language.'

Then she laughs deeply and you can tell you've made her day.

He has a girlfriend. They are in the gossip mags, on the entertainment channels.

She is beautiful. Blonde and blue-eyed, a model, a law graduate, perfect in every way, like an earth-bound angel. A man couldn't hope for a more beautiful girl-friend. She could have her pick of any of them but she chose him. This makes you glad. You follow her on Twitter, alerted to their exchanges, her goodwill messages. She is sweet and optimistic, just what he needs. You have watched him all year and, while you have seen him win some races, you have seen him lose more and you have witnessed his anger when it happens. The Paralympics was the worst, a tantrum on camera, flared nostrils, accusations, excuses. He apologised afterwards but it didn't seem sincere. You remembered that look. You worried for him but now you are sure he will be happy, like you are.

You spend New Year's Eve at Luca's with his extended Italian family; brothers, sisters, cousins. There are so many of them you can slip away unnoticed to his room. You kiss under his duvet, remove layers, fumble, not quite ready for the next step but it makes you happy and you can't stop smiling.

Today is Valentine's Day. It will be the first time in your life you will get a card from someone who isn't your mum. You have bought chocolates for her, because you know no one else will, and you take them, and the single red rose and card you got Luca, from their hiding place in your wardrobe. You were careful about what you wrote; you didn't want to be too sickly. After school you are going to the cinema. You read her tweet last night as you got into bed. It was the last thing you saw before you turned out the light.

What do you have up your sleeve for your love tomorrow??? #getexcited #ValentinesDay

You wanted to reply but didn't have the nerve.

A few birds sing into the pitch dark. From downstairs you can hear the radio, muffled music and the 7am news jingle. You get dressed and put on your running shoes and you smell pancakes sizzling – a Valentine's Day treat. Then the smoke alarm goes off and the air is suddenly acrid, catching in your throat. You run into the kitchen.

'Mum, what are you doing?'

But she's just standing there shrouded in smoke listening to the news. You see her expression and hear words like gun, shots, bathroom, *murder*. You hear his name and you run. You run from the kitchen, out of the front door and onto the street. Your mum calls after you.

You keep running. You don't stop.

It's freezing out and cloudy. The wind swirls around you, biting. It's so early and the dawn light makes the road dim. A couple of the regulars say hello but you keep your eyes forward, following the trail of orange street lamps uphill. Your feet pound the pavement and all you can hear is them and your laboured breath. You forget about pace. Forget everything you've learnt. This is a sprint.

You run 3 miles, full pelt – up and out of the suburbs and onto the edge of the moors. By the time you are clear of the stone-wall boundary, you are in agony. Pain grips your sides, your legs, your hand. You leap over the stile and fall to the grass, frost crunching under your weight, so puffed your breath is a rasping call for help. You lie on your back in the cold looking up at tree branches like writing across the sky, spelling out a story you don't want to be told. He is either a murderer or a coward, maybe even both. You feel sick. Your vision blurs; tears and sweat sting your eyes as you sob. You stay like this for ages, then you stop suddenly. Your breath slows and your vision clears. You sit up, aware of the icy wind on your arms. You hug yourself and look down at the city waking below, car lights edging through the streets, street lamps dimming as the day breaks. You breathe in through your nose. A moment of stillness. Then – you run.

19

Underneath

Jack pulls the plastic apart with a satisfying pop. He shakes out the fresh golden flakes up to the rim of his bowl and pours on ice-cold milk and a dessertspoon of sugar. It has to be in that order, milk then sugar, and then they have to be eaten quickly before the sugar dissolves or the flakes go soft: maximum crunch – nothing else will do. The second spoonful has just gone into his mouth when he hears footsteps on the stairs. He chews quickly and rushes the third spoonful. The fourth doesn't make it into his mouth, hovering just below his lips as Rosa walks into the kitchen and glares in his direction. She picks up the kettle and shakes it, sighs heavily and carries it to the sink to refill it. She has her back to him and he forgets all about his cornflakes as he takes in the view.

'What are you wearing?' he asks.

She looks over her shoulder. The flame silk of her hair cascades down her back.

'It's what I wear in bed.' She frowns at him and turns back to the sink.

The cornflakes no longer hold any interest for Jack. He puts down his spoon and rests his hands flat on the table. Rosa glides around the kitchen, making tea and looking in cupboards, seemingly unaware of his presence.

'Since when did you wear that in bed?'

She doesn't look at him.

'When you were in my bed,' she answers, 'you kept me warm. I didn't need to wear anything. This is what I like to wear when I'm alone.'

'Why would you wear that when you are alone?' he says. 'It's not designed for just one person.'

'There they are,' she says, walking over to the table and reaching across for the cornflakes.

The camisole is silk, with red lace trim and straps and it is printed with red and pink roses. It flows over her body like water, and the look is finished off with matching knickers that rest lightly at the top of her thighs. Jack's mouth is slack. As she leans over the table he glances down between the lace; her breasts are fully visible, whiter beneath the tan line, small pink nipples mimicking the rosebuds on the silk. He waves a hand at her indignantly.

'You can't wear that around the house – it's not decent.'

She sits down opposite him and pours herself some cornflakes, then fixes him with a Paddington stare.

'I'll wear what I want. If you don't like it – move out.'

She crunches loudly on her cereal.

'So much nicer when they're fresh, don't you think?'

'Ah, so that's what this is about, is it?' He shoves his bowl away. 'I'm not giving up my sea view for you. I don't mind sleeping on the couch till you find somewhere else… But please, don't walk around like that while you're still here. You wouldn't prance around like that in front of Spike – so don't do it with me.'

She puts down her spoon and smiles sweetly at his stony face.

'Firstly, I am not moving out. Yes, you and Spike found the flat, but we all moved in together, equal deposits, so it's not actually yours.'

He opens his mouth to protest.

'I'm speaking now,' she says like a teacher to a naughty child. 'And for your information, Spike doesn't care what I wear because, just like you and me since you decided you prefer Colleen, we are just friends.'

She stands up, scraping the chair across the lino with a short backward push of her knees. As she does so one of the lace straps falls off her shoulder and hangs halfway down her arm. They fix each other with furious eyes.

'It was just once. I was drunk. It didn't mean anything.'

'So you said.'

She flicks her hair from her face and takes her bowl to the dishwasher. As she dips down to pull it open, her French knickers ride up over her buttock. She straightens, then bends again to put the bowl inside the machine's gaping mouth.

'For God's sake, can't you put a dressing gown on or something?'

She turns round to face him and gives a little snorting laugh.

'Why? If we were on the beach, it wouldn't bother you at all.'

'That's different and you know it. A bikini is more… solid. What you've got on… It's designed to turn men on, all that swooshing.'

She unfolds her arms, takes a tube of lip balm from the kitchen counter and runs some over her bottom lip with her forefinger.

'Do you remember what I was wearing the night we got together?'

He looks down at his cornflakes; they've gone mushy. He mutters into them. 'A black dress.'

'And underneath? What was I wearing underneath?'

He swirls the pale flakes with his spoon, then looks up at her.

'I don't remember.'

She raises an eyebrow.

He does remember. It had taken his breath away – a turquoise silk bra and pants edged in orange lace. She'd looked like a Hollywood starlet. The bra was old-fashioned and had creaked as his fingers moved over it. His hands were shaking so much she'd had to help him with the clasp. The memory of it moves over his face – and elsewhere.

'See,' she says, 'you do remember.'

He nods dumbly, looking at the freckles on her breastbone. She returns the lip balm to the counter.

'That night I didn't expect to be going home with you, or anyone else,' she says. 'I just like to wear stuff like that. It has nothing to do with you, or any man. I like the feel of it. I like knowing that whatever I've got on, even paint-splattered overalls, there's a bit of glamour underneath.'

She looks sad, as if she might cry again. He never meant to make her cry.

'Please, just go and put a dressing gown on.'

'Fine.'

She slams the dishwasher door shut with her foot and strops away upstairs.

Jack sighs and carries his bowl of cornflakes to the bin; he throws away the mush, then makes himself a new bowl.

'There's no way I'm moving out,' he mutters to Rosa's absent form. As he stands at the kitchen window watching rain clouds scuttle across the sky, he thinks about what she said.

It was true; she always had worn incredible underwear. In their first few weeks together, when they'd spent most of their time taking each other's clothes off, he'd been stunned by the array of unusual undergarments. Every day brought a new experience of silk and coloured lace. He remembered the roses, so many roses, embroidered buds and leaves cupping creamy breasts, or swirling prints on loose satin that bewitched his fingers. Jack had thought girls only wore things like that in movies.

Sometimes he'd watch her try them on, one after another, looking at herself in her full-length mirror, lifting her hair and tilting her head. He'd sit on her bed in a room of perfumed candles and scarf-dimmed table lamps and marvel at how lucky he was. It was never trampy; she never teamed it with obvious fetishes like suspenders or spike heels. Rosa was pure class.

He went shopping with her a few times to tiny boutiques hidden down little streets he didn't know existed. These were the only times in his life he truly enjoyed shopping. He remembered one afternoon in particular. Inside, the shop was draped with heavy velvet curtains and there was a table with a huge vase of Georgia O'Keeffe lilies, their blossoms reflected in a floor-length mirror. The flowers gave off a smell you could almost touch. An immaculately dressed woman whisked Rosa away through gilded saloon doors, leaving him to sit on a spongy armchair and wait. As he listened to their pointy-heeled footsteps echo across the pious tiles, he felt as though he'd somehow sneaked in to the inner sanctum – somewhere forbidden to country boys like himself.

While she was gone, he looked at the rows of fairy garments pegged on padded hangers, in every colour imaginable. The scent from the lilies drugged his senses; he stood and tiptoed across the floor to where the silk and lace were calling him. He checked to make sure he was really alone and then lifted a pair of chartreuse knickers to his face and inhaled deeply. The saloon door swung open and he'd been caught red-nosed and laughed at. It was worth it though.

Rosa had told him that most of her underwear was second-hand. Some of it had even belonged to movie stars. The set she wore on their first night together had once belonged to Brigitte Bardot. There had been a fierce eBay battle over it but Rosa had been willing to pay more than anyone because she wanted it so much. She had a slip from Audrey Hepburn, a Natalie Wood corset, the bra worn by Cybill Shepherd in *The Last Picture Show*. Not everything fitted her perfectly but it fitted her enough. The pieces Rosa liked best didn't belong to anyone famous. She bought them in vintage shops and antique markets. There, she found pants that belonged to other people; people who were probably dead. At first Jack was freaked out by the idea of second-hand underwear, but to Rosa each piece was special. She said there was something sexy in it, as if a little bit of the previous owner's life force had been left behind for her to use. He remembered the delight that crossed her face when she found something beautiful. One time in particular came to mind now; she'd taken him to an antique fair in the old Pentecostal church.

'Look at this,' she said, pulling some filigree out of a wooden barrel of rags. She'd shaken it out and held it up to the light filtering through the cloudy windows. It was a powder blue all-in-one; you could see the stitches down the seams. She gasped with pleasure.

'I think it's original – 1930s or something. Feel the silk,' she said, handing it to him. 'It's like tissue paper.'

He held it in his hand, wary of rubbing it too much in case it dissolved, and thought how he'd like to feel the life force in it when it was stretched over her body. He remembered what it felt like when he did.

She never stopped wearing the stuff, never reverted to period pants and sports bras because she'd caught him and didn't have to try any more. He wondered when exactly in the last two years he'd got so used to it he'd stopped noticing.

Then there was Colleen and her legs, and Rosa's weekend away at her sister's when she came back early because she couldn't bear to be without him. She'd found them together in their bed, Colleen's serviceable knickers flung onto Rosa's armchair among Rosa's special things. What an idiot he was.

A seagull lifts off from the rain-slicked roof tiles of the house opposite and flies gracefully into the grey skies. There are light footsteps in the hall and he turns to see her enter the room. She's put lipstick on and her hair is mussed up. He hasn't seen the dressing gown before. It's minuscule, a kimono that barely covers her bottom – black satin with printed cosmic butterflies and embroidered cherry blossoms. It's tied loosely on her hips, open to her waist, exposing the printed roses of her camisole. They lock eyes again.

'What's that?'

'A dressing gown. You asked me to cover up.'

'Jesus, Rosa. It doesn't cover much up, does it? And it's all swishy.'

'Swishy?'

'Yeah – it's worse. It just makes me think there are more layers to take off.'

'Get over it,' she says quietly and leaves the room. He follows, carried along in her current as he has been from their first meeting. In the living room, darkened by undrawn curtains, she fishes some vinyl from its sleeve and places it on the turntable, lifting the needle carefully into crackles. Billie Holiday, 'I'm a Fool to Want You', one of Rosa's favourites. Jack's not keen on ancient heartbreak jazz; he thinks it's like something his nan would listen to, and he remembers the stinging humiliation on their first night when Rosa asked him if he liked Billie Holiday and he'd said, 'He's alright.' She'd laughed at him and told him that he shouldn't pretend to know about things he didn't; then she'd played him this song. This song is special. This song, their song, brings with it the memory of another life. He remembers dancing in her room – close behind the closed door – she'd laid her head on his chest and then, when the song was over, she'd kissed him properly for the first time.

Rosa hums and sways to the lilting rhythm, her eyes lightly shut, lips closing and parting with the words. She looks both angelic and wanton at the same time, like an exotic animal. He daren't breathe or make a sound. Her kimono rustles as she moves, almost inaudibly. He can't take any more. He walks up to her and grabs her waist, turning her in his arms. The satin slicks under his touch. He buries his face in her chest, his nose rests on a breast and he can smell the softness of the roses. She stiffens in his arms; a corpse against desire.

'Please,' he whispers, the word muffled by her flesh.

'No.'

He moves away, tears in his eyes, and staggers towards the front door and out into the cold, bright air of the street outside.

He's gone for over two hours. She's in the hall when he gets back, about to go out, fully dressed in jeans and a T-shirt with no hint of what might be underneath. He feels green, sweat beads prick his forehead and his heart beats over-fast. She stares at him with a welcome hint of concern in her eyes.

'Are you feeling all right?'

'I'm sorry,' he says, swallowing back the lump in his throat. 'I made a mistake. I don't want Colleen. I just want you. Please take me back, please. I promise I'll be good. I had this done for you.'

He pulls off his T-shirt, wincing with pain. On his chest is the blue–black outline of a full-bloomed rose, complete with thorny stem and the name *Rosa* traced in a florid script. His skin is raw underneath.

Rosa gasps.

'I'm supposed to go back in a few days to get the red filled in but I don't think I can do it without you.'

She laughs and touches her name with cold fingertips. He sways.

'Take me back – please.'

She smiles and looks into his eyes.

'Maybe.'

The earth rushes from under him, and he falls, head first, into the scent of a million roses placed at her feet by his longing.

20

Ruby of the Desert

Ruby was just 16 when Mr Simms built the Coyote Diner on the edge of town, where Main Street seamlessly transforms into Route 58. The town was small and perpetually covered with a thin layer of pale desert dust, as if it had been kept in storage for a long, long time. Entertainment was provided by one bar on the outskirts, frequented by drunks and farmhands, and no place for kids or women. The excitement among the bored backyard teenagers grew with the building site, as out-of-town workmen levelled the one-pump gas station and erected eatery Eden. The kids watched its progress from porches and pushbikes, standing in huddles to gawp at the passing trucks and rising walls and speculate on how the place would look when it was finished. It was 1962, and those workmen left behind more than just a building, they left the tiny dirt-track town the much-needed hope of rock 'n' roll glamour (and more than one illegitimate child).

Ruby went to see Mr Simms before the work was completed, the main shell having been constructed but the inside not yet beautified. She peered through the glass door, still with its protective plastic, and watched him scan the local paper and slurp back coffee. He was a big, grey-haired Texan, complete with the regulation Stetson and spurs, even though his Chevrolet Impala was parked outside.

Men were a mystery to Ruby. Her daddy had left when she was nine – preferring hard liquor and gambling to providing for a family – and then it was just her and her momma, who spent her life sitting silently on the porch in her rocking chair, mending the town's clothes for a meagre living. From this spot Ruby's momma squinted at the desert, which stretched out between the peaks punctuating the town, as if she were waiting for somebody to ride over the horizon. Somebody she knew, deep down, would never come. Money was tight. Sometimes Ruby dreamt of going to Vegas and winning big on the gaming tables she'd seen in the movies so that she and her momma wouldn't want for anything. Whenever she mentioned this, her momma would reply that 'money was better when it was earned' and that Ruby should 'concentrate on her studies instead of spending her time daydreaming about things she'd never have'. Ruby never was one for schooling. Her momma was right, she did spend most of her time in the classroom gazing out of the window, the teachers' words getting lost in the mist of her daydreams. She wouldn't ever be college material, but she did have the savvy to walk up to the Coyote's door before any of the other girls in town and ask for a job. She stood a good while at that door before Mr Simms got the feeling he was being watched and spilt his coffee on himself as he started up and beckoned her in. As soon as she stepped over the threshold she knew she belonged.

In 1962 the Coyote seated 150. It had the smooth chrome lines of an express train complemented by red leather booths and bar stools. Each table had a mini jukebox, ensuring that the music was always on. When Ruby arrived for her first day, in her short pink uniform and matching lipstick, the Tornados blasted through the outdoor speakers and grease monkeys in newly pressed overalls tuned up cars on the parking lot. They stopped and whistled as she passed and she felt more like she was in an Elvis movie than starting work in her home town.

In the back room, in a fog of competing perfumes, the girls fixed their make-up and hair for the grand opening. Ruby knew a couple of them – Cherry, Marlene – but mostly they were from out of town, and Ruby blushed with pride when they complimented her on her legs as she tied the laces of her roller skates. They became the sisters she never had and Chet, the grill cook with movie-star looks, became her first husband, though none of them knew what they would mean to each other on that first day. Back then, they shared an unconscious immortality, certain only that the next day would be better than the last.

The Coyote's fame spread. The last stop before the desert, it drew customers from far and wide on their way to the natural wonders of the valley. It was also the place to hang out if you were young and looking for love. Ruby was its star, a whizz on roller skates, Mr Simms's favourite girl, popular with customers and co-workers alike. It was no wonder; she was very striking, tall and thin with the friendliest of ice-cream smiles. Her hair flowed in unruly auburn curls that kept coming loose from the bobby pins she used to keep them up. She considered it her best feature, even if it did smell of burger grease.

All that was nearly 50 years ago; and on almost every day since – barring the few taken for funerals, childbirth and holidays – Ruby has looked out across the parking lot to the desert at sunset. There is a particular moment she likes best, when dusk begins to dissolve into night and the sun tucks itself beneath the covers of the horizon. She always takes a minute to stand and watch its progress, awestruck as the orange light casts lengthening cactus shadows across the plain. The Coyote's vast windows give her the full Panavision experience. In these moments, she feels at one with the world. Today is the last day she will witness this spectacle as a waitress and she has a lump in her throat as she watches a lone car move slowly away towards the infinite.

From her first day at the Coyote, Ruby remembered everybody's name. It came naturally to her, as if the brainpower needed to retain all the arithmetic and fancy words in school was just waiting for a purpose. She added up cheques in her head and remembered the favourite dishes of her customers, even if they had only visited once or twice. If folks were new to town, she greeted them warmly as they settled into a booth and made sure to ask how they were doing. Sometimes it was hard. Sometimes her heart felt like it would break. In her time at the Coyote, she has gone through two husbands (and her fair share of lovers). Chet ran off with another waitress after 10 years together. Her second husband, a refined older man named Mitch, died of lung cancer a few years after they wed. Each left her a son, Eddie and little Mitchell. Even when they were babies she managed to work full-time, night shifts and afternoons, leaving them with their gramma until they were old enough for school. Later, they came to the diner after class and Mr Simms always gave them a jawbreaker while they picked something from the menu for supper and did their homework in the back room. Mr Simms was a sympathetic boss, more like a grandaddy to her boys. He said they were as cute as pie with their mother's red hair and Opie Griffith freckles, and he taught them their first magic tricks, and then poker, over the counter as Ruby worked.

Mitchell was killed in Iraq. He was 29. They flew him home in a coffin wrapped in the stars and stripes. The army presented her with the flag at the funeral. A young man with a straight back and a square jaw placed it on her upturned hands and then saluted her. She had no tears left to cry. She keeps Mitchell's flag folded in her dresser drawer, out of sight but never quite out of mind.

Eddie didn't cope too well. He got deep into drugs, and the crimes that go with them, and ended up with a 15-year prison sentence for armed robbery. Neither son had married. There are no grandkiddies to dote on. Eddie isn't young any more; his red hair was shaved to the skin last time she visited and his face was puffy and grey. Ruby wishes she could visit him more often but he's in a cross-state penitentiary and the bus fare is more than she can afford. That's her business though. The customers don't need to know about her personal dramas. For them, she has only a smile and a few words of encouragement when it looks like they might be suffering.

In the 1970s the music changed. Approaching 30, Ruby adapted her roller-skating technique, swishing in time to heavy disco beats with a tray poised preternaturally on one hand. The diner still buzzed and Ruby still wore her smile. Mr Simms bought a new sign; as well as the original roller-skating coyote he had the words *Ruby of the Desert* added in flashing red neon. He said he wanted people to see the place as they drove across the plain at night. He said that Ruby deserved recognition for all the years' service she'd put in. Ruby was speechless. She stood below the sign and squeezed Mr Simms's arm as the electrician flicked the switch for the first time and bathed them in a scarlet glow. Sometimes (and this was one of those times) she wondered if Mr Simms wanted more from her than friendship, but if he did, he never said anything about it. He watched her work her way through a few of the Coyote's regulars, and some of those passing through, and he never judged her, never told her to stop. He was more than 20 years older than her and she didn't want to offend him by suggesting his motives were anything but honourable. When she looked back on her life in the cold, lonely nights of old age she figured that if Mr Simms had wanted more it would have been below that neon sign that he would've told her.

The sands seemed to shift under Ruby's feet. Most of the original Coyote girls had left, married or gone South to seek fame and fortune. Ruby was older than the new girls and more like a mother than a sister. She gave them advice when they had man trouble – God knows she'd had enough herself – and provided a shoulder to cry on when they needed it. Mr Simms looked after her; made sure she was eating right and had enough shifts to pay the rent. She thought of him as the father she never had, another bond unspoken but acknowledged in the cheery 'Mornin', how are you?' they exchanged each day. When Ruby's momma passed, he paid for the funeral and afterwards sat with her until dawn sharing bourbon and memories.

Another decade passed under the unforgiving desert sun and Ruby's skin began to wrinkle. She had good genes but the laughter lines ran deep, turning her mouth down at the edges so, unless she was fully smiling, she carried an air of sadness about her. She still loved her job, though it wasn't the same after Mr Simms had his heart attack. Right there in the spot she'd first seen him, almost 30 years to the day. He slumped to the floor and his coffee spilt on the table, seeping into his newspaper and blurring all the stories into one. The Coyote passed to a nephew, who never came near, and the management of the place was taken over by a young man called Gregory, who had a sour face and a silent manner. A Starbucks opened on Main Street and a drive-thru McDonald's across the road. People wanted their food fast. Custom dwindled quickly and within a year of Mr Simms's death, half of the booth space in the Coyote was given over to slot machines. The music was turned way down.

Today, Ruby shows her replacement the ropes. Carmine is her name; it doesn't suit her. She is a tiny, mousy thing with glasses and acne, just out of school. She has to be shown how the staff lockers work several times. God knows how she'll cope out front, but that's not Ruby's problem any more. At least the roller skates have long been replaced by sensible sneakers, rubber-soled so as not to mark the floor. As Carmine stows her outdoor shoes in her locker, Ruby looks at herself in the back-room mirror. She smooths her hands over her belly, noting how her uniform stretches across her bulging middle, and then touches the tight grey perm peeking from under her hat. The auburn curls are gone. For some time now she has been squinting at her order pad through bifocal lenses. Her smile is the same though, a little puckered around the edges maybe, but still as radiant as a desert morning.

Ruby's last order is a rush. At 6.30 the door is opened by a stranger wearing blue jeans and a pressed white shirt. She saw his pick-up drive in from the valley, sunlight reflecting off the wing mirrors like fallen stars. It's unusual to see an unfamiliar face at the Coyote these days. He carries a Stetson and, though he bears no physical resemblance to Mr Simms (he's too short and dark), he reminds Ruby a great deal of her former boss – perhaps it's his soft Texan accent and twinkling eyes. He orders coffee and blueberry pancakes with canned cream and, as she pours, Ruby asks on the off chance if he is related to Mr Simms. 'Wouldn't that be something on my last day?' she says. But the stranger smiles and tells her he's just passing through and there's no connection at all.

Ruby is as attentive as ever but her co-workers spring a Happy Retirement cake on her so she doesn't have as much time to talk to him as she would like.

Gregory – now middle-aged but no more communicative – makes a short, embarrassed speech about her being their longest-serving employee. There is applause and tears and they present her with their gift – a china model of a cowgirl riding bareback. It's pretty, hand-painted, with fine detail on the long red curls sticking out under the cowgirl's hat. Perhaps they thought it looked like her in the old photographs that now adorn the Coyote's walls. It's a lovely gift, planned, thoughtful and completely useless. Ruby hides her disappointment under her usual enormous smile. A Greyhound pass was what she wanted, so she could visit Eddie more often. She was sure she had dropped enough hints.

After the party, she places her cowgirl safely under the counter and insists on clearing her last table. The Texan is long gone. He smiled and tipped his hat to her during the celebrations. She watched him walk to his car as the waitresses set off party poppers and sang 'For She's a Jolly Good Fellow'. Ruby pocketed his tip with barely a glance, assuming from his smile that it was a more than generous note. She goes out for a farewell beer with her colleagues, knowing she will see them rarely. She doesn't think she could bear to come back as a customer. The Coyote is as much her diner as it is anyone's; it wouldn't be right to be waited on.

It is only when she is home, sitting alone in front of the TV rubbing her feet, that her mind returns to the tip. She sits up and fishes into her coverall pocket. She is surprised to find that the folded paper in her palm isn't the twenty-dollar bill she was expecting but a lottery ticket for that night's county draw. She thinks about her momma, sitting on the porch mending clothes, telling her that money is better when it's earned. She remembers her teenage dream of winning big in Vegas, a city her momma never got to visit. A smile crosses her lips as she reaches for the TV remote and changes the channel just in time to catch the jackpot draw.

21

How Malcolm Malone Became the First Punk in Pontefract

When I got to Malcolm lying limp on the grass by the fish pond, the make-up was lodged in streaks inside the cuts to his face. Beige, gold, pearlised blue, smeared into jagged red flesh and filming the blood droplets that oozed from the wounds. He was a total mess. My first thought, when I saw him from the park gate, was that he was dead. Helen had run into the art room as I was packing up. I'd spent an hour after school practising watercolour shading for my A-level portfolio, dropping water on saturated colour and brushing it out delicately until the paper swallowed it clear. My theme was birds of paradise. It's the males that are colourful. The females are uniformly brown. They didn't interest me. I wanted preening Paradisaeidae, glossy manucodes, puffball parotia. I combined them with sketches of movie stars and models, artificial colour overlaying natural embellishment.

Helen was out of breath when she burst in red-faced, her eyes frenzied.

'Elaine, quick, they've got your brother,' she huffed, holding her side. 'They're kicking the shit out of him in the park!'

I dropped my work on the floor. I'd known he was doomed all along. He was too ethereal for our Northern town, too delicate and spry. I was doing *The Tempest* in English and I knew that Malcolm was Ariel as soon as I read it:

> *What is't? a spirit?*
> *Lord, how it looks about! Believe me, sir,*
> *It carries a brave form. But 'tis a spirit.*

If he still did drama, he'd be a shoo-in for the role, only they'd scared him off all that years ago. Now I seriously worried that Malcolm wouldn't live long enough to be set free like Ariel.

The rest of the park was deserted; unusual for a post-school afternoon in

July – as if the town had run indoors and pulled the curtains shut, afraid of being called to witness. I ran over to him calling his name. I stood for a second in shock, looking down at him mashed onto the ground. One leg was twisted underneath him, one arm bent back on itself, the fingers of the hand covered in dirt and blood. A dangly earring lay broken on the floor, his ear lobe ripped in half. There was a boot mark on his school shirt, grass stains on the starched white collar. I knelt beside him, flustered, unsure what to do. Remember first-aid training, two days in the Temperance Hall? Check pulse and airways. Place the patient into the recovery position. He looked so still. Fearful, I put my ear to his chest and heard his heart, its defiant one two one two. A cough crackled in his throat. A moan. I held his hand.

'I'm here, Malcy. I've got you. Helen's getting an ambulance.'

His hair was hacked on top and long at his shoulders, dyed sunset orange, eyebrows plucked. I couldn't tell if it was blusher on his cheeks or bruises.

'What the fuck have you done?' I said.

He opened one eye, the other a blossoming golf ball, and actually laughed, scarlet snot bubbling from a blackened nostril.

I heard footsteps across the grass and looked up. An elderly man with a little white Westie stood beside us. He was dressed in a coat and trilby despite the heat, the dog whimpering and licking Malcolm's trousers.

'I've called the police,' he said. 'And an ambulance. Gang of boys it was. All bigger than him. I didn't know what was going on at first. Thought it was football or something. Like wild animals they were.'

Malcolm murmured – his voice faint and sticky.

'He's trying to say something,' said the man. 'Tell us who it wa' mebbe.'

I leant in closer.

Malcolm began to sing. His voice, no more than a whisper, somehow contained triumph. I recognised the song immediately.

We'd watched it on *Top of the Pops* the night before. It was our Thursday ritual. We had tea, then me and Malcolm washed up while Mum and Dad watched *Emmerdale Farm* over a cuppa in the sitting room. He'd tell me about his day, what had happened at school, that sort of thing. He was a watcher. He stood quietly on the sidelines taking it all in. It hadn't always been like this. When he was little he was the centre of attention; he sang all the time, was surrounded by little girls and always got the lead role in school plays – Gabriel in the nativity, the lion in *The Wizard of Oz*. Things changed when they got to the age of 10 or so. The girls all went off to bitch with other girls, the boys all thought he was weird because he didn't play football. Malcolm went quiet. He stayed home, holed up in his room with the curtains drawn. He sketched and read and sometimes came downstairs to watch old movies when the sport wasn't on. There was bullying, of course, a couple of bloody noses, a bit of name-calling and casual tripping up. There was one kid in particular, Eric Caine, in the year above. He was a right bastard, geed everyone else up to torment our Malcolm. Got so bad he didn't want to go to school any more, kept inventing stomach aches and migraines. He was at the doctor's more than he was at home. Then he came home one day with a black eye. It was one thing too many for Dad. He went mental. He was up at that school and when the head said it was just boys being boys he hauled him up from his desk and shoved him against the wall.

'What's this, then?' he said. 'Men being men?'

The physical stuff stopped after that but they still called him names. Poof. Ponce. Woolley-woofter. Shut that door. Not original. Not clever. No threat to our Malcolm. Freed from the fear of physical abuse he shrugged them off with his delicate shoulders and spent his time waiting it out in his bedroom, ripping out pictures from the *NME* to stick on his wall.

The blue guitar came first, all curves and shade, then the face, powdery and indistinct, images overlaid like a dream.

'Look at the state of that,' said Dad. 'What is he wearing?'

I was in the middle, me and Malcolm wedged on one sofa cushion while Dad took one up by himself. As soon as the camera focused on David Bowie I felt Malcolm tense. He suspended his breathing on the in. I looked at the face on the screen, clown white and high-cheekboned, smoky eyeshadow on the lids, the faintest gloss on the lips, parrot-red hair, spiked and glossy. His tongue slipped slowly along his top lip. Malcolm still hadn't breathed out.

'They get weirder by the day,' said Mum, slurping her tea.

I looked at the tall coat-hanger frame draped in its bright patterned catsuit and smiled.

'I think he looks smashing,' I said and nudged Malcolm in the ribs. 'What about you, our kid?'

He let out his breath in a puffball and looking at me with wide, startled eyes, opened his mouth but didn't close it around any words.

When he looked back at the TV, David Bowie had his arm draped around Mick Ronson and was gazing into his eyes as he sang. There was a shocked silence in our living room. Dad coughed and slurped his tea. The arm was removed. Mum tutted. David Bowie stared directly at me and Malcolm and pointed his finger as if to say you, yes you, you and me – our time has come. Malcolm still hadn't closed his mouth, though he was breathing in and out now at least. That stopped a second later when Bowie draped his arm around Ronson again, more deliberately this time, lingering over it, his polished nails brushing the gold of the other man's clinging catsuit. Malcolm slumped against the back of the sofa in surrender.

'There's no need for that, is there?' said Dad. 'Are they poofs or what?'

Mum nodded. 'Shouldn't be on telly, should it? In't there a law against it?'

I forget who was on next. It all seemed so irrelevant after that. Malcolm's face was burning and he was actually crying.

'You all right, luv?' said Mum.

'Not well,' he spluttered, standing unsteadily and running from the room.

Dad pulled a face. 'What's up with him? Is it PE tomorrow?'

'Go and see, luv,' said Mum, looking at me.

He was lying on his bed face down, his arms over his head.

'Malcolm?'

He tensed. I went in and sat next to him, my hand on his skinny back.

'What is it, luv? It's just the telly, you know. It's not real life.'

He looked up at me, his eyes darting.

'Don't say that, Elaine. That was the most real thing I have ever seen.'

He sat up and hugged his knees. I could see a pulse in his neck, as fast as a hummingbird.

'What I mean though is…' What did I mean? 'It's just for the telly, not for Market Street or school or owt. It's all right for them, they're pop stars. You're not.'

He frowned, then, sensing my concern, smiled and nodded.

'I'll take you into town on Saturday and you can buy it. Just us two. We can have a Wimpy after the record shop.'

Helen handed me a biscuit. Mum and Dad were on their way. Malcolm was in surgery. Internal bleeding, a broken leg and collarbone, a fractured skull. The doctors said he'd be okay but he needed fixing up and they'd need to keep an eye on the skull fracture.

I sipped the lukewarm milk that passed for tea at the hospital.

'What happened, Helen? Why today? I mean we all know he's different but I thought it had stopped. This, this was so brutal.'

'You didn't see him this morning, then?'

'What? No. He was up early. Left before I was even awake.'

'He's a brave little bugger, I'll give him that. He came to school in full make-up with his hair dyed, nail polish on. I thought you must have helped him. Our Kevin said it went quiet when he walked into class. He just sat down as if he looked like it every day, then when Mr Matthews came in he sent him straight to the head who suspended him on the spot. Everyone thought he'd gone home but he was in the park after school. Kevin said it was like he was waiting for them. That's when he came and got me.'

I couldn't swallow my tea, had to spit it back out into the cup. I put it down on the floor under the chair and tried to piece everything together.

He must have waited till we were all asleep. Mum kept henna in the bathroom cupboard for when the greys threatened to take over, and my make-up bag had been downstairs in the lounge all night. It would have taken him hours to get his hair that bright and to hack it into shape. There are hairdressing scissors under the sink. I never heard a thing. I was dreaming of pop stars and catsuits and I suspect he was too, even though he was wide awake.

'David Bowie,' I said.

'Right,' said Helen. 'I saw it too. Like nothing else.'

'It made a big impression on our Malcolm. He ran upstairs crying.'

Helen smiled sadly and sipped her tea. The double doors swung open and Mum and Dad walked in, flustered and full of questions.

They were right about the recovery. It was July already so he wouldn't be finishing the school year. They kept him sedated for two weeks. Me and Mum and Dad took it in turns to sit by his bed. Gradually, the cuts healed and the bruises faded. He looked so small and white, lying still in the bed, his pallor matching the starched sheets the nurses changed daily, lifting his plastered limbs carefully in their arms. He'd moan and roll his eyes but he didn't open them. The doctors said he was in shock and that he needed sleep to get over it. They'd repaired his battered insides with layers of stitches and all there was to tell the story was a thin red scar across his belly.

His hair was still orange though, shaved on one side for the stitches, and he had wonky teeth now, just like his idol. His eye shrank down to its normal size and the purple went blue and then yellow. I'd sit and talk to him about David

Bowie, read from the *NME* and *Melody Maker*, tell him who was on *Top of the Pops* and what the latest trend was, the summer's hits and the new dance craze. I only did it when we were alone though. Mum and Dad wouldn't have liked it.

Our parents never mentioned why he'd been attacked, not even when the police came round. A copper and a plain-clothes man, DI Glover, quite attractive for a policeman, Mum said. The copper drank tea and ate biscuits. DI Glover refused.

'Was there anything unusual about Malcolm's behaviour on the day of the attack?'

Dad shook his head. 'No more than any other day,' he said.

I looked at him open-mouthed.

'He isn't like the other boys,' said Mum, 'but we thought the bullying had stopped.'

'Was there any boy in particular, anyone who had it in for Malcolm?'

'Not that I know of.'

I knew though. I waited until the police had left before I confronted them.

'Eric Caine, Dad! Why didn't you tell them about Eric Caine?'

Dad told me to leave it, that Malcolm would be better off if we let it go, that he was asking for it, going around done up like a fairy. What did he expect?

I went to the police station the next day, asked to see DI Glover in person, told him I knew it was Eric Caine and his mates and that they'd always had it in for Malcolm. I told them where they lived. I didn't think it would be better for Malcolm if they got away with it. How could it be? How could it be better for anyone?

They took Eric Caine in for a line-up with the old man with the Westie. He picked out the undercover copper. I don't know if the Caine family got to him first or if his eyes really were that bad. Eric Caine's cousin gave him an alibi and that was it. No one else actually saw the crime. Helen and her brother went looking for me as soon as the beating started, didn't see enough to be reliable witnesses and nobody else came forward. Scared, I suppose; you wouldn't want to get on the wrong side of the Caines. The case was closed. DI Glover said he was sorry.

We spent the summer at home. The back garden was our beach. For the first few weeks I pushed Malcolm outside in his wheelchair and I'd sit on a deckchair while we listened to Radio Caroline, and if the ice-cream van came around I'd go and get us Strawberry Mivvies to keep us cool. Malcolm had a plaster up to his thigh; he used to scratch inside it with Mum's toaster fork. By mid-August, he was walking again, but the only time he was away from the house was to go to physio at the hospital. His hair started to grow back on the side they'd shaved but it still looked funny, half mousy brown and half orange. I helped him dye it as it came through, much to Mum's disgust.

We grew even closer that summer, our bond bathed in sunlight and birdsong, the paved square of the backyard our little fortress against the knob ends. We even got a little bit of a tan on our faces and T-shirt arms. We didn't talk about the attack, just the recovery – how his bones were, how many steps he'd done, how far he'd swum at physio. Mostly we talked about music and fashion. David Bowie was on the telly again, and I bought *Ziggy Stardust* and *Hunky Dory* with my Saturday job wages. We played them over and over, singing along every time. 'Five Years' was Malcolm's favourite. The end of the school holidays loomed like rain clouds in a blue sky.

He didn't have to go back in September. He could have stayed off. The doctor said he'd write him a note. He was fixed physically but he'd not seen a soul from school since his beating. I was worried because I was due to start art college in October and I wouldn't be there to keep an eye on him. Still, on the first of the month Malcolm said he'd be ready for the first day of school on the fourth.

'No point putting it off,' he said. 'Best get it over with.'

He came downstairs in his uniform; he'd kept his orange hair but he wasn't wearing any make-up.

'Do you want me to walk you to the gate?' I asked.

'Nah, that'll look worse. They won't touch me. I'm last year's news.'

I watched him walk down the path, a slight limp from his broken leg but his head held high.

Me and Mum fretted all day, cleaned everything in sight, drank sweet tea by the bucket-load. At 3.30, a little late back, Malcolm rushed in and ran straight upstairs into the bathroom, slamming the door behind him.

Mum and I looked at each other startled.

'What now?' she sighed. 'That boy'll be the death of me. You go, Elaine, luv. He won't want me.'

I banged on the door.

'Malcolm. It's me. Open up.'

It was quiet inside. I tried the handle but he'd locked it.

'Malcolm.'

I banged and rattled the door.

'C'mon, luv. Did they hurt you? Don't do anything stupid, will you? They're not worth it.'

He still didn't say anything. I began to fear the worst and banged flat on the door so hard my hand hurt. Finally, I heard the lock click.

Malcolm opened the door and stood frowning at me, a towel over his shoulders and black hair dye dripping down his face. The empty packet was ripped open, the pieces scattered behind him on the floor. He pushed past me into my bedroom. I turned and saw Mum looking anxiously up the stairs.

Malcolm was sitting at my dressing table checking his blackbird hair in the mirror.

'What happened Malcy?' I asked from the door. 'Did they hurt you?'

He dabbed at his hairline with the towel.

'Huh? God, no. It was awful though, Elaine. Why didn't you tell me? They all had dyed hair! Even Eric Caine. And earrings. And I'm sure some of them had lippy on. The whole feckin' school. Hard lads playing football in flares and eyeliner. Why didn't you tell me? No one even noticed me.'

He leant forward to scrutinise his rapidly changing hair colour, pulled the flesh of his cheeks tight underneath his eyes.

'Will you cut me hair for me, Elaine? I fancy it short and spiky. And can you help me take me jeans in too? Drainpipes, like the rockers.'

22

Evolution

What would he say?

That was what everybody wanted to know.

I first saw him on the short clip sent with the notes by the university. I watched in wonder, not expecting it to live up to the lofty promises made by the sender. I was wrong. He walked in the countryside holding hands with his infant son, like some mythical throwback of lumbering fur. They collected wood together, he directing the child into the trees while he built the campfire in a clearing. He took some matches from his backpack, struck one and held it to the ball of tinder cupped in his hand. The spark ignited, a red glow bathed in grey smoke. He placed it under the pyramid of sticks, crouched and blew until it took. When the wood burnt ferociously, he took marshmallows, plump and pink, from a packet in his bag, skewered them on a stick and toasted them over the flames, turning to ensure an even cook. When they were done, he blew them cool and passed the stick to his excited offspring, who was jumping up and down in his seat, making the palm signal for give. His lips curled with pleasure as his son ate, his deep, unblinking eyes full of love.

Most men I knew would struggle to make a campfire from scratch. Most men I knew would struggle without room service.

Could I teach him to talk?

The request was blunt.

I wasn't sure.

I knew it wouldn't be easy – that it would take years of my life.

I wondered if it would be worth it. It was such a long shot but if I could do it, I would be the first one – the only one – to succeed.

I mulled it over for weeks. They were willing to wait. I was doing the best work in the field, but I knew they wouldn't wait for ever. They were offering me unlimited funding and a new facility, but in the end it was his eyes that clinched it – I couldn't forget his big, dark eyes.

It was, as suspected, a laborious 12 years.

I moved to California, set up his classroom and threw myself into work. He was wary at first but eventually a trust built up. I taught him through repetition. Repetition after repetition after repetition after repetition. He was a watcher, not a talker; even his own noises were used sparingly. He was strangely quiet. Unnervingly quiet.

I used a system of images and rewards. Point and get a treat. His eyes would widen but no sounds came. He quickly mastered simple nouns, expressions of want. We brought in hand signals too. He liked those – he got quite theatrical – but he wouldn't attempt to mouth anything.

I spent hours exaggerating syllables, making ows and eeez with my lips while he just shook his head from side to side. I wondered if movies would help. We made a cosy TV room for him, complete with armchairs and beanbags and a curved HDTV so he could see the lip patterns as clearly as possible. Every Friday, after working hard all week, we sat together and binge-watched movies with Diet Pepsi and a bucket of butter popcorn. Action movies were his favourites, *The Avengers*, *Batman*, etc. And westerns, lots of westerns. He loved horses and he used to mime riding whenever Clint Eastwood set out in the saddle. When I showed him THE movie, the one everyone said I shouldn't, his eyes filled with tears and he curled foetally on the cushion with his thumb in his mouth. It took him a few days to get over it. He sat quietly in his enclosure, hardly moving. I got the impression he was thinking about what he'd seen, trying to work it all out.

His first utterance was 'pear', coming on the day I'd decided, with a heavy heart, that it couldn't be done. I don't know if he sensed what was at stake but when I presented him with the menu board and asked what he wanted for dinner he simply told me as if it was what he'd always done. His voice was deep and growly. At first I thought I'd imagined it but he said it again, clearly, and pointed to the symbol at the same time. Then he said his name, 'Benny'.

Pear. Benny. Pear.

Around the end of the fifth year his skills suddenly sky-rocketed, a match ignited, and by the time of our press conference he'd mastered around 10,000 words.

The university invited every scientist in the field, the press, local dignitaries, even a Hollywood actress researching a role.

No one believed it. *Evolution doesn't work like that.*

He sat nervously with his back to the room as it buzzed with questions and whispered *Planet of the Apes* scenarios. Security was tight; threats had been issued by several organisations. An abomination they called him. We engaged a unit of armed guards. They were positioned at strategic points around the lecture theatre. I patted his back as I went to start the PowerPoint. He eyed me sadly, his arms hugging his knees. When it all kicked off I had my back to the action.

He was strong and stealthy. He had the gun off the nearest guard before anyone knew what was happening.

'Behold your new king!' he roared, waving the weapon above his head.

The humans cowered, crouching by their chairs, holding their Press files as shields, as if that would work. Even I hunched instinctively, made myself smaller, less noticeable.

The guards had been instructed to protect him above everything else, even the spectators. They sighted him but didn't shoot.

Stand-off seconds ticked slowly through fear and anticipation. The clock on the wall the loudest noise in the room. I crouched further and watched, shuffled forward, willing him to look at me, my hands raised in placation. He turned his head and when I saw his eyes I knew it was going to be okay.

He pulled his lips back over his top set of teeth, a gesture I recognised as a smile.

'Just kidding,' he said, tossing the weapon to the floor. 'Guns are too stupid for words.'

Acknowledgements

For Mum and Sharon and Val. To those who read these stories in their infancy and helped make them into what they are today: Amanda Welby-Everard, Ed Rowe, Alice Cuninghame, Lonny Pop, Stephanie Lam, Karen Hubert, Ursula Robson, Katherine Doggrell and Linda McVeigh. To all the members of the Rattle Tales and Brighton Prize teams who are inspiring and talented in equal measure. Thanks also to the Beach Hut Writers for their support during the funding stage of this collection and to Safia Moore for reminding me to land those big bids. Thank you to Lucy Moffatt for her invaluable help with Mexican swearing. Special thanks to the team at Unbound because without them this collection would not have been published by anyone.

Above all, love and thanks to the famous Mettler boys, Rob, Noah and Gillespie, because it's not easy having a writer in the family!

I would also like to thank the following prizes, publications and events for their generosity and encouragement:

'Sourdough' was shortlisted for *The Writers' & Artists' Yearbook* Arvon Award 2013 and was later published by *New London Writers* in 2016.

'Miley Cyrus Fault' was published in the *Manchester Review*, issue 14, 2015.

'Tea and Frankenstein' was published on the One Million Stories website and included in their Best of 2011 anthology.

'What Me and Pa Saw in the Meadow' was shortlisted for the Bristol Prize, 2013, and is in their wonderful anthology.

'Jackson Was Good' was runner-up in the Guildford Book Festival short-story prize and was included in their 2010 anthology. It was also published in *Swamp Writing – Time & Memory Issue*, 2010 (in both cases as 'Clarkson Was Good').

'You Run' was shortlisted for the Fish short-story prize, 2016 under the title 'ARMSTRONG'.

'How Malcolm Malone Became the First Punk in Pontefract' was published by Jotters United in 2016.

'Evolution' was shortlisted for the Fish Flash Fiction Contest, 2016 and was read at Brighton City Reads in 2015.

'Ruby of the Desert' was shortlisted for Huddersfield University's *Grist* competition in 2017 and was published in *Grist: He, She, They, It* with the title

'A Greyhound Pass'. The story was reduced to 140 characters and published in *Tales on Tweet* (Harper Collins India 2016)

'Underneath' was performed by WordTheatre at Latitude Festival, 2012 and at their Anaphylaxis Campaign benefit the week before. Both times the story was read by Gethin Anthony (*Game of Thrones*) and Diana Vickers and they were a joy to listen to! It was also expertly performed at Liar's League in 2012 by Elizabeth Bower.

'Sleeping in a Coffin' and 'The Tenderness of Constraint' were both performed at Are You Sitting Comfortably? in Brighton in 2011.

'Sourdough', 'Underneath', 'Carbon in its Purest Form', 'What Me and Pa Saw in the Meadow', 'Ruby of the Desert' and 'A Spring Wedding' were all performed at Rattle Tales.

Patrons

Belle Amatt
Louise Amos
June Amos
Tim Atkinson
Julia Baker
Gill Balfour
Jo Bloom
Sonia Boon
Jacqueline Burns
James Burt
Louisa Campbell
Kathy Carter
Gina Challen
Sam Chara
Susy Churchill
Jane Lythell Clarke
Debbie Clifton
Jan Coggins
Dr Suzanne Conboy-Hill
Kate Conto
Hilary Cooke
Isabel Costello
Tamsin Cottis
Sara Crowley
Alice Cuninghame
Louisa Damant
Elts De Boer
Rachael de Moravia
Dominique De-Light
Lisa Dickson
Katie Dixon
Sharon Dixon
Emma Dixon
Katherine Doggrell

Juliet Doyle
Corinna Edwards-Colledge
James Ellis
Nick Evans
David Evans
Clare Fazal
Charlotte Feld
Tracy Fells
Andrew Fenwick
Alison Francis
Frances Gapper
Nick Gerrard
Pia Ghosh-Roy
Darren Gibson
Joanne Greenway
Sophie Gregory
Susan Griffin
Elaine Groome
Karen Guthrie
Araminta Hall
Louise Halvardsson
Ali Harker
Paula Harward
Richard Hearn
David Hebblethwaite
Sarah Hegarty
Jude Higgins
Paul Holbrook
Emma Hopkin
Amanda Horlington
Georgina Jeffery
Marc Owen Jones
Neil Jones
Elena Kaufman
James Kerr
Ayesha Khan
David King
Shona Kinsella

Emmanuel Lachlan
Stephanie Lam
Jenny Lamb
Ewan Lawrie
Pete Lawson
Giselle Leeb
Linda Legters
Soreh Levy
Sophie Lewis
Fiona Linday
Melissa Lucas
Jane Lineker Marshall
Pip Martin
Peter Mason
Stephen McGowan
Louise McGowan
Catherine McNamara
Paul McVeigh
John Mettler
Roland Miles
Edana Minghella
Virginia Moffatt
Penny Montague
Jess Moriarty
Alison Neads
Sara Newman
Helen Nicholls
Valerie O'Riordan
Amanda Oosthuizen
Mel Owen
Sarah Palmer
Richard Partridge
Ann Perrin
Jennifer Pierce
Lonny Pop
Sarah Rayner
Joanna Rees
Jo Rickhards

Vivienne Ridley
Nicolas Ridley
Caroline Ridley
Chris Roche
Allie Rogers
Bernadette Russell
Sarah Salway
Chris Sanders
Jeanette Sheppard
Janet Simpson
Becky Smith
Ann Smith
Catherine Smith
Gilly Smith
Glenn Stevens
Sharon Sutherland
Marianne Talbot
Ellie Tatum
Justine Taylor
Kathleen thomas
Mike Scott Thomson
Claire Thurlow
Monica Timms
Maxine Toff
Neil Towns
Deborah Turnbull
Hannah Vincent
Phil Viner
Jane Waller
Sandy Walsh
Steven Walsh
Benjamin Webb
Bridget Whelan
Hannah Whelan
Melanie whipman
Kristina Whitaker
Laura Wilkinson
Ian Williams

Matthew Wood
Eleanor Wood
James Woolf
Susie Zaleski